CW01215874

Inges

A DISCOURSE ON WITCHCRAFT
AS IT WAS ACTED ON ME, INGES
THE CAT, OF FUYSTON, IN THE
COUNTY OF YORK, IN
THE YEAR 1621

ALONG WITH THE VERITABLE HISTORY OF
MY JOURNY TO LONDON IN THE
PURSUIT OF JUSTICE, AND MY
THOUGHTS ON THE MATTER OF
HUMANE UNDERSTANDING

John Brunsdon asserts the moral right to be identified as the author of this work.

All rights reserved. No part of this publication may be reproduced, stored or transmitted in any form or by any means, electronic, mechanical, photocopying, recording, scanning, or otherwise without written permission from the publisher. It is illegal to copy this book, post it to a website, or distribute it by any other means without permission.

This novel is entirely a work of fiction. The names, characters and incidents portrayed in it are the work of the author's imagination. Any resemblance to actual persons, living or dead, events or localities is entirely coincidental.

Copyright © 2021 John Brunsdon

All rights reserved.

ISBN: 9798577925703

Inges

John Brunsdon

tewhit

For Pi, Jasper, Aethel & their souls

The intelligible forms of ancient poets,
The fair humanities of old religion,
The power, the beauty, and the majesty,
That have their haunts in dale or piny mountain,
Or forest, by slow stream or pebbly spring,
Or chasms and wat'ry depths; all these have vanished;
They live no longer in the faith of reason!
But still the heart doth need — a language,
still Doth the old instinct bring back the old names.

— Coleridge, from Schiller

Overture: *On Imps & Other Matters*

MY NAME is Inges, so you'll already know I'm not a good cat – no cat of moral standing would own up to such a name.

This is my story. I didn't write it for you. I had it taken down – the most part, anyway – at the house of a great man in London, long ago. It was to help me remember, at a time when I knew that I might soon forget. It's very easy to forget, and some things must be remembered.

If you are to read this tale, then we should probably get some things clear from the start. Our world – the cats and the other imps – is not like yours, so I have made some changes to help you make sense of it.

For your understanding, I live in a parish you call Fewston, in a place you call Yorkshire, in a country you call England. And everything I'm going to tell you about took place a little while back in a year you call 1621 – which is a year I call Nine, because that's how many years it was since I was born and I really don't have much need of the other 1,612 that came before.

That is your world, not mine. But in this particular year some things happened. Bad things. Things that made your world cross over into mine. And that is never a good thing.

To cut a long story short, I saved some humans from a horrible fate, uncovered a sinister plot that went to the very highest top of society, met two kings, some marquesses and bishops, a great playwright, and all manner of imps. I fell in love, had my heart broke, fought a great battle, and generally put everything right in the end. Some others were involved too, but it was mostly me.

Now, I know what you're thinking. 'But Inges,' you're going to say, 'you said you weren't a good cat – so how come you ended up saving the day and playing the part of hero?' Well – here's the thing. My fur might be black and white, but morality – for a cat of my nature – is always a little more tabby. Why did I do it? Because there was something in it for me.

You people have a lot of names for us: 'imps', 'familiars'; 'pets' – if you're one of those sorts of humans. But the reality is, we own you. If you're going to read my story you will need to come to terms with that for a start.

Every imp (that's the term I prefer, but 'familiar' is acceptable too. Not pet. Never pet) selects their human just as soon as they are old enough to make a decision for themselves. For us cats, that's about a week old, when we first open our eyes. In the case of dogs… no, I'm kidding you, they never make a decision for themselves.

You see, the thing about being a cat – or any sort of imp – is that we don't have souls. Now that's a good thing and a bad thing. A good thing because we don't have to deal with all the hand-wringing that goes with it – and try doing that without opposable thumbs. A bad thing, because without a soul you can't move on. When you die, you die. But if you have a borrowed soul you can keep coming back, just as long as the person who holds that soul is still alive, that is. So, our humans are very important to us. That means we need to keep them alive as long as possible.

When my human was facing a particularly nasty end at the hands of some rather intense pyromaniacs, I needed to step in.

Inges

The others I saved? The other things I put right? Put those down to collateral virtue.

Anyhow, that's all by way of letting you know what was behind all my troubles. When I told my old friend Vinegar Tom I would be making a human version of the tale of my adventures, he said two things to me. 'Inges,' he said, 'make sure you don't forget my part in it all.'

That was one thing he said, and the other was: 'Humans are proud, stubborn creatures who won't take the word of a cat, so you have to show them what happened, not tell them.'

So, I'll start in the year One, and I'll show you what happened.

ACT 1: IN YORKSHIRE

'The road to Hell is paved with good intentions'

–Ben Jonson

Inges

A Murder

I LIKE to take my time before making important decisions. Some say it's a fault of mine, and I say to them go ask little Cowpea, who was kicked by John Pullein's heifer, about a choice in haste. Or ask Coney Fishbone, who couldn't wait for dark to try the greens in Mr Franckland's garden.

Go and ask them, I say. And they say: 'Oh but Inges, we can't.' And I ask why, and they say: 'On account of they're dead.' And I say well now whose fault is that?

So, I take my time. And that's how it was with Peg. I could have chosen little Ellie, the Tanner's child – she was of an age with me and newborn six months when I opened my eyes. She was a fat little thing and always crying. And a good choice she would have been too, as she is fat and crying still – loud enough to scare off death itself, I'd say. I could have chosen Tam Mouncy, who Cowpea took in such a hurry – all gurgles and dimply grin, until the kinkcough did for him.

But I took my own time. A whole year I waited; while all those around me warned me that – just like that – I might be taken by that big hound Barghest that belongs to Mrs Dickenson and has a taste for cats. Or I could be thrown from the church tower, as is the tradition of the Flemings they say, or else turn sick and die in diverse ways. And if I waited too long there'd be no going back. But I waited. And then I picked Peg.

I picked Peg and I picked her mother, you see, as they are both cunning women and if you have one you can be sure you have the other. You have Peg's soul, and you have her mother's heart. If you have Peg's mother's heart, you have her healing – and that is a good thing to have.

There are those that live in York or London, or in the big houses, or even at the very King's court – those who have money to buy the world, and who have the learning of Aristotle and Plato and all the old ones. And they would look down on Maggie Waite and her daughter and clack their tongues and shake their heads at her unctions and poultices, and her herbs and bile and bitters.

Then when their child sickens they will call out for Dr Astrologia, who knows the stars so well he need not visit the house, nor even see the child, to know how much the cure will cost; or Dr Episteme who will tell the mother to feed her child the skin and blood of some poor weasel his boy had trapped, while he returns home to eat custard spiced with nutmeg. Only then – when they have paid the learned men to play the quack and their child just gets sicker – they come down from their high houses and knock on Maggie Waite's door.

And I wouldn't give a hundred dead Greeks for Maggie's knowing. She will make up a draught of mother's daisy and mistletoe for a child that has the fits; or willow and St John's herb for one who melancholia keeps all day in bed.

When the child is better the mother will put a penny down on the table and turn away, for fear of Maggie's touch. Then the next time her child sickens she will pay a hundred times that again for a man who knows the name of a leech in old Latin.

So, I thought to myself, I would be glad if my soul was tended by a woman who knew flax for sickness and celandine for the sores. And that is why I chose Peg, and why I didn't choose Lizzie Fairfax – though she was the right age and as bright and bonny as any human I've seen; and who knows how different things might have been had I done so.

Peg was ten years old when I chose her. She was, I am told by those who know how such things should look, an awkward child in manner and appearance, and even I could see she had a mouth whose front teeth paid their tithe in a different parish to her back.

But those same folk say that by the time of our troubles she had grown to be a woman that human men think highly of – at least in how they steal looks at her when sat in church, if not in how they talk of her and her mother outside it.

And Peg is a kind one. We don't expect much of our humans – just that they don't beat us, or scald us with water, or stuff us to burn for a Queen's birthday. Some food is nice, a warm place to sleep is better – then we mind our own way.

Well, we cats will. Barghest – the dog that hates cats – he will barely put one foot in front of the other unless his human gives him leave. And Tewhit – who came from the far Indies with Widow Thorpe's husband – he sits on her shoulder half the day and whistles his own name while he fixes you with his red eyes, asking that you admire his golden feathers.

But me, I like to be left in peace. And Peg, even as a bairn, would feed me and close her eyes at me then walk away.

Which is how I like it as I'm not like those cats who have grown soft from table meat and petting – nor like those that live only in the fields and the grain store and freeze to death in winter rather than let a human look them in the eye.

When it is cold I will sometimes sit beside her if she has a rabbit fur on the bench, or lie on her bed when it is stuffed with woodruff and the scent coddles my head and sends me to hunt mice in the clouds. And if it gives her comfort to scratch at my ear those times, or rub my chin, then I will tolerate it and make pretence of pleasure, for I would not wish to upset her by showing my indifference.

I would say all was peace and comfort in my house, with Maggie about her business all day, or out gathering herbs and flowers in the fields and forests, and Peg mixing up her mother's brews, or sat at weaving, or some such handiwork. But there was one more of us living there. And he gave me such trouble that sometimes I thought maybe I should have gone with Lizzie Fairfax or the fat Tanner's child after all.

Quin was his name. A great black cat with fur so thick and rough you could have used him to scour the boiling pot, as I sometimes wished they would.

How old he was, I don't know – I wasn't about to ask and he wasn't going to tell – but he was old enough that when I saw him asleep on the rushes by the fire I would think him dead sometimes. Or maybe I'd just think to hope that.

But I did hear Maggie Waite one time say to Jennit Dibble – when they were sharing their aches and pains and cursing at the injuries time had done them – that she and Quin had been together close on 20 years. Jennit laughed at that and said her and Gybbe had had 40 years; which seemed peculiar to me at the time, but which now I understand better.

In defence of Quin, I suppose being so long the only imp in the household makes you proud and aloof. It certainly makes you put up your back and put back your ears when a handsome young tom steps over the threshold and finds your spot by the fire.

Now, I know you might say: 'Inges, I do not think it is your place to say you are handsome – let others do that for you.' But there are no others to tell you that and, as you cannot see me through the words, and as this is a true history, I must put aside modesty in the name of thoroughness or else you might miss some important detail of all that happened.

The first night I came to live with Peg I found a spot among the rushes, just close enough to the hearth so my back could stand the heat a minute and no more, and then I turned so my belly got the same.

Looking back, I should perhaps have been wise to it, but the rushes were pressed down just so – sweet-flag, newly cut so it still had its scent. The hollow was just the right size for me, just the right nearness to the fire. Perfect. Just a little too perfect, as it turned out.

Inges

I was on my back when Quin attacked. I didn't even hear him, and he didn't even have the courtesy to spit and howl before. It is an unspoken rule that you give your opponent fair warning, and I still hold him in dishonour for that even though it is not good to speak ill of the dead.

My belly was there for the world to see; I'd stretched my legs out to capture the warm air all settled in the softest of my fur, and my eyes were closed, defences down. He was on me before I knew it — his front claws about my neck and his thick back legs a-raking at my side. I swear, if my fur weren't so lush and healthy, I would have been hurt far worse than I was.

Maggie had to close me up with a red-hot poke and bind me with egg yolk, rosemary and turpentine where, to this day, if you look close on my left side, you will still see where the fur won't grow.

As if that weren't enough, Maggie put around my neck something like a funnel that stopped me from cleaning my wound. Truth be told — and I did promise to hold back no detail — it stopped me cleaning any part of me. For a good fortnight I was not in a state that I should wish anyone to see and even now, when I think about it, it gives me the urge to put up my leg and take my ablutions, even though I'm not one to do that in good company.

Of course, Quin, he would just mark me with that look of his. It would have been better if he had thrown scorn at me, or mocked me. I knew what he was thinking. I knew what I looked like. 'Just say it Quin,' I'd say to myself. But he didn't — and that made it worse.

So, we didn't get off to a good start, and it got no better. He would lay in wait for me sometimes as I came through the door and he'd swipe at me or go to chase me. He wasn't so bold when I had my eyes open and my belly down as he had been that day by the fire, and a few sharp swipes at the soft part of his nose had taught him to play with more caution.

But still, he was there always to tell me he was the boss of the house. And Maggie — for all her virtues — loved that cat so that, when she had cause to scold him, her voice was soft so if you did not know the words you'd swear she was calling him 'Sweet

'Mr Pusskins' or 'Kitty Mine', instead of 'brute' or 'villain' as he should have been named.

As time went by, we did come to more of an understanding. I knew to keep away from the places that he claimed as his own, and he knew that he could glare at me or spit a warning, but he knew better than to give chase or follow through on his taunts. Especially as the years took the strength of our limbs and the sharpness of our claws in opposite directions.

Right before the end, you could say we were almost friends. I say almost, because there was something in the pride of us both that would not allow it to be any nearer.

There was one day when, as I lay upon it, he had jumped up on Peg's bed – which was my place, but he would make sure to leave his scent there when he knew I wasn't around. Only this time he had erred; this time I was there. He landed right by me and, in a flash, my mind went back to our first meeting by the fire. Now this time I was prepared. I pulled back into the softness of the bed to cover my belly, and my claws were out ready to strike before he had found his balance.

He looked at the bed, then at me, then at the hard floor, and I think he weighed them each against the other and I thought I saw the weight of years in his eyes. He sat down next to me and turned so his back was pushed against my legs. And there we stayed a while, until the soothing of his purrs ran through me and calmed my head into peaceful sleep.

That was just before the start of the time of my troubles, but I wasn't to know it then, and for the next month the house was more a home than it had ever been. We even spoke. Nine years of near silence and now we spoke.

We talked of this and that, of how to catch a mole by listening with your feet – which he had never learned in all his years. And we played at naming those who came calling for Maggie, such as 'Peter Piles' or 'Bilious Bett', and the like, on account of what ailed them. And the one that always tried to pet us when she came – we schemed to put a vole liver in the pot that was boiling for her ointment. She came back scarcely four weeks later and was singing of how Maggie had cured her, and she laid down her money for more of the same while she picked me up and scratched at my belly; so that didn't work.

Then one night, about the time of the full moon, when the blackthorn flowers were first open for Peg to gather, we had the most peculiar conversation, Quin and I.

'Inges,' old Quin said, 'do you ever think of what would be if you had not Peg's soul?'

'Well,' I said, 'then I should keep out of the way of cows and hope to live as long as you. And I dare say I should miss her.'

'No,' Quin said, 'not if she were dead, if you just had not her soul?'

I didn't know his meaning so I implored him to tell more and he then said this, which made me most curious: 'I will tell you my meaning Inges, but first I must be sure of it. I must go to Timble Gill tonight, will you come with me?'

I asked what we would be doing at Timble Gill, as it is a long way from Maggie's house and at night that little glen is full of red foxes and great white owls, or you can fall in the beck that runs through it and hides its tricksy edges in bur-reed. Or, in that dark place among the trees, you might get taken by a boggart if such things do exist – and I had no desire to find out the truth of those stories.

'I can't tell you, as it is not allowed to talk of it, but come with me Inges and see for yourself my meaning,' he said, and he had a look in those orange eyes of his that at once made me in equal parts cautious and curious.

'No,' I said. For, ashamed as I am to admit it now, caution played the stronger card that night. 'I think I shan't as Peg was searching just this last hour for a rat that had got into the pantry and I have sworn to myself to catch it for her.'

Which was true. At least Peg had been looking for a rat, but not that hour. Nor that day. Nor week. But there was some truth in it at least.

'Well then Inges,' said Quin, 'I will go myself, but tomorrow I will talk to you more of it, for there is much that I must say, and by then I am hopeful that I will be free to say it.'

'On your way then, Quin,' I said. 'Leave the rat to me, and mind you don't get taken by the boggart.'

And those were the last words that I spoke to him, for the next morning I woke to the sound of Maggie weeping and wailing, and Peg had her arms around her, comforting her as she sobbed.

At the church in Fewston, across the way, there was a new gate put there just four years before. And across the top of that gate was a beam of oak from the old tree that blew down at Cobby Syke the year Widow Thorpe's husband died – a sturdy piece as thick as a blacksmith's forearm.

They found old Quin there, hanging from that beam by a yard of rope. His orange eyes had gone and, where they had been, empty black hollows now seemed to stare right through me and into the darkest depths of my heart.

They pulled him down and spread him out there on the dirt of the road, so that all the world could see. Peg wrapped him up in her shawl and held him as I'd seen Maggie hold the little ones when they come to us with the colic.

'They have done him murder!' Maggie cried. 'My Quin, my lovely boy, they have done him murder!'

And with that murder was the start of all the troubles. For me, for Maggie, for Peg, for Widow Thorpe and the other cunning folk; for the poet Fairfax and poor little Anne, for Ellen and Lizzie. And for all of those, high and low, who would be touched by all that followed the death of a sorrowful, grumpy old cat: all; from a humble frog to the King of England.

The Poet in the Valley

I DON'T know much of poetry. Those that know me say I have a turn of phrase, and I flatter myself – simple country cat that I am – that I can shape words to make a heart race or a tear swell, change a mind or alter a trajectory.

'Inges,' they tell me, 'your tongue is as quick to draw fine words as it is to draw up milk.' But I would never talk that way of myself, and certainly I never earned such praise as Edward Fairfax, nor got to kiss the hand of a Queen, for my words. Though it should be said – and I am just an honest reporter of facts – that his great work, for which he received his royal blessing, was dismissed by my good friend and esteemed playwright Ben Jonson as 'not well done'.

Be that as it may, this poet did receive praise elsewhere and he was, for a time, a man in great demand – feted at court, and by those that fancy themselves lovers of art.

Godfrey of Bulloigne, or the Recoverie of Jerusalem. Done into English Heroicall Verse: it is a bit of a mouthful, and, in truth, is simply a translation of another man's work. But I will not think any less of it for that. It is not a piece I have read, I must admit. From what I learned in the time that followed Quin's murder, it would seem to deal with the typical comings and goings of human life outside my little forest home. And I have seen enough of that now, because of this ill-starred poet, so it shall remain unread.

Whatever its merits, this great work of his saw the finest doors in the land opened to him. He would dine with earls, share tales with Shakespeare, dance with countesses and attend upon queens: a treasured guest and a generous host, the toast of London and the pride of his friends. It would have seemed that the whole world was his to conquer and enjoy.

Yet here we were, he and I. Two poets singing our verse not at Court, nor for Italian princes, nor in the great hall of Whitehall Palace, but in the dark sylvan green of Knaresborough Forest. Our stage: the simple Yorkshire earth; our Herculean Pillars: the great elms that girdle our sunken lanes; our Heavens: the… heavens.

Anyhow, you get the picture. Just four years after old Queen Bess herself accepted his poetic dedication, Edward was huddled in the cold of New Hall, hidden from the world by the slopes of Swinsty Moor and the thick forest that shrouded his door.

You might think for such a man, who carried the name of one of the great families of Yorkshire, New Hall was an ill-fitting home. It's a dark and dismal place, right at the lowest point of the valley, and shut in by hills all around; not even a cart road runs down there.

The rooms – for I have seen them, though not as well as it was thought when my life was to be forfeit for it – are simple. The roof is low, the windows small. One has a picture in coloured glass, though it is cracked and ill-repaired: a pelican pecking at its own breast to draw blood with which to feed its young. I was told it was the coat of arms of one that once owned the hall.

That the home of a man of the famous Fairfax line would carry the shattered Arms of another man's family was not such a great surprise as you might think. New Hall was less a home, and more a sanctuary for a man who seemed tired of life; a place where he could hide from the troubles of the world.

'So Inges,' I hear you ask, 'what should cause such a fall? What cruel game did fate play to pull the poet from his pedestal and bring him to the valley floor?' Well, I shall do my best to recount the tale just as I was told it:

Edward was born into the family of Sir Thomas Fairfax of Denton, who had been knighted by Queen Bess, for some gallantry I suppose. However it was done, Sir Thomas was to see his family fortunes rise and his sons grow towards fame.

His most famous son, and his favourite, was born of his wife and named Tom for himself, as is the way with humans. But two more were carried by another woman – of great beauty, but low birth – and these were Charles and Edward. It is the fate of these two brothers that you will see crosses with my own.

Maybe it was because they shared a mother, or were more distant from their father, but Charles and Edward had a bond that was strong even for brothers, they say. I often thought they must have been like Peg and I, like an imp and its soul, so neither was whole without the other.

Now, though Charles loved Edward best, he most wished to be like his other brother, Tom, and follow him into battle. Perhaps he sought his father's love too? Or he simply had that same longing for glory they say runs in that side of the family.

Charles would become a great soldier and win fame on the battlefield in the wars between those people they call the Dutch and those they call the Spanish.

I won't pretend to really know the difference, but it is supposed the Spanish were the enemy and the Dutch were friends. Though I knew only one Dutch human and no Spanish, and if the Dutch are friends then the Spanish must be a terrible foe.

When Charles left to fight his first campaign, still so young he didn't yet have fur on his face, Edward was heartbroken. And on Charles' return – with a reputation won as a bold soldier, unafraid to face the hardest danger – Edward swore that at the next campaign he would join him so that he could keep him safe.

But Charles laughed at this and told his brother he was a poet and not a warrior, and that every man should follow his calling. So instead, Edward wrote a poem for Charles and asked that he keep it about his person in battle so that, in spirit at least, he could be there at his brother's side.

And this charm seemed to work, as Charles fought many a great and fierce battle and it seems fortune was always with him. At a place they call Nieuwpoort, which is a long way from here, he rallied his men to join a desperate fight against Spanish pikemen when all had seemed lost. And again, at Sluis, he led 300 men into the trenches to route the enemy, pushing them to drown in the swamps or to huddle where he cut them down as they crouched in terror. This, I am told, is how men fight, and I am glad to be a cat that only needs to show an enemy he is beaten then let him walk away.

But then one day, in September of the year called 1604, Charles seems to have misplaced his charm. At least they say Edward later asked after it and was told no piece of poetry was found on his body.

Having won his great fight at Sluis, Charles was ordered back to Ostend, which the Spanish had long been trying to capture. He was to lead the English there as they fought to keep the city, as they had done for the three years before.

He was not to know this but, as Charles was fighting there, his commander, Prince Maurits of Orange, was preparing the papers of surrender – for he had what he wanted in Sluis and saw no need to continue the defence of Ostend.

I would assume that Charles would have liked to have known this sooner, for, just three days before the siege was to end, he was sat at the city walls in conversation with a soldier of France and, I imagine, said something the man did not like, as moments later that soldier gave Charles a piece of his mind.

That is to say, the soldier's head exploded, and poor luckless Charles took a nice part of it to his face. And that was the end of Edward's brother.

Needless to say, Edward took this badly; especially when he found his brother had not kept his poem with him. He blamed himself for not being there, or for not writing more often, or sending more poems, or for some other fault he saw in himself. Though I should think he would have done better than to blame himself; and while I do not know how common such incidents are, the lesson I would have taken from it is not to stand too close to a Frenchman.

But that same day that news came from Ostend, they say Edward changed so much as you would hardly recognise him as the man he was one day if you had seen him the next.

He took his sorrows and his broken soul and hid them away behind the heavy doors of New Hall and under the dark hills of Fewston. And there he poured all that he had left in his cracked heart into the love of his family, and he shut out the world; I think in the hope he could protect them in a way he never could his brother.

Yet sad to say, all his love would not be enough, and his pain and his desperation would turn this man of learning to believe such base things as would bring a curse on me and my family. Such is what happens, I think, when we try to control that we were never meant to.

We imps – most of us – we are happy to be ignorant of what fate awaits us. We have no charms or prayers or curses. We know what we cannot know, and we accept that which comes. And maybe that is why we have no souls of our own and must borrow them from people. But I would rather it were that way, as I have seen what sorrows souls bring – for those that have them, those that lose them and those that desire them.

But now I think I've become too melancholy, and you are not here to listen to the sorrows of Edward Fairfax the poet, you are here to follow the adventures of Inges the cat.

And yet, impatient as you are to hear more of me, I must stay a little while with the Fairfax family, for the thread of their lives shortly joins with mine.

Edward had two sons, but we need not trouble ourselves with them. The girls were far more interesting. Ellen was the eldest, and it seems she was known for her charm and beauty, her gentle, trusting ways and naive heart. All these things, apparently, are prized in human girls. The younger sister was one called Lizzie – who I might have bonded with, and who in many ways reminded me of Peg. She was fierce and bright, bold and inquisitive, quick of wit and temper. All these things, apparently, are frowned upon in human girls.

And then there was Anne. I only wish I could tell you of her gifts or faults, but she did not live long enough to reveal any. She lived only long enough to be bonded with Fillie – and while I need instruction in what is deemed desirable in a human female, I know only too well that which is best in a cat, and everything I could list there was to be found in Fillie.

Her fur was as white as the snow that caps Barden Fell in winter, and her eyes were as blue as… well nothing; there is nothing as blue as Fillie's eyes. Her coat shone and sparkled as she moved, shimmering like the summer breeze through barley. And the way she shook her tail when… well, it's a cat thing. We won't talk more of it. It's not that kind of book.

Anyhow, that was Fillie. She had arrived in the village a few months before, not bonded to anyone. While I had seen her around, she kept herself to herself for the most part, and I would have thought her one of the barn cats if she were not so clean and well-mannered.

She was young and, like me, she had waited before she made her choice. When I first saw her come from New Hall I thought she must have bonded with Lizzie Fairfax, which pleased me as I thought them well matched. I saw her again shortly afterwards, (and whatever that beak-brained Tewhit might tell you I wasn't following her, I just like to walk that way up to Fewston some days as there are a good lot of voles about in the wood there). Anyway, by then she had chosen Anne.

It seemed a wise choice, as Anne was of a good family. The stock was strong and healthy, the home a good shelter, the father a wise man with wealth enough to feed and clothe her well. I was pleased for her, and glad she would be able to stay at such a home, which wasn't too far from mine.

For the first month or so, it seemed all was well. Anne grew quickly and Fillie would sometimes sleep at her feet where she was swaddled, and they would keep each other warm. They were bonded well. Some imps bond and the human does not even know them. It is possible to be bonded to a human and spend your whole life out of their sight, and for many imps that is exactly how they like it. But for Fillie, she was always there, and I thought the bond must be almost as strong as that with me and Peg. So, it was a terrible day when I heard the cries from New Hall; cries that seemed to echo through the whole valley.

Anne was just three months old when she took sick. Fairfax called all the physicks and surgeons that he knew from York and London, and they took his gold to shake their heads. I urged Fillie to draw them to Maggie, and finally, when poor Anne grew sicker, her mother came to our door.

'Oh Maggie,' she cried, as she was wont to be familiar with her when she suffered, even if she would pass her by when all was well. 'Maggie, my poor Anne ails so terribly. Is there nothing you can do? Edward will pay you any price if you can only save her.'

So, Maggie stepped into New Hall and she looked at Anne. There was no illness nor malady she had seen before in that child and, though she knew every herb and root and every alchemist's trick, nothing would seem to bring the colour back to her cheek. I saw her work all night by the tallow light, mixing as she hummed healing words, tasting and smelling, grinding and steeping, until she would fall asleep at her stool and the wick would burn down and coat the air with that bitter tang that lets you know it is the end of light.

But for all her wisdom, none of this was enough. And four months after she had come into the world – just as the early June apples began to shed from the tree outside her window – Anne left it.

The poet learned that no hideaway, no matter how far it was from the world he had turned his back on, could keep death from his door. And for Fillie, I knew this meant only one thing; her soul was gone.

Now I must do what Fairfax had failed at: to keep those I care about safe. And that – hard is it was – should have been all that was taken from that day, and that should have been enough.

Fate, though, had more in store for all of us, and it started to show us just what mischief it had planned the very next day.

I had taken Fillie to rest at Maggie's house, as there were too many memories at New Hall and, if truth be told, I wished to keep her under my watch at this time for I had a great dread in my heart. I could see that Maggie had taken Anne's death badly, and the house was quiet and still. Quin had been dead just three months and now this had put heartache on heartache.

The first we knew of it was a banging on our door that came just after dawn. Peg rose to answer and was startled to see old Bess Dickenson there, her hair as wet and matted as that of her great dog Barghest when he has been chasing mallards in the beck.

'Have you heard?' she said to Peg, though it was clear she was being sure to be the one who told her first. 'Have you heard about Anne?'

Peg rubbed her eyes and shook her head. She was still in her nightgown and dared not open the door more than a crack, but Bess leaned her weight into it and was in the room shaking down the water from her sleeves before Peg could speak.

'Shocking it is – the reverend has heard of it and is to talk of it on Sunday.'

Peg shook her head. 'We know Bess. Everyone knows about poor Anne. Maggie did her best and is sore-hearted by it as anyone but the poor girl's family.'

Bess skipped up and down as she waited for Peg to finish speaking, as though the words were kicking at her to be let out. 'No, not that. It's what they found. In her room. When they were a-clearing it up of her things.'

'What did they find?' Peg asked, for things unknown should not be found in a dead girl's room.

'A simlicum they called it.'

Peg shook her head.

'A smilicrum – that's what Reverend Smythson said.'

'It's called a simulacrum.' Maggie had awoken, and whatever it was, it was clear it troubled her greatly.

'That's it – that's what he said. A samilcrum.'

Inges

Peg looked as puzzled as I felt at that moment, and her mother lowered her voice to talk.

'A doll. An image. It will be made of clay no doubt, to look like Anne.'

'And who would make such a thing?' Peg cried.

'A witch,' said Maggie.

'And why would a witch do that?'

Maggie closed her eyes and put her hands together at her waist. 'For to kill her,' she said.

Inges

Barghest

NOW YOU would think I had worries enough at this time. Quin had been murdered and now it seemed Anne, too, had been taken. And people were saying it was by a witch, which would mean only one thing for the likes of my Peg.

Folk will come to a house like ours calling for a tonic to ease their stomach from worms, or an ointment for the mites. Wives will ask for mandrake draught to make their husbands come to them, or one of verbena to make them keep away. And all the time they will hail the likes of Peg and call them 'cunning women' or 'wise'.

But if the crop fails, or the milk sours; if the weather is too dry in Spring or too wet at harvest; if the stool leg breaks or a child gets the pox: well then, she is now called a witch. If there is a falling out over where to sit at church, or over who looked the wrong way at who, or over money owed or any little thing: she is called a witch. And in those days – with King James on the throne – that dark word was blacker and more deadly than the berries of the nightshade.

You see, they say that when James chased his little Danish mate like a lovesick spaniel across the water, a coven of witches conjured up a storm in a sieve that nearly drowned him – and that, in terror from that day, he became obsessed with the destruction of all their kind.

I have no great knowledge of the ways of such things, but it always struck me as an odd thing that a witch would have the power to call down the heavens and rise up the sea against the King of England, yet be powerless to shut the mouths of local gossips.

By the time of our troubles, his fever for witches had cooled a little and he now looked under his bed each night instead for those called Catholics. But still, to be called witch by your neighbours was to face the near certainty of joining the hundreds of cunning women who had gone to the gallows or the flames for a lot less than the death of a great poet's child.

But this was not all that troubled me. Fillie was without a soul and I must keep her safe while a murderer was at large in Fewston. And one who had taken not only Anne, it seemed, but most certainly had taken Quin.

And, despite all these new troubles, it was the taking of Quin that occupied my mind the most at this time. Not so much his death, nor even the manner of it, but the fact that months had passed and he had not returned. While Maggie lived, Quin should have returned.

Sometimes it can be hard to tell at first. You see, when you come back you are reborn. You come back into the world furless and blind as you came into it before. And – while your life before is still in you – just as you cannot see the light until your eyes are open, you cannot remember the past until you open your mind. Even then, it only comes to you as a half-remembered story. But over time it should return, enough at least that you seek out your soul, even if you do not know why.

And by now he should have come back. Gintsy, the calico barn cat from Jenner's farm, gave birth to a litter of six in the hazel coppice across from Fewston bridge just three months after Quin died. By rights, Quin should have been among them. I went by to see them soon as their eyes opened – which caused some gossip in the village, especially with one of the litter having something of my colouring about them. But as an honest storyteller I will tell you what I told Fillie – Gintsy and I are just good friends.

Anyhow, that is by the by. Quin was not there, that was sure. You can always tell a returning imp before it has bonded as there is a twinkle in its eye – not like any normal twinkle, mind. One that shimmers with life and memory. They say what you see is the thread that ties you to a soul – the soul binding, they call it. And it is beautiful, and it is unmistakable.

But it was not there, in any of those kittens' eyes. And if Quin was coming back it should have been. So now I knew, Quin was dead. Dead and gone for good. And he shouldn't have been. And that troubled me greatly. For if he were truly dead it must mean he no longer had Maggie's soul. And if he did not have her soul – well, I thought back to that conversation we had the night he left for Timble Gill, when he spoke of souls in such a way that, now I thought on it, seemed more peculiar still.

And now Anne was dead, and another cat was without a soul. Did the black-hearted murderer now have Fillie for a target? Was this the cause of poor Anne's sickness? To sever another soul and take another imp?

There was a puzzle here, and it struck me that there was but one in all of Fewston who could best put their mind to unpicking such a puzzle. One who was sharp enough of mind and claw. Perhaps there was a reason that all this had happened under the eyes of Inges, I thought to myself. And if that were pride, so be it, for in the end it was Inges who unpicked it – albeit the mystery was deeper than even I could imagine then, and its trail stretched far beyond our quiet hills and vales.

But at that time I was not to know that, and so I started my search in our parish.

There was something in particular that puzzled me about the discovery of poor dead Quin. Something that did not make sense. Maggie's house lies in the homestead of Timble, which is but a little clutter of houses to the south part of Fewston parish. From that side of our house runs a narrow path that is called the Bridle Road on account of the pack horses that have walked it since time began, wearing down the path so the ground rises up and the hedges embrace above.

At the bottom of this road, a half mile from Timble, the beck runs across the pathway. Once you step through that water you are in Timble Gill. Though, I should say, I am not one to get my feet wet, and I climb around through the verge. Except in late summer when the stickybob gets in my fur. That is no fun to tease out as you have to get it in your teeth and make soft, fast little pulls – not hard, sharp ones as I've seen some do.

Anyhow, that's not important. All this is just by way of letting you know the layout of the land. For the peculiarity of Quin's finding was this: he was at the church gate, which is at Fewston village – a good mile or more to the north of our home.

I reasoned if Quin were going to Timble Gill, he would not have headed north. I had no reason to believe he had been untrue about his destination, as he had asked me to accompany him – and perhaps if I had he would still be here now; but there was a business with a rat, and we cannot undo what has been done.

So then, did he go back north to Fewston and meet his end there? Or was his fate sealed in Timble Gill and he was then carried north by those that had done the deed? The answer to this, I thought, might tell me how he had come to be murdered.

I determined to start first with the place old Quin had been found – the church at Fewston. And the best time to visit, it seemed to me, was when all the people of the parish would be there and I might catch a nervous glance at the gate, or spot a grimace of regret, or else see other signs of guilt upon the murderer's face.

Nicholas Smythson, that folk call Reverend, was to talk of the death of Anne at church that Sunday – that is what Bess Dickenson had told Peg when she came-a-calling in her excitement. So, it was on Sunday that I too went to church.

And with me I took witnesses. For when a crime is done it is for all the community to uncover and witness it, and I thought, if Fillie were to be kept from harm, it would be best for there to be safety in numbers. I gathered together those of the imps I knew best – Fillie of course, but also Gybbe. I had hoped to

Inges

call on Tewhit too, but due to a misunderstanding some months before when I had mistook him for a finch — as anyone might do with the winter sun in their eyes — he still seemed to have some distrust of me.

There were others too, but of no use to me then. One was Barbara, the frog who was bonded with Mother Fletcher. She stayed out at The Tarn, which is a pond just behind the inn, and makes a poor choice of home, from all the drunkards that would stumble out to piss in it.

And then there was Barghest. And of him, I had learned something troubling that day.

It was Gybbe who told me. For you see Barghest, as you know, is a dog. And like all dogs he has no mind of his own, but instead waits on his human to decide which way he will walk, what he shall eat and how he should sit, or roll over or beg. And Barghest would never be found without his mistress, Bess.

Bess and her hound live next door to Gybbe, which troubles him often, as Barghest will take to barking at him as he does his morning business, and he fears would eat him if his mistress did not tie him to a stake beside the door. His mistress's house is bigger by half than most in the village, so why they find no room for him indoors I don't know, except perhaps they have as little love for the smell of a dog as I do.

Be that as it may, there had been two occasions in recent times, Gybbe told me, when he had risen in the morning and Barghest had not been there to bark. He had, in curiosity, dared to peek at the window of the Dickenson's house and had seen Bess and her husband Thomas there asleep; but of Barghest, no sight, sound nor smell.

'And what days were these, Gybbe?' I had asked him.

'Well, that is the worrisome thing, Inges,' he answered. 'The first was the day they found poor Quin a-hanging at the gate.'

'And the second?' I asked, already suspecting the answer.

'That was the day little Anne perished.'

And so it was we gathered there at the church that Sunday. Fillie and I hid ourselves away behind the aumbry door to witness the sermon, while Gybbe kept watch on the Dickenson house lest Barghest – knowing all good folk were gathered at the church – should slip his lead again.

In the world of cats, a fellow's standing is not always clear at first. You can maybe tell in a walk, or in the way we hold our tails, who is the first in the village and who is the last. But if there is doubt, then there might be need to make notice of it with a good spray of piss. And if that is still not enough, we can posture and raise our backs and make a great caterwauling until one will acknowledge the other as his better. Not that in my village there is need for such posturing, but this is just the way it is with our kind.

For humans, it appears all this work is done more simply. All is apparently decided in where a person sits in church. At the front sit those who are the highest. There you'll find Hal Robinson – that they say found his gold in the empty houses of the plague dead of London – that is when he comes down from Swinsty Hall, which is not often. Alongside sits Edward Fairfax and his family. Behind are the likes of Henry Graver and John Jeffray, who made their money through toil or enterprise and so must look at the backs of their betters.

The rows go back, through farmers and thatchers, the keeper of the inn and the shoe-er of horses, until you get to the likes of Bess Dickenson and Widow Thorpe. Then, at the far back, or standing when the pews are full, will be Maggie and Peg, Jennit and Mother Fletcher.

At the back they need not be looked on or thought of by those in front. That is, most of the time they aren't. But this day it seemed the good people of Fewston would honour them with their attention, for heads would turn all through the sermon.

'The evil that these creatures do…' Reverend Smythson coughed to draw attention back to himself. 'The evil they do is at the bidding of Satan, and it is from Satan that it comes. And be warned, for is not the witch also alike as the Papist that hides in our midst in the guise of decent folk?

'Do they not show themselves in the form of some good woman, but hide their true, hideous form save from their master?

Inges

And do they not – like the great Antichrist that is in Rome – seek to have all power in Heaven and Earth and blasphemously claim it for themselves? Do they not claim to heal – be that soul or body – yet send you to bodily death, or worse yet the damnation of your soul?'

There is a way with some humans that they can change colour depending on their mood. I have seen it with my own eyes, yet some cats deny it can be done. I know it is possible, as Tewhit told me there was in his home lands an imp he calls Giragit that turns blue when angry.

Reverend Smythson had the same trick it seemed. He is usually that same dull puce of all the humans here in Fewston, yet today his hairless head was as purple and round as Bramberry Hill when the ling heather is out. And the spit and froth was flying from his mouth so that I thought Hal Robinson might wish he'd taken a little less from the dead so he could sit a few rows back.

Peg, too, I saw could change colour, as her face – which usually had a flush of pink about her cheeks – was as white as Fillie's fur, and even her eyes reddened. But the holy man had not stopped his ravings, and now came the greatest injustice.

'But they cannot hide from the sight of the Lord, nor shall they stay hidden from his judgement. For he has given us the power that we may see them in the cunning that they do. For just as the Lord marked Cain for his sin, so are these foul creatures marked. They have about them devils in the form of beasts who suckle…'

No, I'm sorry. I can't do it. I won't repeat what he said. But let us just say that of the many slanders and shameful libels put against me in my time, this was by far the lowest and most debased.

Fillie had to stop me from jumping out from behind the aumbry door and setting my claws to his purple face. I won't speak of it again, but even now – when I recall it – I feel the fur along my back a-setting up and I find I must pull in my claws.

It was clear that now the folk of Fewston were to be on the lookout for women who kept close to them animals such as cats, frogs and birds. Well even the simplest fool in the far pews knew who he meant, and now all eyes turned to the back walls.

Yet some humans surprise me. Some, I think, might even have made good cats had fortune been kind enough to bless them with that incarnation.

One of these was Henry Graver, and he stood to call out the minister. Those around him sat open-mouthed, save Ellen Fairfax who smiled, then put down her gaze as he looked back at her. That gesture in humans I do understand.

'Forgive me Reverend Smythson,' he said, 'but such talk will do nought but turn us on each other. You speak of witchcraft and all here know of whom you speak, yet there is no cause nor reason but base superstition and folk tales. You are a learned man – you, Mr Fairfax, are a great learned man. Surely reason must be our guiding light, not tales of witches and imps and such fairy stories?'

There was silence for a moment, but for murmurs, then the minister spoke again. His words I do not remember as well. Though he claimed them to be the very epitome of modern thinking – and he quoted some great French thinker as he said was named Bodin. And I wonder if perhaps this is why these Frenchmen's heads explode – for I would find it hard to contain such thoughts in mine.

This scholar, he said, reasoned the accusation of witchcraft was so serious, yet the guilt of a witch so hard to prove, that the proper thing to do is simply to burn anyone accused, as otherwise none would ever be punished. And further, anyone who argued against this must be in league with witches themselves.

Well, that silenced Mr Graver, and no one else spoke up neither, so it was assumed that was the end of that. The minister read some words of his grand old book that spoke of stormy seas and promised no peace for the wicked, and he sent the folk on their way.

Outside the church I saw Mr Graver look again at Ellen, but she kept her eyes in front this time and took her father's hand.

We waited – Fillie and I – behind one of the old dead stones till all the people had made their way back to their great halls, their homes or their hovels. We waited, as we had planned, for Gybbe to bring news of the goings-on at Bess Dickenson's house. And when he came, he came with a great look of worry on his face.

'How goes it?' I asked him, and he answered me straight.

'Not well I fear, for Barghest has slipped his rope and, though I followed him, I lost sight of him as he crossed Fewston bridge.'

With Barghest on the loose, and the light now fading, I feared a little. For Fillie, and for Gybbe. And my concern rose when Fillie herself spoke up.

'Inges – look here,' she cried, and she was by a dead stone set just to the back of where we stood, pushing aside the green that was growing over it. 'Someone has been digging at this place.'

It seemed an ancient stone, as it was thick with moss and its etchings faded and flaked. And sure enough, though the earth was covered with ivy, bramble and brake, under the leaves I could see where a small hollow had been dug and the clay taken away.

'I have heard of this,' said Gybbe. 'My Jennit she said, when she heard of the child Anne, that the devil doll would have been fashioned from the clay of a grave long forgotten.'

Fillie had the notion that we should lay in wait to see if the digger would return, and we thought it a good one as we believed he might be about that night. If murder was to be done again, as we knew it must, he would be back to claim the earth that had worked so well on little Anne.

We hid ourselves in the old yew tree, whose branches are thick and dark so even a cat would not see into them. Then we rolled ourselves in a fresh posy that had been left at poor Anne's new-dug grave; which some persons have since told me was a little insensitive, but we needed to hide our scent.

And we waited. The clouds were thick that night and there was little moonlight, but we could see the furrowed grave from our hidey place well enough. Enough, certainly, that when it happened, we saw him clear as you like.

The first we knew was the sound of feet landing as he jumped the bars of the gate, then the padding of paws on grass. The panting seemed to grow heavier as he moved towards us, a rising excitement to it; as though he were nearing his wicked goal. The branches of our yew tree swayed as a dark brown body brushed hard against it, a giant of a dog, sniffing, hunting – and Fillie's paw went instinctively to mine.

And there, just a short jump in front of us, scenting and scratching at the defiled clay of that ancient grave, was the hater of cats, the beast of Fewston: the slavering hound Barghest.

Inges

The Fairfax Litter

WE HAD watched Barghest a while as he dug at the earth. Though we now had our suspect, we knew that he would not have worked alone. Someone would have fashioned that doll, and someone would have plucked out Quin's eyes so neatly. And that someone would not be this flat-padded, dribble-jawed, droop-eyed furry marionette; that much was clear.

And we would maybe have seen the mastermind of the evil doings, I thought, if not for an unfortunate moment for which I bear no responsibility. Gybbe had wanted to confront the hound there and then, but Fillie was afraid and – from respect for her – I agreed it best to stay hidden. Besides, I reasoned, Barghest must be waiting for his accomplice, and what better chance would there be to catch them both about their deadly business?

Well, we never got the chance as Fillie, in her terror, pulled back to where I – to keep her safe and calm her nerves – had just that second moved myself next to her. She claimed it was me who moved too close to her, but there were witnesses. Anyhow, she moved back into me, I lost my footing, and I tumbled from the tree. I landed as softly and lightly as I could, but that beast's flapping ears pricked up at once at the sound. In an instant I found myself staring into his great maw; the warm stench of dog-breath tickling my whiskers in the most unpleasant way.

I was ready to defend myself, and Fillie, and my claws were unsheathed. He was a hound of prodigious size, with teeth like a row of sharpened war hammers waiting to strike me down, and even I, I must confess, felt a frisson of fear run down my back as I arched it in readiness.

And then, to my great surprise, he simply barked once in my face and ran off. Perhaps, I thought, he had heard of my reputation as a clawsman? Or else he was hurrying to warn his accomplice he had been discovered. Either way, we had lost our chance of discovering his true master, and lost the element of surprise. Now it would be known we were on their trail and they would be ready for us.

Sure enough, the wheels were now in motion that would see the hunters soon become the hunted. And when they came for us, we fell into the killers' trap all too easily.

That trap was set and sprung on a day that had started out so unremarkable that, even though its end is etched upon my mind now, I still struggle to remember the details of all that passed before.

I imagine the sky was grey, as it usually is. I imagine the cows were in the lower pasture, as they always are. I imagine Fillie walking, with her tail in the air, down the narrow road that passes in front of Peg's home – as I always do, even now.

But where my mind sharpens from imagining into reality is at New Hall, the home of the Fairfax litter, and the place we had come – Fillie, Gybbe and I – as we continued our search for the truth. We had spent most days since the events of the graveyard in watching the Fairfax house – certain that it was here the killer meant to strike again. And we – or at least I, who took an interest in such things – had learned much of the family.

There was an unusual bustle about the place this day as there was to be an entertainment for the Fairfax children. The great bull that had been raised in Fairfax's paddock the last 12 months was to be slaughtered, and the barn had been set aside as an arena for the pleasure of viewing the act.

Now I have heard it said by your kind that we cats are cruel in our killing. That we toy with our food and cause great fear and pain before the kill. But this is unfair.

To you – up there on your two legs, with your traps and your bags and your hammers – a mouse may not seem much of a thing to fear. But trust me – and I have the scars to show it – it is a different story when you are a cat, and the little buggers are fighting for their lives. Fear is a great potion for a warrior, and they will nip and scratch and try any means to make you back off and to free themselves.

So, we do what we can to wear them down before the kill. A quick scratch, a bite to the neck, a pad with the claw – all these things weaken the prey until the time comes to strike the final blow. In that way, we protect ourselves from harm. It is, in truth, no different to when Maggie Waite uses an old oilskin to take off the pot from the fire – we are both making sure our dinner doesn't bite us.

It seems to me only humans make sport of their food. I have since seen how great theatres are built just so men can enjoy the cruel death of an animal. And this I do not understand, for none of them will even eat of it afterwards. Knowing what I now know of the human passion for death, it surprises me less. At that time, though, I was a less worldly cat.

All the Fairfax litter were invited to the slaughter, but for Ellen and the eldest boy, William, it was a spectacle they had seen often before, and they had no interest.

Ellen had taken herself to walk down to the river as it was a laundry day, and the sheets were to be wetted and then hung up on the hoarwithy bush to whiten in the sun.

It was a task she seemed to relish, and it always struck me that if Henry Graver had been born a cat he may not be so fond of Ellen, as she would surely have been a dog. She took great delight in obedience and loyalty and the pleasing of her betters, and other such contemptible traits.

William was, in his father's eyes, the inheritor of his genius. He thought himself, and was thought of by Mr Fairfax, as a scholar and a poet. That day, he had taken himself away to the room he called his study — which in truth was simply the room he shared with his young brother Eddie, transformed temporarily by his brother's absence.

He had the use of his father's books, which the other children were forbidden to touch — Eddie by reason of his age, Ellen and Lizzie by reason of their sex.

In my trips to New Hall I had seen Mr Fairfax on occasion through the west window as he cast a look of fatherly pride on discovering the bookcase disturbed and that his child had taken down Holinshed's Chronicles, or perhaps annotated an attempted translation on Astronomia Nova.

And I wondered if that pride would hold had he known that it was young Lizzie who had done both those things. Or that it was she who righted the hexameter in William's poem on Venus and Adonis, and that William had given her a half penny to keep that to herself.

Either way, William was the great favourite and even Eddie lived in his shadow, despite himself having all the qualities that his father seemed to value tucked neatly between his legs

Ellen I was fond of, as she had a love for cats and treated them well. William I could take or leave, he was rarely out of the house, so I had no great opinion of him. Eddie was well loved by his sister Lizzie, but I have never quite forgiven him for throwing beech nuts at me when he spotted me at the back door one evening. He chased me around the square of grass that made a garden, and I was forced to take refuge in a tree that lacked for lower branches and so made for an undignified descent that was witnessed by both Fillie and Gybbe.

Lizzie, though, was the best of the litter to my mind. She was quick of thought and not afraid to speak her mind, even though that was seen as the worst sin one of her kind could commit short of murder or witchcraft. And she had a way with cats that few humans do.

Inges

I'm no great lover of human company, but some cats seem to crave it. Gybbe was one of those, yet he was shy and afraid of those he did not know. But Lizzie, it seemed, was learned not only in the old tongues of humans but had some of the language of the cat about her and would blink and set down so as to let Gybbe know she meant no harm. He would then approach, cautious at first, before dropping to his side and flipping over to show his belly as a sign of trust. Not my kind of behaviour, you know, but I respected Lizzie for her way with Gybbe.

She would sometimes leave out titbits for us to eat – as she had seen us about the place and may have thought us wild and hungry. Eventually, when the days were hot and her window was ajar, we were able to enter the house where she would shelter us and keep us from sight – whether for our safety, or for her father's dislike of cats, we weren't quite sure. But it gave us a place to stay hidden while we kept watch for any dark deeds, and I first understood just how much the softness of a human bed could vary between the house of a rich man and that of a poor widow.

And so it was we were about early that morning and rose as Lizzie did. The bull was to be slaughtered after breakfast and one of Fairfax's men was sent to bring it from the paddock. John Spence, the butcher who would sometimes chase me off from his house front when I tried to pick at an offcut that would otherwise be waste, was waiting at the barn when the family arrived. I hid myself away in the hollow of the great hay mow that filled the back of the barn, and on top of which Lizzie and her brother Eddie had settled to watch the proceedings.

The bull was pulling at the rope about its neck and I could see it was much afraid, as I suspect – like me – it could smell the blood around butcher Spence's apron, even though he must have tried hard to scrub it before coming up to the house.

This poor bull was a mute animal – no imp, and I know not whether imps take the form of bulls, though I've never met one, so I think not.

Yet it needed no words to express its terror, and Mr Fairfax, the butcher and some other men there pushed and pulled at the creature as it bellowed and snorted. The men struggled to tie the frightened beeve to a stake for its throat to be cut, and it began to froth at the mouth and toss its head about wildly.

Lizzie leaned forward and called out to calm the beast and, in that second, from behind her came a great whoosh of wings that caught her about the head and down she fell – from the full height of the mow and onto the stone of the barn floor below. Still as the dead on the hard ground.

'My Lizzie – what has been done!' cried Mr Fairfax, and I thought his heart would break there and then as, to all the world, she was surely dead.

John Spence grabbed at the bucket of water that had been put aside to wash the blood and he dipped his rag in it to press against her head. A stream of red ran from it as he wrang at it and dunked again.

We dare not set foot outside the mow, but we could see – and so now could Fairfax – circling the roof of the barn: the winged assassin who had struck down little Lizzie. A golden bird, no bigger than a crow.

'Tewhit. What has he done?' Gybbe whispered. But I stopped him. Sure enough it had the look of Tewhit – but the flight was wrong. I had seen him fly close up when the unfortunate finch incident occurred – and this was not his flight, though someone had gone to great trouble to find a bird that had the look of Tewhit. And Gybbe was not the only one fooled.

'That bird – I've seen it before. That's the one that Widow Thorpe keeps!' butcher Spence called.

'I think you're right,' said another of the men there. 'She surely must have sent it. I knew she wasn't right.'

But Mr Fairfax gave attention only to his daughter, who he now held – his eyes filled with water that ran down his cheeks. And in a sudden Lizzie gave a little cough and opened her eyes, and the tears flowed out like I've never seen from a man before.

'Oh my daughter, God be praised, you live!' He called to his men. 'Be quick, take her to the house, put her to bed. Someone call the physick.'

Inges

Mrs Fairfax and Ellen had heard the commotion as the men brought her up to the house – and we kept close behind but out of sight. They made a great fuss of her and cursed the name of poor Tewhit when Spence maligned him.

Gybbe and I made our way ahead of them to the room of Lizzie, as her window was still ajar, and hid ourselves under her bed so we could hear more of what was to be regarding Tewhit.

Fillie made her way back to Timble to warn Tewhit – as we feared that there might be calls for revenge upon him, for there was much anger among the men there.

From our hiding place, Gybbe and I heard the talk of the Fairfaxes on the meaning of Tewhit's action, and Mr Fairfax said that there was a curse upon his family and that 'they' would not rest until all were dead, to which Mrs Fairfax cried and told him that she did not think anyone wished them ill.

Who 'they' were he was not clear on – though both Gybbe and I looked at each other with the surety that we knew who he meant.

It was then the more surprise that Mrs Fairfax decided to send Ellen to my home – to Maggie and her poultices for the great bruise that now rounded out the forehead of poor Lizzie. Mr Fairfax protested, yet his wife said Maggie had done them much good and it was not her fault what happened to little Anne. I felt that, in matters of care of the children, Mrs Fairfax held the reins – if in nothing else.

And so Ellen was sent and presently returned with the poultice and a powder that was made into a draught to ease Lizzie into a peaceful sleep.

Mr Fairfax was the last to leave, and gently kissed Lizzie on her forehead before saying goodnight. We waited as he stood by the door, for now would be the time to make our own way to our beds and away from the house. But then something most unfortunate happened, that perhaps I should have considered.

'Ah Lizzie – you will catch your death with the window open,' Mr Fairfax whispered to her – and to our alarm he returned to pull down at the shutters that would keep out the night air, and trap us inside.

'We'll have to stay the night and hope Lizzie wakes before the household,' said I after the bedroom door was shut.

Gybbe agreed that would be better than to try the door, which would perhaps open but with a noise that would wake those in the other rooms.

And so we settled in for the night, at Lizzie's feet where we had sometimes slept before and where it was warmest.

And there we slept peacefully until nearly dawn, when we found that the whole household had awakened – to screams from Ellen's room.

We were trapped in with Lizzie, who was now slowly waking from her deep sleep. From through the wall we could hear muffled words of a tale we could scarcely believe.

'Daddy – help me. The witches!' came the scream, and we heard Mr Fairfax hush Ellen to calm and explain all that had happened.

'They mean to kill me Daddy – the cat told me.'

'Hush now darling, it was a bad dream.'

'No Daddy, it wasn't a dream. A cat came in here and it told me – it said that the witches had cursed me and that I was to be taken by the devil himself as a bride and pass beyond this world. He said if not they would kill me – and Lizzie and Eddie and William – as they killed Anne.'

There was silence for a minute. Then Mr Fairfax asked just what I was wondering too: 'Who are they?'

'The witches,' there was a long sniff. 'The cat told me they are Jennit Dibble and Widow Thorpe.'

Gybbe looked at me in horror.

'And Maggie Waite and her daughter Peg.'

And now he would have seen the shock on my face as she recounted an incident I knew could not be.

'Maggie gave me a penny change for the poultice, and the cat told me. He said the penny was cursed and I had touched it and now I must be taken.'

Mr Fairfax roared: 'I will burn it. Destroy it with brimstone and grind it to dust. Curse that woman, curse those witches – they must pay. They must be made to pay!'

I looked at Gybbe and gestured to the door – maybe in the confusion and anger we could slip out. But right at that moment our attention was caught by a new sound – a tapping at the window. We turned to look and there, pecking at the glass, was that great feathery fool Tewhit.

'Tewhit – what are you doing?' I hissed. 'Get away from here.' But the silly bird had clearly come in some fantasy to clear his name and kept at tapping. Which was the end for our escape plans, for the sound aroused Lizzie's sleepy attention and now she turned and saw at the window the bird she thought had nearly taken her life.

'Help! The bird. It's come to get me. Help me!'

The noise rattled and hummed at our ears and the door sprang open, revealing an unfortunate scene to the Fairfaxes: Lizzie sat against her bed head with her legs pulled to her chin; Tewhit's head tilted at the window with his great gormless face and blood red eyes; Gybbe halfway up the curtains; and me sat at the end of Lizzie's bed with my paws upon the bed knob, trying to look a bird in the eye.

We were caught red-handed and I thought that the worst had happened, yet there was more, and we had not even come close to our nadir, it seemed.

'Oh my Lord preserve us. It's him.' It was Ellen, her face as white as the long nightdress that covered her.

'Him?' her father frowned.

'The cat,' she was screaming now, 'the cat who came to my room and told me of the witches and the curse. That is him, there on Lizzie's bed.'

And she was pointing at me.

Confession

QUITE HOW Gybbe and I made our escape from the room I do not fully recollect. It was something of a blur.

How I remember it best was that Lizzie threw her pillow at the window where Tewhit – oblivious to the chaos in the room – was still a-pecking. This caused him to fly up and Ellen to begin her screaming again.

Mrs Fairfax had about her a long sash with which she seemed determined to whip down old Gybbe from the curtains. Mr Fairfax was torn between comforting his wailing children and taking hold of me, so that I slipped through his legs and dashed down the turning stairs to the front door of that house. My way was still barred and now the housemaid saw me, and she too began her screaming and chased me into the kitchen, where she took to hurling whatever instruments she could lay her hands on in my direction.

By chance, a great copper pot she had hurled missed me by a whisker length, as I ran along the worktop, and shattered the window of the kitchen. I leapt through it and ran as fast as I might, back through the woods toward Timble. I arrived back at Peg's house with the sun just rising, and slipped under the door to find my place by the hearth, that still had some glow of last night's fire about it. And there I waited – my mind now full of dread of what had become of Gybbe and of what must now await poor Peg.

My first fear was soon assuaged, as Gybbe strolled in, sure as you like, to tell me that he too had got away. It seemed Mrs Fairfax had dislodged him from the curtains just enough that he then climbed her nightdress and that, in terror, she tore it off and threw it, and him, through the bedroom window.

Of Tewhit there was no sign, but even his hollow bird head must have picked up the danger he was in, and it seemed he had made his escape to who knows where.

Now Gybbe and I turned our thoughts to our borrowed souls. Both Jennit and Peg were accused by Ellen of witchcraft, and the shadows of the noose or the stake hung over us.

'There cannot be cause enough for a hanging from some soft girl's dream,' Gybbe said, though it seemed he was trying to convince himself as much as he was me.

'Perhaps,' said I, 'yet she accused me direct, and it is known I am Peg's cat.'

It rattled at my head that Ellen had been so sure that it was me she had seen. I did think for a moment could she be the one who worked with Barghest? But I knew her to be no killer and that she loved her sisters dearly. She did not have the art to make a play of something like that.

Then I thought that if the killers had gone to such trouble to find a false Tewhit, then they could have done the same to me. But to talk as that one did to Ellen, any cat must be an imp, and in league with Barghest; and that made less sense still. And, though I say it myself, no cat can look like me. I am what you might call striking: white with black spots, a black patch above one eye. Most notable of all – that same eye is blue, while the other is black. There are not many cats that look like me.

'We cannot wait here, nor at my home, you know that, Inges,' Gybbe said, and I did know – for they would surely soon come knocking to accuse our people, and we must be out of sight when they did.

Inges

We made our way to the old yew tree by the church, where we had uncovered Barghest's digging. There we had agreed to meet Fillie, before we had been caught by the closed window, but we were a whole night late now and she was not there.

And so we took ourselves to a place we knew would at least give us shelter until we could decide our next move. The crypt of the church can be accessed by a grate that is set into its northern side, just behind a briar bush.

The place is cold and wet, and rarely visited, and it has a good supply of mice and rats that like to pick at the bones and the rags of the dead that are still laid there from time to time if their family holds a key.

It would do for now. And we would make our way under cover of the bushes and briars to keep our eyes and ears on the fate of our souls as best we could.

As fortune would have it, it soon turned out to be the best of all vantage points for that: for the accused women, fearing for their safety, took themselves later that same day to the church to make a plea to Reverend Smythson.

Maggie and Peg came, their dresses pressed by the fire I could see, as they had pushed in the deep creases that would not fold out and it looked like they wore the leaves of a well-loved book.

Widow Thorpe was there too, though her mother Jennit was not with her. This troubled Gybbe greatly, and I was not surprised at this, as she was much troubled with age and I feared her mind and body would not stand the strain of accusation.

With her, instead, widow Thorpe brought bold Henry Graver, who it seemed had not been cowed by Smythson's admonishment and dared still to trust reason. Though he would have known fear was that virtue's greatest enemy and that there was, in those times, much fear in the parish.

We had made our way into the chancel and beneath the heavy table they called the altar, tucked behind its drapery so as to see the proceedings. Peg and the widow were upon their knees at the feet of the vicar, who was making some play with the candles so as not to look upon them.

Maggie stood against the wall, her arms folded; a gesture I had seen in her before when a customer had accused her of making bad medicine or pocketing their change.

Mr Graver spoke first. 'Reverend, these women have implored me to talk again with you. They fear for their lives against the unjust accusations made upon them and believe only you have the ears of the parish – and of Mr Fairfax – enough to make them heard.'

The vicar looked up at this now, and I thought I saw a sadness in his eyes. 'Mr Graver, the accusations are grave, and I cannot in good faith overlook the seriousness of them. Offence has been done to one of the best men of our parish, and accusation made by the same. This is a matter, I fear, that must be decided by higher authority.'

Mr Graver shook his head. 'They are accused on the dream of a... of that unfortunate young lady. Her baby sister recently dead, her other that day feared, for a while, the same. Is it any wonder that her dreams are full of devils and omens and talking cats? We cannot prosecute witchcraft on such lurid tales.'

Reverend Smythson sighed. 'Indeed, you may be right Mr Graver. An hysterical girl, much troubled by events, is not a reliable witness.'

Mr Graver nodded and Peg looked up hopefully at him.

'Unfortunately,' the vicar continued, 'she is not the only witness, nor the worst offended.'

Peg now looked in panic at her mother who shook her head with a look of cold anger. Mr Graver questioned the meaning of this, but the vicar simply raised his hand to hold him there as he stepped from the chancel and gestured at the door of the sacristy to the side. Out from that little cubby room of his stepped young Maud Jeffray, her lip a-tremble and her hand clasped in that of her father.

Gybbe shifted awkwardly beneath the altar curtain and his tail, which was swinging greatly, pushed at it so that it ruffled for a second. I caught sight of Maggie who, it seemed, must have seen the movement, as she looked down curiously to where we crouched. I gave Gybbe one of my fiercest stares, and he dropped his eyes in apology.

Inges

It seemed, thankfully, that no others had seen it as they were now transfixed by the sight of the tearful little girl.

'Do you want to tell Mr Graver what you told me and your daddy, Maud?' The vicar poured out his words soft as honey. Maud, a scrappy little girl with a face as round and freckled as a wren's egg, looked at her father pleadingly and he nodded to her to speak.

'Tell him what you told me, darling. About the bad cat,' John Jeffray told her, and my claws extended.

Her voice shook as she spoke. 'There was a cat and a lady.'

'A lady?' Reverend Smythson asked in a way that suggested this was a new part of whatever tale the girl may have rehearsed. 'What sort of lady? Do you mean one of these women here?'

She shook her head. 'A pretty lady, sir, with golden hair. She had a cat with her, and the cat spoke to me. It made me much afraid.' She started to sob, and her father knelt down and put his hand to her back until she could speak again.

'And what did this cat say, dear?' Reverend Smythson spoke to Maud but looked at the father, who shook his head.

'He said that I was to fetch a cane for him. That I should give the cane to Ellen the next time we are at the river to wash, and that it would curse her and cause her to die. He told me if I didn't do it, then Satan himself would come and drag me down to the depths of Hell, where I would be eaten by imps.'

Now the sobbing really took hold, and it was a good five minutes before she could speak again.

I gestured to Gybbe that he should leave – back to the crypt and out the grate. He would know that he must find Fillie, and Tewhit if he could, for I now had great fear not just for Peg and the women but for all the animals that were known to associate with them.

Finally, Maud's chest slowed its heaving and the vicar asked if she could continue. She nodded.

'And what did you say to the cat, Maud?'

'I said "no, you must go back to Hell with your master for I believe in the Lord that is our God and he will protect me from evil so as you have no power over me".'

The Reverend smiled at these words. 'And then what happened?'

'Well, he turned his tail and hissed at me, and he told me that a witch of Fewston was his mistress as well as Satan his master, and that this witch would curse me so that my limbs would rot, and my eyes all fall out.'

I expected her to sob again at this point, but it seemed her well had now run dry.

Smythson put his arm on Maud's shoulder and gently turned her to face the women. 'Is the one he named as witch among those here, Maud?'

The women looked at each other and I saw Peg close her eyes as if she could not bear to see hope depart.

'Yes sir. She is there. She is Peg Waite.'

'And the cat?'

'He was her cat, sir.'

'Are you sure of that, dear.'

'Yes sir – I recognised him, sir. A most distinctive cat, all white with black marks and curious eyes – one of black and one of blue. That cat what belongs to Peg, sir. He boasted his name was Inges and that he was the greatest of imps and most favoured of Satan.'

'And the pretty lady?' Mr Graver now spoke, and John Jeffray stood from his daughter's side to face him. Maud shook her head.

'I think we've put you through enough, dear,' Rev Smythson said softly. 'Thank you so much for your help, your father will take you home now. But keep your faith in Christ, child, and no imp nor witch can harm you.'

Well, I thought, I knew of one imp who would happily give her a scratch on that freckled nose. I had never heard such calumny and untruth in my life. I am distinctive, granted. And there may be those, who know no better, who think me the greatest imp, but I would never make such a boast myself. Nor harm a young girl, unprovoked, I should add.

It was clear now that someone was trying to make a case against the cunning women of Fewston and their imps besides. And the Rev Smythson, if he were not one of them himself, was certainly ready to play into their hands.

Inges

'The women must be tried. The evidence is too strong now and the risk, if we are to leave them in our midst, too great for the children of Fewston,' he said. Peg gave out a great wail as her mother moved to her side and held her, all the while her eyes burning at the vicar.

Mr Graver was silent for a moment, then nodded. 'They must be given fair trial at the Assizes and I will speak for them.' His voice dropped, and he now spoke to Rev Smythson as if to a friend. 'Nicholas – you know these women. You know they would no more harm a baby or a little girl than they would their own children or mothers. If they are accused so, you must speak for them when the time comes.'

Rev Smythson shook his head, then his face for a moment softened. 'Henry, you are a man who sees the best in all, and I wish sometimes I had your faith in man as I have mine in the Lord. The law will decide upon their guilt and we must have faith in the process of law, as it is conducted under unfailing God, who is the judge of all.'

He put his hand upon the shoulder of Mr Graver, who dropped his head in response. Henry Graver spoke to the women to stand and leave the church with him.

That they would be taken to York Castle now to await trial was certain, and that they would be condemned more certain still. And any forlorn hope they may be acquitted now vanished at what happened next.

The poor women were barely at the church door when there came a knocking upon it, although it was open already. And there at the door stood Jennit Dibble, banging at it with her hazel stick.

Widow Thorpe, seeing her mother there, ran to her side and put her arms about her, at which Jennit looked about her, saying: 'Has anyone seen Margaret. That naughty girl is meant to be at home now, where is she.'

Widow Thorpe took her mother's face in her hands and cried that it was her, her Margaret, and that she should be home herself, not walking about alone in such a state. But Jennit shook her head free and stepped forward as surely as her old legs were able.

'I must see the Reverend Father; my Margaret has been a wicked girl.'

Henry Graver went to help her as she hobbled towards the chancery, but she put him aside with a feeble shove and called out to Rev Smythson. 'You there – I must see you. I have to make my confession.'

Smythson smiled uncomfortably. 'We have no use of confession here lady – that is between you and the Lord, or to those you have wronged. I have no power to forgive.'

'Well, I have wronged you, so you will do,' she said as firmly as she could.

'Speak then Jennit – let it be heard.'

Well then she spoke and not I, nor Peg nor Maggie nor, most of all, Jennit's daughter could believe that she spoke of such things. She was, she confessed, a witch of the worst kind, and her Gybbe was an imp that would feed on her and dance with her, and all their kind, to Satan's tune up at Timble Gill.

She named Peg, and Maggie and her daughter and said they too would dance with the Devil and do such things as are not fit to put down here. And then, to my great surprise, she named also poor Mother Fletcher and even Mrs Dickenson – and it seemed if Barghest had a part in all this then his treachery was complete, as his own soul would now surely die.

What madness I was seeing I could not comprehend. Yet, before the end came, I would see that what I thought lunacy now was but a simple head-cold before the great fever of insanity that would take hold and shake apart the body of reason and justice.

Even the Rev Smythson, it seemed, was shaken and he put his hand upon a pew end to steady himself. 'Take them away!' he cried. 'Take them from my sight, from this sacred place that they despoil. Get out!'

Henry Graver put his arm on Jennit's shoulder and pleaded to Smythson, 'Nicholas, can't you see – she is confused and old. Someone has put her up to this, exploited her. She does not even recognise her own daughter's face, yet her tale is full of rehearsed detail. It's not believable.'

Inges

'Just take her out Henry, out of my sight.'

Mr Graver put his arm to lift Jennit, who now asked why the vicar was shouting and if he was her husband, and he led her and her fellow 'witches' from the church. As Henry moved to close the door, he looked back darkly at Rev Smythson, who paced the stone floor of the aisle.

The vicar looked to him for a second and then called out. 'And make sure you put those foul beasts to death. Find that damned cat Inges and drown him in The Tarn. Find them all and kill them on sight – let all the parish know they must die!'

Lord Pumpkin

I SPOKE of Hal Robinson and his work with the dead of London, but now I should tell you more of him, for we were to have dealings with his great house at Swinsty Hall, and that is a place of ghosts and legends.

Yet of all the fancy tales of that grim pile, one I know to be true. That of the beast that patrols its grounds – a merciless ball of teeth, claws and ginger fur. The one they call Lord Pumpkin.

If you listen to the silly gossip of the cats around Fewston you may have heard tales of my prowess with the claw, and my reputation as a cat who can hold his own as much with the toms as he does with the queens. Cats are given to spin such stories, but it is true that I have had my fair share of times when I needed to stand my ground, and I dare say I held firm when required.

But even I must dip my head to one in that field. Lord Pumpkin is no imp, he is a simple cat – slow of wit, big of head and prone to licking himself in a most undignified manner, even in the best of company.

However, in one regard he is impressive. His great paws are the size of teasel heads, his eyes burn with copper fire and, even covered in thick orange fur, his sturdy limbs and broad chest impress as those of a cat who need not spray his borders to let you know that he is Lord of Swinsty. Of all the cats I knew, of all the places I could go, Lord Pumpkin and Swinsty Hall were among the few that I might hesitate to visit.

And yet, in our dark days, it was to Swinsty I was now heading, with Gybbe, Fillie, Tewhit, and Barbara – the frog imp of Mother Fletcher – who we had come to know since the taking of her soul.

The accused women had been imprisoned, we heard, at the Castle in York. It is not a place I have seen, but I am told by those that have that it barely deserved the name and is but a miserable, dank tower set on a muddy heap, surrounded by some crumbling buildings into which those awaiting trial or execution are thrown.

Its walls are half gone from the habit of the recent keeper there of selling off the stones in secret – at least until the locals spotted the holes and beat his arse around town with a barrel stave. Now the prisoners are closed in with great wooden beams that let through the rain and the cold and the wind. It is no place for old women, and no place for Peg.

We needed to find out how they fared there. Gybbe, in particular, worried for his soul as she grew older and weaker daily even before her taking. I thought perhaps, if we could hear from Maggie, she might let us know what they would need to keep her and the others well, and that we could fetch that for them.

I have learned that prison is a terrible place. There is nothing like it in the world of imps. We deal justice swiftly and decisively, and when death is needed it comes in an instant.

In prison, justice is more often found lagging wheezily behind Death, who races ahead in his greed to claim what might not even by rights be his.

As often as a villain is put to the scaffold, an innocent accused of some slight crime will be consumed by the prison fever and die; not hanging high from a rope, but soaked in their own filth down upon a cold, wet floor.

If you have money and connection, you may pay the jailer to provide some comfort; food that is not rotten, straw to make a bed. And then perhaps you may make it to the scaffold, or else – if you are so well connected – buy yourself out.

But Maggie and Peg, and the others? Their only connection was with us imps, and we had no money to buy their lives. So instead we must bring what we could: our wisdom and cunning.

To get to York was the problem. Tewhit knew the way and offered to fly. His enthusiasm, as ever, outweighed his wit as he is a great golden bird who would be spotted from Harrogate, and surely netted and no doubt roasted in a pie. We needed stealth if we were to get in and out.

Fillie was not known, but she had no soul now and we could not risk her. Gybbe and I were marked as outlaws and would barely make it out of Fewston alive.

Besides, the journey was too long and too full of risk. The only hope was to go as the humans do – by the coach road – and do so unnoticed. And so, that is where Barbara came in.

All the women who had been taken had their imps. It is no surprise, as they were all well-versed in the healing ways and so were good choices for those who value long life.

For all those now in gaol, their imps stood accused alongside them. All but one. Barbara.

I have never had much dealings with frogs. I half-heartedly chase them sometimes, but they are tricksy and fond of water, which I very much am not. So, I knew nothing of Barbara – and neither, it turned out to our great fortune, did anyone else.

She was one of those imps we call shadows. Whether for fear, or shyness, or for reasons of living space (a burrower or a water beast would not find a house to their liking) some imps have nothing to do with their souls beyond the binding. They will stay close by, as you should, but will not share a house or even make themselves known. Barbara was a shadow imp.

It is possible Mother Fletcher knew nothing at all of her and would be greatly surprised when she turned up at the prison. That meant that none of the guards would suspect a thing, and she might slip in and out easily. So it was decided, Barbara would be the one to go to York.

She had come to us seeking help when her soul was taken, and I think was greatly surprised that we now put our trust in her. For she was a kind and gentle frog, but one who thought much higher of other folk than she was ever able to think of herself.

'I'm not sure I can do this you know, it's a very big adventure for one such as me,' she had told me. 'I've never been beyond The Tarn before, except out on the banks when the ferns are grown.' And to that I said I had the greatest faith in her or else I would not have asked.

'Well,' she had said, 'if one such as you thinks I can do it, then maybe I can. I shall try my very, very best not to let you down.'

I admired her spirit, but I could see my doubts reflected in the azure blue of Fillie's eyes as she gestured me to join her.

'Inges – let me go,' she whispered. 'Barbara means well, but this is too much for her and you know it. I am unknown too. To the humans I am Anne's cat and a victim also, they think, of those they call witches. It should be me.'

Well, that was not something I would let happen. Not only as Fillie had lost her soul, and so was at more risk than any of us, but because only Barbara could hope to get in and out unnoticed.

'Fillie,' I said, 'you are brave no doubt, but also you are beautiful.'

Well, she made a show of not accepting that, but I caught the way her eyes held mine and blinked. However, much as I enjoyed charming her, that was not my point at this time.

'I mean, Fillie, that you are too beautiful. You are snow white with eyes like sapphires – and every cat between here and York would take note of you, and so too the guards. A cat such as you belongs in a fine house, at least such as the Fairfaxes, not in some stinking prison. You would be found out at once.'

She agreed, though reluctantly and modestly. And so it was set: we would get Barbara aboard the York-bound cart that passes each morning from Skipton. Yet to get to that we would need to travel a good distance to the pass at Blubberhouses – and with the whole of Fewston on the lookout for us, and it being too great a distance for a lone frog to travel, we would need a lift from somewhere closer to home.

The only place we knew of where we could catch such a ride unseen was down through the woods to that place of great, grey gables and dark solitude: Swinsty Hall. There we would find a horse that is known to Tewhit and is ridden each Monday to Blubberhouses by Hal Robinson's man, when he takes all correspondence for his master to and from the York cart. We would need to make our way into the grounds and into the stable in time to smuggle Barbara into the saddle bag and then make our way back out again unseen.

The hall is not that old, certainly not as old as some of the great houses in this part of the world. Yet in a short time it has become a place of mystery and legend that would put even old John O'Gaunt's Castle to shame.

The house is the finest in the valley – great tall gables filled with windows all of glass, and stone mullions tall as a man. The chimneys raise their smoke high up in the air so that the tops can be seen above the trees that otherwise hide all the house from any view.

No true road leads there, not even a trackway for laden horses, and no quarry stands near. Yet this great house had seemingly appeared here from thin air – as though transported by some wizard or sorcerer from far across the valley.

The owning of it by Mr Robinson too came with a dark tale, told often at the inn when any new traveller stops the night and has had more than they should of Mr Tanner's ale.

Young Hal, it is said, had left Fewston as a poor weaver many years ago and looked to London to make his fortune. As it happened, he arrived in London at the same time as the great plague that laid low so many of its people of both the lowest and highest birth. And Hal, who was apprenticed there to a clothsman in Smithfield, was sent to call with his wares at one of the better houses to the north of the city. On arrival he found the house awry, and no rattling at the doors or window could raise a soul. And no wonder for all – master and servant – lay dead from the pestilence.

Hal entered that house of death, and there he found – unneeded now by its owner – a great fortune in gold and silver, which he wrapped in the length of cloth he carried and took for himself.

For the next weeks he searched the city for those houses now empty – either from the death of their inhabitants or else from them fleeing the city in terror at the unseen miasma. And so he took what they left behind and returned at last to Fewston, a wealthy man.

Yet word of his ways had reached the village, and none would deal with him. Not for any thought on his method of enrichment, but for fear of touching the gold that they thought must carry the death with it.

Hal, it is said, then took the gold to wash at Greenwell Spring, that is at the back of the hall – and there first saw that building. A place that would fit a man of his new-found status, yet keep him secure away from jealous eyes or the view of those that might have thought their claim on his wealth greater than his own. And so, with his ill-gotten gold, he made purchase of it and hid himself there ever since.

Of course, there are others who say such a tale is nonsense and that the hall became his through default of a loan – but the darker tale stuck best so that few people ever visited, and it would be a safe place for us to show our faces.

Safe, that is, from all but Lord Pumpkin.

We had walked just a little way into the dark woods that surround the hall when Tewhit first alerted us to his presence. He had taken a position high up on top of one of the tall poplar trees that shield the stables on the south side of the big house.

He gave his call – a sweet chirp and then a throaty squawk. Though perhaps I was hard on him sometimes, Tewhit did have the most beautiful call and, though I knew it was a warning of danger, still it lifted my spirits a little.

The plan was this. Barbara would sit on Gybbe's back, watched by Fillie, while I would scout the perimeter of their path and, if needed, hold off Lord Pumpkin long enough for them to make it to the stable. Tewhit would warn again if Pumpkin was near.

That was the plan at least, but like many in such adventures, it fell apart almost as soon as it began. For Tewhit, alas, was quite as witless as I had thought him and more short-sighted still. He had been singing his fine song to warn us of a patch of orange hawkweed growing close by the woodland path.

The real Lord Pumpkin, I now found, was standing directly in front of me, his eyes burning into mine and his back risen so that he appeared even more vast than he already was.

'Well, Inges,' I thought to myself, 'you have had a good run and now if you must give your life it will not be cheaply.' And I readied myself for his move, my claws now loosed from their sheaths ready to take blood for any I must give. And he moved towards me and then, quite unexpectedly, past me.

I stood there for a moment and must have looked quite foolish as I had my back arched and my claws at the ready staring into the space that had once been filled by Pumpkin. He, on the other hand, was staring at something quite different. There, behind me, stood Fillie – and right at that moment I thought I might rather fight ten Lord Pumpkins than witness the display that had caught his eye.

My Fillie had dropped her front paws and was rubbing her cheeks in the most suggestive fashion against a tree stump, her tail raised, as she treaded her rear paws to the back – all the while calling out in the softest fashion to Pumpkin.

I did not know which way to look. I knew that this was all display for my benefit – for the plan. At least I thought I knew that. But it was enough to get the blood up of any tom worthy of the name and had proved too much for Pumpkin – and also, I thought for a moment, for me.

Fillie snapped me from my daze with a sharp look and nod towards the trees where Gybbe and Barbara hid, and I made my move – nearly running into a tree as I glanced back over my shoulder to where Pumpkin was now moving far too close to her for my comfort.

'Come on – be quick,' I called to Gybbe, and as Barbara clung tighter we raced through the leafy forest floor to where the trees opened on a hard gravel yard. Behind me, from the woods, I heard Fillie cry out and my heart raced so I thought it would burst.

There was the stable in front of us, and now walking into the stable yard was Robinson's man. He saw us and for a moment I thought the game was up. But clearly, tucked away in the deep woods, word had not yet reached Swinsty Hall of our outlaw status and he merely glanced at us as if to wonder where we had come from, then carried on to open the stable door.

By now my turbulent thoughts would not leave me alone. They ran upon ideas of Fillie and Pumpkin and I feared greatly for her safety. 'Gybbe,' I said, 'take Barbara and get her into that saddle bag – then come and find me.'

Well, he was most annoyed at my leaving, and called me out for abandoning him over base jealousy. He could not understand that I simply have a protective spirit when it comes to my friends and would never leave them in danger.

I wished Barbara luck then turned toward the trees, when out of the shadows I saw the flash of white as Fillie tore from the undergrowth.

'Run Inges, Gybbe – he's very angry,' she cried, and I could see a deep cut upon her nose where Lord Pumpkin must have struck in his frustration at her ruse. Behind her came thundering a great storm of orange fury.

Gybbe leapt onto the bar of the horse's stall, but too close to the stable man who took a swing at him with his crop, and Barbara fell from his back into the straw bedding.

For a moment I thought she might be trampled – but the horse moved forward a step and she had just time to hop away from its reach.

Pumpkin was upon us now and I thought would take us for certain, but in that moment Tewhit did quite the bravest thing I had ever seen a bird do, and I happily forgave his poor eyesight and judgement from earlier.

He flew at the head of Pumpkin, who swung wildly at him – a flash of orange and gold, the flapping of wings and spitting of anger. But it was enough for us to make our escape. We were away and now Tewhit disengaged. But to our horror, instead of following our disappearing trail into the woods, Pumpkin turned to Barbara who was now on the floor of the stable as the horse began to walk out.

Inges

Pumpkin must have realised she was with us, for he turned all his fury towards her and was on her in a second. It seemed she would be dinner for the ginger demon, but as his fierce claws came down she launched herself with all the force her legs could muster and caught hold of the horse's swinging tail just as it started to break into a steady trot.

We watched as she climbed the tail, and up along the horse's back, Pumpkin swiping wildly at the air in frustration as she slipped quietly down into the saddle bag.

We had put good ground between ourselves and Lord Pumpkin and were now at the boundary wall, with the pastures of Timble spread out before us marking the end of the beast's territory.

'Thank you Gybbe,' I said, 'and thank you, Fillie.' She blinked, and we walked along a short while in silence, until I could hold my thoughts no more. 'Can I ask, did you…'

'Shut up Inges!' she said, 'I don't wish to speak of it again. I did that for Barbara, not for you. I did that for the mission, and I don't want to ever speak of it again, do you hear?'

I dropped my head in apology and she walked off along the wall with Gybbe, who gave me a look I probably deserved.

'And no,' she said, turning back suddenly, 'I didn't, and if I had it would have been my business not yours.'

We walked on, keeping that little distance between us, until we reached the place where the road runs on to Blubberhouses. At that moment the horse – who must have stopped again within the estate as he now carried more bags than before – rode by.

We stopped and watched and, as he passed, saw a small grey-green head pop up from one of the bags and a little webbed foot raised in greeting.

'I did it everyone! I really did it,' Barbara croaked.

I blinked my eyes fondly and I tilted my head in salute, then looked at Fillie. She looked back sternly for a moment, then her blue eyes twinkled, and her tail swished in the way you might say a cat smiles.

Inges

Timble Gill

OF THE many absurdities in that tale of the imps and cunning women and our dealings with the Devil, one could easily be dismissed by anyone who had ever visited Timble Gill.

Jennit, in her addled mind, had seen us dance together in the gill with Satan himself. Well, if we had, then surely we must have done it atop brooms in the air, as the old wives' tales say. For one imp alone would have trouble finding space to dance between the narrow walls of that wooded glen.

There is no track through the gill, other than the crumbling, inconsistent banks of the beck as it winds through the trees and the weeds that grow thick around it at this time of year; tumbling over cobbles and black boulders that clump like the petrified droppings of some monstrous sheep.

The gill is barely wider than the garden at New Hall at its greatest extent, close by where it rises to a sharp, dark cliff, hung with oak, that stands to its north.

There is little need for anyone to visit this place, save to gather the timber for which the Bridle Track was carved many years ago, and that was a winter's job.

For that reason, it was now to be our home. Fillie took us where she knew a place we might be safe, a quiet refuge she said her mother had taken when she brought her first into this world. There beneath the black shale face and hanging ferns, set back from the path and obscured by ash leaves and summer nettles – a hollow that would be called a cave if it was just a little less shallow and a little more deep.

Gybbe, Fillie, Tewhit and I – three of us hunted and one deprived of her soul. We would be mostly dry there, and warm enough by day at that time. At night we would huddle – all save Tewhit who felt safer in a high oak than caught between three cats whose twitching dreams often turned to chasing.

It would be a fortnight at least before Barbara made it back. If she made it back. We would meet the rider again from the first coach after the next full moon and find out then. Until that time, this was to be our home.

Out in the gill the food is plentiful, but so is its cover. Voles, mice and shrew nip and dive into prickly sedge and sharp thistle, so that it is a job to fetch them out and our paws must be well tended with rough tongues at the end of each day.

I thought, in a quiet moment there, I might wish to be a bird like Tewhit, who could fly to the bramble bush or pick a butterfly from the side of a birch trunk. Then I could fly to York – or away from here at least, for, as I thought more on my soul and how it was sure to be lost, I began to think of all I wished I could see before I died.

'Tewhit,' I said one night as I readied myself to pad down my moss bed, 'before you fly to your tree, I wonder – could you tell me something of yourself.'

'Of course, Inges – what would you know?' Tewhit was a bird of clipped speech, not given much to fancy words, and spoke with a whistle in his voice that sometimes took his words to song.

'I have seen little of the world, Tewhit, and may never see more. Tell me what you have seen in all your travels. Tell me of far India.'

Well, that night Tewhit spun a vision of his lands that, had I not known him too simple a fellow to invent such wonders, I might have thought more fanciful than any tale of witches. He had lived where great mountains rose so high they pierced the blue of the sky and were capped forever in snow, which was more of a wonder, he said, as the sun there was hotter than a Sunday morning hearthstone.

A river, wider than the sea, ran down from the mountains to the forest where he dwelled. The trees there were filled with birds whose tails were as broad as the church door at Fewston and more brightly coloured than the glass of its windows at sundown.

'And there were cats, Inges – great orange cats called tyger – that roamed those forests,' he had told me, and I asked if they were as large and fierce as Pumpkin, to which he whistled a laugh and told me they could cover that cat whole with a single paw.

'They will eat people if they can,' he said – and swore he had seen it. I said to him that one day I would see these cats for myself that I might know that was true. And that I did, but that is another story for another time.

'So tell me Tewhit – why did you leave such a wondrous place to come to this dark valley?' I asked him, and he told me a tale that made me wonder, as I sometimes did, why we imps were cursed to bind ourselves to such foul beasts as people.

Tewhit had been born, he said, in that vast forest – below the great white mountains – that spread so far and wide that, even if you were to soar above the mountains' highest peak, you would not see its end in any direction.

His nest was among many other golden birds such as he, and fine black ones too that shone like Whitby jet. All around were beasts and imps such as you could hardly imagine – spotted deer with horns like rapiers, birds whose beaks could crack a stone, spotted cats that hunted in the trees; most curious of all, creatures like a man but covered in fur and who, instead of hands, had a tail with which to climb trees.

I wondered how much of this Tewhit may have imagined only in dreams, for he told me he had not long fledged when he met a human's net set amongst the trees. He was caged and carried with other beasts of the forest, hung in boxes that bounced and rattled on the side of great beasts like walking houses, with carpets on their backs.

They came down from the forest to follow the wide river, then across burning lands where no trees grew and beasts ate only rocks. After many weeks, they reached a vast city and a scented market where a million people came to look at him.

Here he caught the eye of a young woman whose clothes rivalled his own feathers in colour and sheen, he told me – as he was now, it seemed, warming to his theme and spinning it out in brighter hues with each sentence. The woman took him inside a great fortress carved from deep red stone, and there he lived a year inside a golden cage studded with the shiny stones which humans seem to value above life.

His prison room was that of a great lady – perhaps a queen, he said, as she seemed much engaged with affairs of state. She would come to Tewhit only at rare moments to sit on silk pillows and listen to his song, before again busying herself to attend to some matter of money or war.

The queen had a husband, who the others at the fort called Conqueror of the World. Tewhit said it seemed, though, it was he who was conquered each day by a dark wand that looked something like an old harquebus, but with smoke that smelt of easter cake and woodruff instead of sulphur.

One day an Englishman arrived at the fort, and there was much anticipation at his arrival. He brought with him a good deal of gold to buy those things, such as silk and pepper, which he could not get at home. But the Conqueror of the World seemed most taken with the brown bottles he brought, and the men sat and drank for long hours and talked of barley and Dutch hops, until the Conqueror fell to sleep and was carried to his chamber.

The Englishman spent much time then after in conversation with the lady, on matters of trade and embassy, and in their meetings Tewhit's song often caught his ear so that when it came time to depart he asked of him, and our bird was given as a gift.

To get her name, Widow Thorpe was one time married to a man called Thomas, who was cooper aboard the ship of this

Englishman. Thomas had searched both ends of the world, she would say; lost a city of gold in the west and found a golden bird in the east.

Widow Thorpe would say the Englishman gave Tewhit to her husband as thanks for saving his life from privateers close by the Turkey shore. But Tewhit told me a different tale of how Thomas had thought his songs were worth the marks on his back for making a cage so easily broken.

'That's a fine tale, Tewhit,' I told him when he finished, 'yet you travelled half the world and only found your soul in our dark hills, not in the palace of a king?'

'Well,' he said, and fixed me with one red eye, 'that, I think, was my mistake, for no-one had told me of souls until I met your dead friend Quin.'

And it seemed Quin – who caught birds more easily than any cat I knew – had taken Tewhit at the cowberries up on Jeffray's fields. He would have killed him too, but he saw that sign in his eye that tells of an imp yet to find a soul, and so told him to find someone then come back so he may eat him without shame. And Tewhit flew back to his cage and saw his mistress there.

'He did not eat me,' Tewhit said, 'though sometimes I wish he had at the first chance. For now I am bound all my days to the Widow Thorpe and, though she feeds me and is kind, I will never see my forest again, nor the white mountains, nor another bird like me.'

We looked out a while then, Tewhit and I, at the short fall to the beck and the bank beyond. Neither of us spoke, but if I knew his mind I would say we both thought then of what it might be to be free.

Gybbe came by from the back of the hollow to ask what we were looking at. Tewhit spread his wings ready to take flight for his tree, and in that instant Gybbe said: 'Aye – I see it too. I think it's the dog.'

We looked now, Tewhit and I, and wondered how we had not seen it before, except that our mind's eyes had blinded us to what was in front of us. There in the bracken by the edge of the oak wood, nose to the ground, ears dragging through the leaves: the hound Barghest.

'Be. Very. Quiet.' I whispered, but I knew this dog saw with his nose more than his eyes, and the wind would not be in our favour.

Tewhit froze, but Gybbe and I moved slowly, quietly, back so that we were below the lip of the hollow where, with luck, the wind would not pull out our scent.

Fillie, who had been sleeping at the back in the deepest shadow, stirred to wake and I needed to hush her with a look before she spoke. We tried to gesture to Tewhit, but he stayed unmoving at the hollow mouth. Hidden as our den was by leaves and darkness, his bright feathers would shine through any gap at the slightest drop of moonlight, so I moved to pull him back.

Slowly, and close down on my belly, I moved towards him – as I would any bird in different times, but here my intent was to save a life not take one. I edged closer until my head was beside his black wing, and I whispered for him to get back. But that shell-headed bird would not move. Instead, he gave out a song – a sweet, spiralling chirrup and a sharp trumpet call – and at once Barghest looked up.

'You traitorous bird, you cuckoo,' I cried and straight away pulled out my claws, but Tewhit was already away to the tree top before I could strike.

Barghest had seen him, and now he turned. Not to the hollow where we crouched, but away towards the trees that backed the narrow gill and through which Tewhit now skitted close above him. Fillie was now beside me and I pulled back in my claws that I had hung in the air as I watched him fly.

'He betrayed us Fillie. Tewhit. I thought–'

'You should have killed him,' she said coldly. 'Gybbe should go after him. He will tell others.'

'She's right,' Gybbe, who was now standing beside us, put in. 'They will bring the killers; someone should go after them and it should be me.'

I refused and said if anyone went it would be me, but Fillie pleaded to let Gybbe go as she would be afraid without me. But now it seemed it would make little difference, for there at the edge of the trees that faced our cliff was a dark horse, and on him sat a hooded rider.

The horse was pulled short by where we had last seen Barghest, and paused a second before he was geed across to where the narrow woods sloped down towards the beck below our hollow. The rider dismounted and in their hand we could see: the moonlight broke through the trees just enough to catch its sharp light on a blade's edge.

'I fear it is too late,' I said. 'Fillie, I will distract him – you make a run for the trees. Gybbe – go with Fillie and I will meet you all at the top of the gill, if I get away. It will be too thick with bramble and dog rose there for a human to get through easily, and may give us time.'

But Gybbe now pulled out his claws and looked at Fillie first, then me. 'There is no time,' he said. And at that he jumped from the cover of our hollow and towards the hooded figure who was now dismounting.

I moved to join him, but Fillie pushed her flank against me to bar my way. 'He's giving us time, Inges, we should use it. Come – back in the hollow, in the shadow, we can hide–'

But I would not hide, not while Gybbe risked his life for me. 'Fillie, I'm sorry. Run now, and remember me fondly.'

I did not look at her to test her reaction, it would have tested me more. And with those words I leapt from the hollow, and I was still in the air when I saw it.

Time, they say, is a river that flows through all our lives, pulling us with the flow whether we would go or not. But it does not run even. In those moments where the streams of life and death meet they form a maelstrom – turning and twisting you with greater force than you have ever known, yet you move not an inch forward. I was suspended in the air as I saw Gybbe, his back arched and fur risen, and I saw the swing of the blade, and I saw his head take its leave of his body.

The slope below the hollow was steep, and the sight took my thoughts from landing so that I tumbled and slid with the shale to the gill bottom. And now the hooded rider saw me, and the blade was raised again.

To die when you still have a soul is still to die. You return, but you are not the same imp. You have the memories of another, but you are not the same. If it was not so, perhaps we would not fear death. The humans, they say, have souls that live on forever, yet they run from death as fast as any beast I have ever seen. I faced my death with acceptance, but I am not ashamed to say also with fear.

Then it hit. I wondered at first if it was the horse: that it had somehow bolted in fright from the sound of my defiant hiss and found its way down through the trees. A crash of muscle and bone that pushed all down and tied us up – me, the rider and this new force. We tumbled together and I thought I might be crushed before I was cut, if I had not learned the way to become a shadow on the ground when you feel the sky falling.

Then I heard the snarl and felt that warm stench again that I had felt at the graveyard, and once more I was face to face with Barghest. But in that instant I saw those hammer teeth were not for me.

'Step aside Inges, I must kill this demon,' he growled.

And in the madness of it all, with the world full of witches and great orange tygers and magic wands, I thought perhaps the rider was indeed some fiend from the depths of Hell. And, with all that I now know, perhaps I should say that she was. But this demon – with her hood now pulled aside – was a human. A woman. A pretty lady with golden hair.

She screamed out as she swung her sword at Barghest, and he fell back just before it could bite. Now she advanced towards him as he growled, and she held her blade in front to keep him back. Then Tewhit was on her in an instant, pecking at her head and flapping in her face so that she lashed at him with the bladed hand, and in that instant Barghest struck.

His great jaws clamped around her arm and the blade fell. I pulled at it with my teeth to drag it away from any hope of her regaining it, as she kicked out at Barghest and tried to pull her arm free, Tewhit still troubling her head and now aiming that red beak like a bodkin at her eye. The woman, with great effort, pulled herself over and unbalanced Barghest, pinning him for a moment on the ground. Then she reached her hand into his daggered mouth and punched. He loosed his grip a second and her arm was free, but not quick enough as his jaws snapped down on her open hand.

The woman let out a scream that might have shook the trees from their roots and brought them down from the cliff above us. She tugged with all her weight to pull the hand out and was up and across the beck in a moment; one leap onto the back of her horse and she kicked him to run, crashing through the tree line and back towards Timble as if Barghest, behind her, was the Devil's own hound.

Tewhit sat in his branch and looked down at me, tilting his head to watch me with an expressionless eye. Fillie was down by the beck now. I had not seen her arrive, but I could tell she was badly shaken. Her tail tucked and her ears down. I promised it was over, but I could see she knew it was not.

'Inges,' Barghest's voice boomed and I jolted at his loud return. 'She got away.'

'Thank you Barghest. I... I may have misjudged you,' I looked up to Tewhit too. 'I may have misjudged both of you.'

Tewhit chirped. Barghest simply swished his tail, then spat: 'You might find a use for this,' he said.

On the ground before me, wet with drool and blood, white with bone, and bound with a heavy gold ring, lay a woman's finger.

Fillie let out a sharp hiss.

INTERLUDE: *In Ostend*

MY NAME is Fillie, so you'll already know I'm not a good cat. If I was, why would I be here now?

I might as well tell you before he does; give my side of the story, let you be my judge. He didn't give me time to tell it, you see. Maybe he did; maybe time wasn't the problem.

Inges – whatever he tells you – he is a good cat. That is if any being can be good. That is if goodness is not just a rudderless bark that moves which way the tide flows that day.

The people who burned our town were good. They served their country and their queen and their God; all that was expected of them. They poured down fire and iron and pestilence for three years, so that when they brought their Queen Isabelle to see what they had made of her wedding present she rode on sand roads cobbled with skulls and wept at what good men had done. Three years of death so the mother of Ostend could reclaim all that was left of her wayward children: a bootlegger's whore and her blacksmith lover – two souls bought at the cost of 100,000.

He was good too. The man who killed my Anna, the man who took my soul.

Inges

I was born on Midsummer's Day in the year of the plague, as was Anna, who saved me. She did not remember it, as a human must learn memory, but I know all that happened from the moment I first felt the cold air cloak my wet fur.

We were born and we were bound in a town people call Doetinchem, a long way from the place where we parted. It was my first year, but for Anna it was 1,580 years since people started counting.

Doetinchem had once been a place of great bounty for cats, they say. The markets drew farmers from far and wide, and the farmers bought grain and cheese; and the grain and cheese fed mice and rats; and the mice and rats fed us.

But not that year. That year the town was broken by the war that has no beginning or end, and there was barely enough for the rats to eat. Anna was born crying for food, and would do so for many years more.

She had been born just an hour after I was, in the same room, in the same house. Her mother cried out for her God and cursed all men, but most of all the man who had put that life in her belly. He did not hear her cursing as he had long since left that town, it seems, for she cursed him for living and for leaving and for being a Spaniard.

There were four in that house the day Anna was born, and when it came time to open my eyes and choose a soul there were but two the sickness had spared, and neither would suit me. Anna's mother was too broken by her birth, and Anna – I feared – too young, what with the plague now cutting down the people of Doetinchem as fast as I could count them.

I thought of six others before I chose Anna. The butcher's boy whose name I cannot place – red-cheeked and fat. The young priest who looked like a fighter, but who I knew would be kept far from any battlefield. Four more who I forgot almost at once and certainly cannot bring back now.

It was fortunate that I was not decisive then, as all six fell from rude health to the plague pit before the week was out. But Anna's mother still lived, and so did her child.

Inges

She was pale, sickly – her skin that same piss-stain yellow as Dutch painters name in honour of boastful Isabelle, who would not change her undergarments until Ostend fell. She seemed a poor choice.

Yet young men as broad as oxheads were falling each day in the street, while Anna and her mother refused to die; and I wondered if Death saw them so sickly he thought he must have reaped them already.

So, I chose her. I chose Anna, and I chose well. Many imps – perhaps most – do not care for the person who holds their soul any more than a man cares for the bag that holds his coin; they care only for what is contained.

But for some – and I would count Inges and Peg in this also – the bond is as close as any mother and child, or any sisters. And so it was for me and Anna. We would play together, and share a bed, share what little food we had. I watched her – before she died – grow from a child too frail to hold her own head up, to a woman who turned the head of every human man who saw her pass.

We had ten years together in our own world, and then Matilda joined us. Anna's mother, who had shunned the company of men since her daughter's birth, was in the end won over by a plain shoemaker who had seen her child's bare feet and carved shoes of wood and leather for the price of the mother's attention.

They married in Autumn of Anna's ninth year and by the time of her tenth birthday there was a new life in the house.

I consider myself foolish now, and look back with some shame on it, but I was jealous. More jealous even than that soft-head Inges when I played the queen for Lord Pumpkin. I even thought to scratch baby Matilda so she might get a fever, or I wished for the plague to return and do it for me.

Don't judge me; yet. Love makes us mad. It's the same for you, I know.

But for all I feigned disinterest, or put my attention on the mother to try to stir that same jealousy in Anna, I could not break their bond, and so first I came to accept it, then understand it, then join it.

Inges

I learned to love Matilda too. Not as I loved Anna – as that could not be remade – but maybe I saw even more of myself in her than in my soul.

Anna was a dreamer. A romantic. Oh, she was tough – how could she not be – and stubborn. But she was giving too. She was quick to temper and quicker to forgive; you wouldn't want to cross her, but you would soon forget why you had. She was strong and brave, fiercely loyal; a fighter and a lover. She had all the qualities her mother would want, if she had only been a boy. And in the end she was. In the end, I mean: the very end. She died as a man, and I think that is how she would have liked to have lived. Had she had the choice.

Matilda was a woman before she stopped being a girl. She did not quite have the beauty of her sister, no one did. But she had something in her like a magic charm – if such a thing existed – that when she grew would turn men to dribbling fools, begging like a dog for the scraps of attention she might throw them if they just rolled over and played dead. And she would give them scraps only, and they'd think it a feast yet still be hungry. And hungry men, she would come to learn, will give anything to be fed.

Our shoemaker worked hard, and Anna too put herself to work weaving, and soon we had a house that was more fit for such girls, and for me. There was a time – just a short time – when everything was right in our worlds and it seemed we would all grow old and fat together and have the fortune of a story not worth telling.

But the war that has no beginning and no end, it sucked everyone in, in time. It left no field unploughed, not even our tiny scrap of rough pasture.

The wars of humans make no sense. I was going to say make no sense to me, but that would make it seem the fault was mine and that others could understand them. They can't. They will say they can, but they can't.

And how do I know this? Because human minds, put to the task, can plot the course of the stars, or build wooden ships to tame the seas, or shape great churches that point their fingers at the sky and say 'look at what we can do'.

Inges

But how few men watch the heavens? How few sail the sea? How few work in stone? Whatever their numbers, you may multiply it 10,000 times before you find the number who have been to war. And so you would think men would know war better than they knew any other thing. Yet they cannot predict the course of war, nor ride its storms, nor point which way it will go. They cannot decide its start nor fix its end. They can do nothing but be consumed by it. The thing they should know best, they know nothing of. And it consumed us too.

Just before the old human century turned to the new, Death finally noticed the trick Anna's mother had played on him all those years ago and played her one back. The plague barely touched our town that year, other than to take the mother after she paid a visit to her sister in Winterswijk.

They burnt herbs about the house as she told them, and put onion and oil on the swelling, but all to no avail. As the sickness worsened about her legs, they cut them open and put in a hot poke, which caused such screams that I thought my ears would burst sooner than the boils. But in the end Death had her anyway.

Her sickness, the townsfolk said, was on account of her marriage to the shoemaker. For he thought the wrong way on matters of God and so must be punished, first by Him, and now by the town, which shunned his trade and refused what little coin we had to buy at market, in case they caught his sin.

And so our shoemaker took away to his old home at Ostend, and Matilda with him. But Anna, who, like her mother, thought the right way of God, said she must stay as she was near 20 now and grown and that she must put her mother's home in order and would join us soon. She made a basket for me of withies and kissed my head and told me to care for Matilda until we should meet again. When I met her next she was just one of 1,000 corpses in the wet, bloody sand below the walls of Hell's Mouth.

If the shoemaker had thought he was taking Matilda to safety, he could not have got his presumptions, or his timing, more wrong.

In Ostend, his brother, a small merchant who traded in English wool and Dutch herring, had a good, warm house in which we were made to feel welcome. Within the house was comfort and calm, but without it the town was already full of that hot and close oppression that precedes a storm.

The town was built for war: walls of stone and iron, and all around it a great channel – so that any army that wished to take it must steady their siege guns on quicksand and march across water.

So sure of its strength were they that, even with their enemy at all sides but the sea, they not only sat behind their walls but came out from it to jab and goad and steal. Until the enemy decided that it must put a hot poke to this boil – and I had seen already how that would go.

They came in the summer. Thousands of men from across the world to try themselves against the city walls. They swore to end it by harvest-time, but we watched them as they floundered in the trenchworks just to dig their own graves in sand and mud while the guns of the Half Moon tower laid them down, and the sea covered all they had died for with disdainful ease. Even those red-cassocked bastards they called English – they who would kill an enemy as easily as they robbed a friend – wept at the pointless bravery of these death-loving idiots.

But for all the might of the defences and the waste of the enemy, by winter of that year the end was in sight. The enemy had now built forts of their own outside the walls and their siege batteries laid fire on fire, so that few houses still stood, and the mighty stone walls were held together by their fallen beams and studded like a pomegranate from the enemy's iron. The outer forts were broken or lost, and all the talk in the town was of whether it could hold till Christmas.

That is when we met him. The man who would save us, the man who would kill my soul.

The English were not well loved in Ostend. They fought harder than any men within our walls, and when battle was on the people would think themselves lucky if they were in their sight. In the moments of peace, however, they would wish them far away. These soldiers would drink, and fight, loot our houses and steal from friend or enemy alike – it mattered not to them. Before he died, the shoemaker forbade Matilda to leave the house when the Englishmen were in our quarter.

But there was no shoemaker, nor no house, when she and I met our Englishman. The first had been lost to an arquebusier's shot during one of the regular sorties against the old port. The second to fire: from what direction, we never knew.

So we found ourselves, Matilda and I, alone and hungry in the little that was left of an old accounter's hut upon the dockside. I would hunt for rats and, when I had my fill, that which was left of the hearts and the livers would be tied to a thread from Matilda's breeches and she would haul in crabs from the dock. And that was how we lived for nearly a fortnight; until we saw his boots.

Living with a shoemaker you know the smell and sound of leather so well that you could cost up a man by one glance at his feet. And when Matilda saw those boots pass by our little splintered half-door she knew at once this was a man worth calling to.

'Kind sir, your lordship, your highness, please spare us a half penny for we are starving, and the Catholic devils have took all. I fear we will not last the night for want of food.' She coughed as though she had a furball stuck in her throat, which was well done.

The man turned and lowered his head to look at this girl and her starving cat, and he smiled. "Kind sir' is high enough dear – and I hope to prove kind, though I have no purse upon me now. Will you be here a while? I shall return.'

The truth was, we had nowhere else to go and she told him so. Then he looked again at me.

'What a beautiful cat you have. What beautiful eyes. My mother had one quite like this, though not near as pretty, when I was a child. Does she have a name?'

So Matilda told him, and he was good to his word and returned within the hour. He took us to stay with the cook's wife, who roomed in the officer's quarters, and told her to keep us and feed us well; which she complained about, though not to his face.

In those few moments when the smoke and the thunder ceased, and men returned to lick their wounds or prepare their guns again, he would visit us sometimes.

On the second time he saw us he said: 'Well Matilda – and you, Fillie – I know your names so I have the advantage on you and you should know mine.'

And he said his name was Charles Fairfax. And this Charles Fairfax had no child though he had hoped he would. And he had a niece, who would be just a babe now, but he longed to see her when the fighting was done. And he would tell her all about Matilda and Fillie. And maybe, when the world was at peace again, they would meet her one day.

He stopped by a dozen more times, and on the last he was dressed more finely than we had seen any man before.

'I have to go away for a short while. I have told Cook to keep you well fed – both of you – and that if I am still away at Christmas Day then you can have my share of the figgy pudding.'

'Where are you going?' Matilda had asked him.

'I am going into the enemy camp. But do not be alarmed,' (he had seen Matilda pull me close to her, which was quite uncomfortable for me, but I could hear her heart racing). 'I will be a guest. They will look after me very well, and in return they are sending two of their gentlemen who we will make sure have everything they could ever want here.'

He smiled to himself at that, then reached into his breast pocket to pull out a soft leather sleeve that smelt of money and in which there was an old and yellowed letter, folded over four times.

'Things will go well, Tillie, but if they don't–' she pulled me again, 'if they don't, then this may keep you safe.'

Matilda took the paper and looked at it a moment, turning it in her hand. It was in English and, even if she had reading, would have made no more sense to her than to me at that time.

'It's a poem. It's a lovely poem my brother gave to me a long time ago to keep me safe. It has worked very well so far, but I think maybe I shall live a little longer without it. If I don't come back, I will simply be an honoured guest of the Habsburgs and they will look after me and fatten me up with appeltaerten and sell me back to my family for far more than I am worth. But, if that happens, I want you to keep this – it will keep you safe, as it did me. I hope.'

Inges

Matilda held the paper carefully, tracing her finger along its unfamiliar words. 'Wait, I should give you something to keep you safe too.' She reached into her little woolen bag that had held her whole world for the last few weeks, and pulled out a small portrait picture she carried, no bigger than a goose egg. 'Here, my sister painted this last summer. Keep it; just until you get back.'

Fairfax turned it in his hand and smiled. He left. We waited. Then the honoured guests arrived here, and we saw the start of the game Fairfax was to be a piece in.

I had taken myself to wandering around the headquarters, as the food all about this place was – even in the deprivation of war – finer than any I had tasted in peace elsewhere, and I knew well how to play the men who dined there. Had I chosen to be a spy for the Spaniards, I would have been the best they could employ.

Just the day before Fairfax brought his letter, I had been at sleep on the soft overhang of a curtain in some fine gentleman's room. I was woken by voices at times raised and others hushed, and knew I must be with someone of great importance.

The talk was of walls breached and men so low in numbers they could no longer be held, and of eyes in the Spanish camp that saw a full scale attack was due that next day. These important men spoke of surrender and terms. But the finest of the gentlemen there hushed them and instead chose to speak of time.

And so, when at last the grand old gentlemen of Spain arrived in that same room to discuss the terms of surrender, the game began. Before they could even remove their hats, there came suddenly a great beating of English drums signalling attack on the other side of the city. The English commander roared treachery and dismissed the men, then called them back, then again refused to speak to them.

They insisted most passionately that no attack was taking place, but the Englishman was so put out by events that he ordered them sent home by the west gate.

Yet the tide was now in, which could of course not have been predicted, and so the men had to stay the night. They were taken back through the town in the manner such as I have since seen done by those new Hackney Carriages of London that charge by the mile, so that they were very late to bed.

This charade carried on two more days. The men were sent on fools' errands that wasted the days, then comforted by evening with heavy food and wine. Until at last talk of terms must wait, they were told, as now it was almost Christmas.

And so it was that the whole talk of surrender was put off again until Christmas Day, when the English commander took possession of the gift he had most been looking forward to. 600 troops, fresh from England and eager for the fight, sailed into Ostend harbour and the Spaniards left with shame in their hearts and fire in their belly at having been so duped.

Charles Fairfax was released back to Ostend, where he would prepare for the attack that now must come on our newly fortified defences. And he had a gift for Matilda.

'Anna is alive!' Matilda squealed, and jumped so suddenly she threw me from her lap. 'How did you find her? How is she? Is she well? Have the Spaniards hurt her?'

Fairfax raised his arm and smiled softly, waiting for Matilda to quieten long enough that he could answer at least one of her questions.

'She is well. She was filled with joy to hear of your safety and good health. The Spaniards have not hurt her, she is with them willingly and works as a seamstress for the army, and in helping tend the wounded.'

'Is she coming to see me?'

'That would be difficult. She came in the hope of entering the city, but storms forbade it, and that passage was shut weeks ago; and now, of course there can be no road in. Not yet. She understands.'

Matilda sat down again and dropped her hands. 'Could you not have brought her back?'

Fairfax shook his head. 'I asked, but was refused. They fear what she may have heard from the men she tended at camp, and what she might tell us.'

Matilda was silent now, and Fairfax knelt down in front of her to softly speak the next part. 'Tillie, I told her to leave. I told her

I would keep you safe but she must leave. I gave her something – some trinket I had that has worth – to buy her way back to your own town where you can meet her when–'

Matilda struck Fairfax across the face, though he barely moved but to put his hand to where hers had been. She turned herself over to put her face down on the bed and sobbed. Fairfax looked at me and shrugged. I thought I might tell him she was just upset, but I think that may have made things worse.

The Englishman's ruse had bought time, but not much. Just seven days into the new year and the Spanish came.

Wave upon wave of cannon shot poured down on the town from all sides as the enemy tested the resolve of its new defenders. But the time bought had been spent wisely, shoring up the breaches in the walls with the rubble of fallen buildings, and preparing a hot welcome for the Spanish troops who would follow the day's cannonade.

Then, as the early winter night fell quickly to blackness, the cannons stopped, and the sound of men's battle cries and the bark of small arms was heard all round the city.

The Spanish, it seemed, had meant to confuse the Englishman so that he would not know where the attack was coming from. Then – at the right hour, when the tide had ebbed enough – they would pour their main force, thousands of men, over the shallow bed of the old harbour and against the breach at Sand Hill fort.

They had meant to confuse, but the Englishman's spies had done their work. No sooner did the attack begin than great pyres of wood and tar barrels ignited across the wall tops to throw their light below and present a sight for the thousand guns now pointed into the abyss.

And they fell like orchard apples in an autumn wind. By their thousand, yellow-coated pikeman and hooded arquebusiers, rushing to their death as their iron-clad cavalry stood to the rear and urged them on into the fire of the cannons and culverin.

Those that did make it to the breach found they must lay their ladders across the backs of their dead and scale them to meet the eager end of a Zeeland pike or an English long knife. They were the lucky ones, as hundreds screamed to death in the embrace of burning pitch hoops thrown from the ramparts.

I could not resist but watch: such is the folly sometimes of those who take their souls for granted. There was a cruel beauty in it all, the fire and smoke. But I would run back to comfort Matilda between times, as she huddled in the heart of the officer's quarters. Then I felt it. My soul. It was close. Closer than it should have been; than it had any right to be in this Hell. I leapt from Matilda's arms and back out to the wall beside Sand Hill, drawn by the silent call of it.

And from the embrasure there I saw her. Illuminated in that same ghostly yellow light that burned out all those lives below us: Anna – her familiar face unmistakable even in the confusion of battle and the rough dress of a Spanish pikeman – was pushing her way through the bodies below the breach and towards the knife edge of the battle.

I had no time to think of, nor care about, the laws of imps. I ran back to Matilda and in a second I spoke. 'Your sister is close by the breach – she is trying to get to you. I think she has lost her mind and disguised herself as a Spanish soldier, you must stop her.'

Matilda was stock still for a second and then must have thought that this world had shown her enough of its madness that one talking cat more or less was not to be dwelt on when her sister was in mortal danger.

I followed Matilda as she ran out to the walls, ran past what stood of Hell's Mouth fort, across the scarp and to the breach close by where Anna now crawled her way through blood and entrails, pulling herself up by the limbs of the fallen.

'Anna!' Matilda screamed – but her voice could not be heard down in the mayhem of the breach. Not by her sister at least, but someone heard it.

'Matilda – what in God's name are you doing here? Get back to safety at once – that is an order.'

Charles Fairfax had one eye on his men who were pushing against the rolling wave of Spanish steel now trying to force its way through the breach, and the other on Matilda.

'My Annie – she is there, she is there,' Matilda screamed, and now it seemed Anna could hear her.

'Tillie – I'm so sorry, I had to see you. I knew they were coming to kill you all. I had to do something, I had to try.'

She was close enough to the wall now almost to reach down and pull her up, if you just had one of those Spanish ladders, if the air was not half-filled with shot. Matilda pulled at Fairfax's undercoat, which protruded beneath his bloody armour. 'You have to help her, she's nearly there. Please, please help her!'

But at that moment another, too, wanted Fairfax's attention. A young soldier, lightly armed and red in the face, had come running with news from the great Englishman.

'Sir – Commander Vere's orders, sir. The tide has turned. He sent me to get men to open the flood gates sir, fill the harbour. Drown these bastards.'

Matilda screamed and fell to her knees. 'No you can't! She needs one minute. One minute. You can't. Please, I am begging you!'

Fairfax looked at Matilda and then back at the soldier. 'Take two men and do it quickly.' I saw a single tear wash a clear silver heart in the film of blood on his breastplate, and he stepped back into the breach.

We found her early the next day. Her long golden hair, matted across her face, signalled her from among the thousands. We saw her from across the strand, sitting almost upright against the wall of Hell's Mouth, as though she were in some reverie.

She had been carried back on the wave of retreat as the harbour filled, and pulled with the other doomed into the tide as it rushed in. Her face, blue and cold and swollen with water, was still beautiful, I thought.

Around her neck she wore a gold chain, Fairfax's price for her to leave. Matilda took it from her and threw it to the crabs and sandpipers.

I left her with her sister. My soul was gone and now she was an empty vessel. That sounds cruel, I know, but what is a person but their soul? She was not Anna anymore, and my heart hurt too much to look at some broken facsimile. So I headed back through the bodies and the sand to somewhere I could be alone, where I could be safe now my soul was gone.

'Imp. Where are you going?' The voice startled me, coming as it did from the dead. I looked around and, were I not a cat, I doubt I would have seen it. But there, looking from beneath the long-coat of a dead soldier who still held his pike, was a mouse.

'This is ironic isn't it?' he squeaked.

I looked at him a second, then carried on my way.

'This is ironic isn't it?' he called after me again.

'What is?' I snarled at him, 'the fact that you were about to survive a great slaughter only to be eaten by a pissed-off cat?'

He laughed. 'You can eat me all you like, finish me off. In fact, I wish you would. Look at this,' and he pulled himself out of the jacket to show the blood and matted fur where his hind legs had been. 'Same bullet did for him. I only came out with him to keep him safe. Can't say I didn't try.'

He laughed again, but I couldn't see what was funny.

'What do you want, mouse?' I hissed.

'I want to do you a favour. Build bridges, so to speak. Look at the mess we get ourselves in when we think we have to fight. I want to do something for you. Before I go.'

I moved closer, I hoped with an air of menace, but I am sure he saw my curiosity. 'What do you mean, mouse?'

'You've lost your soul, which is a pretty hazardous situation in the middle of a battlefield, I'd say. And I've just lost mine at a most inconvenient time. If you'd got here five minutes earlier you might have helped me, but he's gone – just this minute. I heard his heart stop.'

'So?'

'So – I'm buggered. But it's your lucky day. I want you to kill me.'

Well, I'd kill him happily, but I could not see why this made me lucky. So, he told me; and in that moment I was doomed.

'Look in my eye, cat. What do you see there?'

I looked, and to my astonishment saw a familiar shimmer – the light of the soul binding which should only be there in a newborn, in a yet-unbonded imp.

'It'll be there another minute if we're lucky, probably less. He's just this minute gone – it's broken now; one end, but not the other. That will break in a moment and vanish with his life. But not if you catch it.'

'Catch it?'

'Just for a second. You'll see it. Kill me, I'm done anyway. Life has left him, but my soul lingers in him just this short while. We will part together then, you see, at that same instant. Kill me now and take it. Be quick, before it disappears.'

And there, on that grim, grey plain of salt, blood and death I learned that terrible secret known only to the few. To the oldest. To those who live.

'Use it quickly – the first person you see, it will be gone before you know it, don't wait, don't think. Don't hesitate.'

I didn't need to wait. I didn't need to think, I didn't hesitate. I bit his neck in one instant, and at the next I bound myself to Matilda.

ACT 2: IN CHEAPSIDE

"Language most shews a man: Speak, that I may see thee'

–Ben Jonson

Inges

The Mermaid

PERHAPS IT was the stench of the river, or the filth of the streets. Perhaps the gauntlet of cartwheels and feet all-in-a-hurry to knock you down, the grasping hands of legless doorway beggars, or just the noise and the smoke and the shit.

Whatever the reason – and any of them would be enough for me – this city, more full of humans than I thought possible, seemed near empty of imps. And who could blame them? This was a place where you might trust a soul to live as much as you would trust warm milk not to sour, and both would likely last as long here.

There were cats. Cats at windows, cats on walls, cats fighting over scraps under carts, cats in the street full of fleas, cats in the rivers bloated like Shrovetide footballs. But they were dumb beasts, not imps. Dogs too – though it would be hard to tell the difference there. My feet were filth-stained to the joints and I gagged at the thought of how to clean them as I tiptoed through the crud that caked the paths of London. Already I was wishing to be back in Timble.

'Then Inges,' I hear you ask, 'why did you travel all this way, so bravely, by yourself, and to such a place of grim streets and smoke and sin?' Well, hard as it is for me to say, Barghest, it turned out, had been ahead of us all in regard to The Woman. I guess every dog has his day, like they say.

She had called at the Dickenson's house a good month before poor Quin died, he told me, asking after some herbs that were then out of season, and which Bess Dickenson kept in store. She had been asking questions about the wise women, and who they were. Barghest had not liked the smell of her, and he had tracked her since, though not so well that he could stop the deaths of Quin and Anne, so I can't be sure his nose is as good as he says.

'She bought a distillation of nightshade,' he told me. and said she smelt of badness. Well, I don't know what badness smells like, but it seems it has the scent of those same men who stay sometimes at the inn when they have come from London to York and on to Skipton.

'They smell of money,' he told me, 'and soap and lime and greenwood smoke.' He thought maybe the nightshade was what she used to kill poor Anne, but I said no, as then Maggie would have known it. More likely, I said, it is what she used to make her eyes so dark and cold, as Maggie said the wealthy ladies would use it for such and call it belladonna – which means 'beautiful lady'. In which case, I thought, her beauty hides an ugly soul.

And it was Tewhit who made it certain. That bird, who couldn't tell Pumpkin from weeds high up, had eyes like a goshawk when it came to seeing close by. He said this was on account of spending so long in a small cage: 'that turned my eyes the wrong side up,' he said, but then he is a bird slow of wit.

He had seen the sign on our severed ring. A crowned cat, pressed into the shining yellow metal. 'I saw that same sign on a ring of the Englishman,' he said, 'and that my lady asked him if it was for a tyger, but he told her no it was a leopard and was to show that such gold was struck in London.' And so that was the sign, also, we agreed, that Inges must go that way.

There had been other marks on that ring too. The top was stamped with an odd shape, like a bird's tail spread, that none of us knew. Within the ring were letterings. These, I could read. I had learned human symbols, human words, sitting at Peg's lap. Imps do not read, but Inges reads: *'AS I DESERVE SO I DESIER +GEORGE'*.

So, I came to London. To the foul air and the fouler water, looking for the history of that ring; a story of it that would find our woman, or else one who knew her well enough to buy her gold. I came also, in truth, as in Timble I was now a wanted cat. In Yorkshire, I would die; in London I might find salvation for us all.

I had with me the two things I would need to accomplish this – my wits, and the ring. The first I have about me always. The latter, I had about my neck in a manner that I wish I did not have to speak of, but again I am a servant of completeness in this tale.

It was Barghest's idea. Of course it was. Mine had been to eat it. I would swallow it, I would jump a cart, I would get to London, I would find a den, I would expel it. Dirty, uncomfortable, but more dignified than his solution.

'I have heard it takes six days to London, Inges, if you even find a coach or cart or willing pack horse at each stop; or are not caught; or jump the right one that is going that same way. You cannot hold it, and I think you wouldn't want to swallow it a second time.'

Was this true, or was this his game to get me to wear the damn collar? I know it to be mostly true now, but I still don't forgive him.

'It was mine when I was but a pup,' he told me, 'so it should fit you well.'

In size, indeed, it did fit me; in every other way it could not have been less fitting. Choked like a dog. I'm not sure – even there in the cloying waste of London's streets – my neck didn't feel more soiled than my paws.

Around the collar, half hidden in my fur so as not to attract the gaze of hungry eyes, the gold ring was secured. I would take it and I would study it and I would try to unravel its mysteries. Quite how it could help me further; well, that had seemed a trivial matter waiting at the coach road back in Yorkshire, but now it was pressing on my mind with each stinking step I took. Perhaps the marks would lead to the one who had it made, but how was I to enquire on that? I could hardly ask for directions. So I had determined to find my way down to the docks where Tewhit had first spied London – for that, he said, was where the gold came in. And if I find gold, perhaps I find the path to our woman.

I had come into London on the eighth day of my journey by way of a stop at a great house outside the walls. I had, at a town some miles to the north that no one knew the name of, made the acquaintance of a packhorse named Abel. He had allowed me to sit among the cargo of smoked eels that he had been bringing down from some great wet place to the east; offering passage in return for a promise I did not eat the goods.

Close by where I stopped I met another imp, a cat whose name I cannot recall. He asked me if I was looking for the Dog House, and if my soul was gone. Which alarmed me a little, with all that had been spoken of in Timble. But instead it seemed some of the cats from the country around here, when they are old and sick and have lost their souls, will go to the Dog House, where the hounds of London are held, to end their lives among the stench of those foul beasts.

I did pass close by, in my error to find More Gate that he said was near. The House was rotten with the dogs' filth, the roof and walls half gone, and around I saw, untended, the bodies of hounds, half eaten by their starving brothers. I thought I would die a hundred times before I let that be my end.

Through the streets of London I headed south towards where the river would be. Tewhit had told me that, from what he had seen between the bars of Thomas Thorpe's cage, the Englishman's ship had set down before the bridge, where the river widened. I should know the way to the river by following the worst of the stench, and to the bridge by following the worst of the crowds.

And so I followed both until I found myself where you found me just now – tiptoeing through the dirt of Thames Street, which seemed a good way to find my destination. Now I just had to follow my nose – and it pointed me towards a sight that I still recall whenever I get that smell of sea and fish.

The street ahead of me opened up into a space that had been filled with scattered carts, each wheeled to the middle with stilts to prop them level. On top of them were all the creatures of the water – I cannot imagine there could be any more not there. Fish of all shapes and sizes, all scents. So many creatures I did not recognise; some like spiky chestnuts, others like giant chuckypigs or huge crayfish the size of a rabbit.

The smell was overwhelming, but also intriguing. I slipped under the stalls, and between the hazards of swinging legs, stopping here and there to sniff at a piece of herring or some odd fish that found its way between the tables. All a little too ripe for my tastes, and besides I was still full of smoked eel. You must try it, if you are ever that way – it's very good, though the bones scratch at your mouth if you eat in too much of a hurry.

So, I passed under the last table – nearly kicked by a fat man in an apron all glistening with fish scale and mucus – and saw that the road sloped down gently a short while. At the bottom was the most extraordinary sight. Rising up between and above the buildings was a forest of wood and rope and linen that seemed to me like the withy bushes by The Tarn on washing day; only I was an emmet, or else the washers were giants, as they towered above all.

There were three ships, one at the very waters' edge and two behind, each with three great masts rising up almost to the sky and tied with yarn like a cat's cradle. Around were others of different sizes, some with two or one masts and many with none at all. Most of all were those small row boats I later heard called wherries, and I thought that – for all the streets had been full – maybe only half the folk of London lived on them as just as many again were riding on the river to and fro.

The waterside was full of shouts and hustle, boxes and bags, and people all about their business loading and unloading, boarding and unboarding, walking planks and hauling ropes. I had never seen a place so busy in all my life, and I wondered how any one person could know another with so many faces.

Moving among them I soon found they had their own ways. The voices spoke in tongues I did not understand, even those who spoke mine did so in a way I'd never heard before. I saw men were not all that shade I had thought them, and wondered how much more of the world there was beyond the green of Yorkshire and England and over the waters. I thought again of what had been on my mind since I spoke with Tewhit – of what other folk, and imps, this world might hold.

I now picked up a most invigorating scent drifting down from just above me. Eel or no eel, this made my mouth water. It smelt of brine and vinegar, but also of sweetbreads and succulents. I was stood below a cart where a man was calling the names of his wares: 'Cockles, fresh cockles. Whelks, mussels, scallop – I have 'em all, fresh just this morning from the sea.'

Well, I thought, I should at least try these – for what is the point of travel unless it is to broaden the mind and show us new experiences. The fishy man was busy now working his knife on some things that looked like little grey rocks, but which popped open with a twist. They smelt good, but I now had my paws up on the stall side and could see the things that had most tickled my nose. These must surely be what cats eat in London, I thought, as they were all laid out in a row inside what I took to be little saucers, such as Peg uses when she feeds me. Well, can you blame me? They looked so sweet, all juicy, orange and white, like little sweetmeats.

'Oy, get your bloody paws off my wares you 'orrible vermin!' The stall owner had taken his eyes off his little grey stones to see me licking up the last little juicy bits from my third saucer. He had maybe meant these for his own cat, as he was not too happy with me, it seemed.

He went to grab me, but I was too quick for him, and he started to chase me – picking up my used saucers and throwing them wildly at me.

I ran between the legs of porters, who twisted and cursed as they half-spilled their load, over crates that smelt of Christmas pudding, under the web of nets strung between gangways, and down into a clutter of broken cases, where I could slide through the gap of missing struts. One of the saucers narrowly missed me and thudded into the wood of the case as I dived into the darkness and safety.

'Don't eat me! I have children! Hundreds of them!'

My eyes took just a second to adjust to the new dark but now it seemed I wasn't the only one who saw the advantage of this hidey hole. Right in front of me, its tail accidentally caught beneath my paw, was a small, very frightened, black rat.

'Don't worry. I've eaten far too much,' I said, pausing just long enough. 'Although I could always save you for later.'

'Please – señor gato, there is so much fish here. I can show you the best places. The very freshest, all my secret larders.'

The rat looked fat enough, which meant he probably spoke the truth, but also that he would taste very good. 'Maybe I'll let you show me, then I'll eat you,' I said, and his whiskers shook so hard they tickled my foot.

'Please – I have lost my soul, if you eat me that is it. I can help you. I know this place; I can help you find anything. Food, cream, las gatas más bonitas–'

I put my other paw on his back and pushed him down so that his legs spread out below him and his belly touched the ground. 'Do you know anything about gold?'

He wheezed a little and his small black eyes looked at me with confusion, then I saw he glanced at my collar. 'I can tell you where you can find it, but it will be well guarded.'

'I've no interest in stealing it. I want to learn about its marks – take this collar off me.'

That little black rat chewed nervously through the collar – which was a great relief, though I was glad to be hidden where no other cats could see a snack chewing at the neck of a proud cat.

The collar and ring fell to the ground, where the little rat now examined them closely, his shiny black nose twitching as he scanned the strange markings.

'I will tell you the truth cat, I do not know how to read these signs, but...' he pulled back on the last word, expecting a claw perhaps, 'I can tell you where this was made, as all such rings are made there.'

Ferdinando – for that, he said, was his name – told me all about the street of gold in London, where the shops are all bright with shining metal and stones. 'At Cheapside, that's where they are.

It is not too far from here, and there are great houses. So many places to hide, so much food…' again he paused, as he perhaps remembered that my food and his would be very different.

'Do you have any more of these?' I asked, showing him just outside the door of our hiding place, where the fish man's saucer had landed, 'they are very…'

The saucer had landed upside down, so that now I saw the back of it. And it looked like something; something I had seen before. It looked like a bird's tail, spread out.

'Do you know what this is, rat?'

'Si – it is the vieira. Very tasty. Like from the Camino de Santiago.' He saw the expression on my face. 'The Camino de Santiago? No?'

'No.'

He sighed. 'Ok – I will tell you a little.'

Well, he told me a lot. First about the Camino – how people travel from across the world to follow these little shells, to a place where they keep the body of a man who was killed many years ago. I'm not sure why, although I store a few old voles I killed under the broken forcing pot that is sunk in the Pullein's garden, and maybe a trail of shells would remind me. I must remember that, now I think on it again.

And he told me how he had come across the sea many years before, from the land of these shells, on a great flock of ships to bring war to this country. He said there had never been so many ships together in one ocean, and it sounds like there were maybe too many, as his ship collided with another and the next day was taken by the English. 'Abandoned we were, a wounded comrade left to their mercy by cobardes – by cowards.' The English took them all – ship, men and rats – into port a long road west of here.

Ferdinando and his soul were locked up like cattle in a barn a while, before they made their way to London, and here they stayed – his soul selling pickled fish at the market and he living well on the scraps that abound here.

'And what happened to your soul?' I asked.

'Well – that is a tragic tale. You see, he lived well – to a good old age – and I thought he still had many more years left in him.

But then I gave him the plague this early summer. Es mi culpa, what can you do?'

Which shows that sometimes there is a reason that imps and their souls should not mix.

'Inges,' he said, 'since I lost my soul my courage has gone too. But if I had a strong and vital cat such as you as my companion, I could once more walk the streets of London. It would be my honour to be your traveling companion and assist you on your quest for gold, and in return, perhaps I could walk in your shadow and be safe from less honourable beasts.'

'Well,' I said, 'I am such a cat, and to have someone who knew these streets would perhaps help me in my search. Very well, rat, you may walk with me.'

I must be fair to Ferdinando, the lodgings he found were well suited and he was a good companion. It was a place he said he knew well, as his soul had often been there after a day had gone well in the market.

'He fancied himself el nuevo Cervantes, I think, and liked to sit and talk the night away here with poets,' Ferdinando told me. 'And he liked one of the ladies who works upstairs.'

Our home was in the roof space of a tavern that was called The Mermaid. It was much different to the inn at Timble, which was simply the man Simon Tanner's house with a great bench and a stone floor that could be swept – straw, piss, blood and vomit – wholesale over the doorstep each morning.

Here were set tables and chairs and paintings on the wall – crudely done, of ships and fish-women and some old men who it seems should be known.

There were great barrels of ale and wine and other such bitter slop that makes men take their masks off. The place would have taken in every drinking soul in Timble, I thought, and still had room for them to dance.

This was a good spot for us, Ferdinando told me, as we would find much to eat here among the overturned dishes, and we could travel through the roof spaces and over the thatch to Cheapside Street, where we would likely find our ring-maker.

We made that trip many nights. Ferdinando and I took rings, chains, brooches, even toadstones and tankards, all to find some mark that would link a gold maker to our woman. The rat found a wooden box where we could keep these pieces close by, and sometimes I wonder if some fortunate fool should ever find it, or an unfortunate one hang for the taking.

On all the gold there was that sign of a crowned cat, but each smith it seemed had their own mark too – though none that we could find on the woman's ring.

We searched each shop until I was quite sure we had covered them all. 'Ah Ferdinando, this is a pretty fix we have ourselves in,' I said, as the days were passing, and with each one was another day in the slow death of prison – or another closer to the quick death of the scaffold – for my soul.

'Do not despair, Inges,' he said. 'When I and my soul were closed up in that barn there was barely enough room to stand, let alone lie down. Some of the prisoners there starved so that they took to eating the soft stalks of ivy that grew through the guttering. Then they saw me and eyed me with greedy intent. I thought all hope was gone, that my soul would die of hunger and I would be eaten. Yet, at the darkest moment came relief, when a kind farmer, in secret, brought us food.'

'So you're saying there's always hope–'

'Then that farmer was found out and hanged from a tree.'

'Thanks, Ferdinando, I feel so much better now.'

'Well you see, what I am saying is, things can always get worse.'

'Yes, much better. Thank you.'

'But here I am, still alive, you see – and even with my soul gone I go on, with my new friend...' (I wouldn't call us friends) '...Inges, and so there is a purpose to all this, I believe. Why we survive when others die. There is a meaning to it, and a reason you found me and I found you.'

Well, I don't believe in such things as fate or meaning. We are born, we live, we die. All that happens in between is from our own action or the chance movements of the world. What fate was there in Cowpea dying before he had grown? What cause did it serve for that greyhound at the Dog House to be disemboweled by his pack? Just the cause of feeding hungry stomachs, I think.

Yet, for all that, had I believed in such a thing as fate, I might have seen its hand in what happened next.

The two of us had taken to making our trips over to Cheapside by day. It was more risky, in that we could not hope to get into a shop and out without being discovered. But we had searched all shops for marks, so now we had a new plan. We would watch who came by the street to buy and sell, and perhaps The Woman might be among them. Though it seemed a forlorn hope, it was the only hope – the only idea – I had at that time. This Cheapside was the place where all of London came, it seemed, so better to wait for her to come to us than us to go out looking.

We had been watching in this way for two days. We watched rough-clothed people walk to the market stalls, picking over fruit and leaves, raising voices and shaking heads. We saw fools beaten and their ears cut at the stone pillory as others mocked them. We saw rich folk holding up their hands to measure their piece of the silk cloths that hung from windows and balconies like a billowing rainbow along the roadside. We saw all of London go in and out among the gilded signs of cow heads, keys and disembodied legs that hung above the doors; or go along and back again the wide, busy space between our rooftop and the great houses far across from us.

So many people, I felt I must have seen all of London twice already when finally I saw it. The street is busy with carts and coaches pulled by horses, paying little attention to people – where the law of the road seems to be that the smallest must give way to the biggest, or to Hell with them. On the second day, just after the bell sounded to end that day's market (a bell no one took the slightest notice of) I saw two men, servants it seemed, as they hauled a weight of cloth into a waiting cart. They were directly below us and, as I watched them, my keen cat eye caught sight of the marking on their coats – a cross, such as you see in the humans' churches. And set within that cross, vieira – those same shells as in the ring.

I looked around for Ferdinando, but he was not there, perhaps out looking for food elsewhere, I thought. But I could not waste this moment. I ran across the flat part of the roof to where I could jump down to the balcony below. A startled woman threw a shoe at me which missed and hit a gentleman in the crowded street below. As the woman and man traded insults I jumped and caught my claws in a length of purple silk that ran to the ground, slowly sliding down with my talons catching hold to slow my fall.

The cart had moved off now, and I must be quick. It turned down by a church and picked up speed on the straight road ahead. I was going as fast as I could, but it was getting away. Then I saw my chance; the door of one of the taverns opened and two men stumbled out, holding onto each other for support. At first I thought they embraced in friendship, but then it was clear they were fighting, right across the street and out in front of the cart.

'Get out of the damn way, you drunken fools, or I'll horse whip you,' one of the servants on the cart yelled, and the one man who was still standing stepped aside and fell backwards into a shallow ditch. The cart driver mumbled some obscenities and moved on. But now with a passenger. I was clinging to the backboard.

Wherever this cart was going, it would have some connection with the shells, and I would find it. It seemed we were heading for a small dock, as I could now see the sails of river boats above the roofs of the smaller houses. We turned onto the riverfront, and the driver reached back to hold some of the cargo that had slipped in turning. And he saw me.

'Christ's boots – it's a bloody cat. Get off you flea-bitten moggie.' He swung his whip at me, and I leapt out of the way, out of the cart, over the quayside, and into the unforgiving waters of the Thames below.

Inges

Jack

I HAD imagined deep water – foul as the thought was – to be soft, yielding and wet; yet it was none of those things. It hit me like a carelessly swung door, taking the wind from me in an instant, then wrapping me in its dark, icy grip; binding my chest so I could barely move.

I could feel only an uncontrolled surge through the water, the strength to resist slapped out by the force of the cold. The detritus of the river, soft parts and hard, swept into and quickly over me – the only indication of the direction I was going – lost in this senseless underworld: down, down, down.

This is how it ends, Inges, I thought. In the cold and the dark and the shit. You will be just another of those bloated cadavers that bob beneath the weirs of the bridge until they finally burst. There you'll stay, rolling in the fetid foam until a great red kite swoops to pick off the expelled fruits of your stinking belly.

Those dark imaginings were knocked out of my head when something far larger and more solid than a floating turd hit me. At first I thought it might be some part of an animal the market butchers had thrown to the Thames – it was firm like muscle; but it was moving still. Then back it came, hitting me again, and now I thought my end would be different. Even in the darkness I could sense its size, its power. This was some great fish, sizing me up for a meal. Well, fish, I am in your world now but know this, you will fight for your supper today.

'Keep still cat, I'm trying to help you.'

It is hard to describe the sound of a voice through water. Barghest asked me about this and I told him to put his head in the beck while I do the same and I would tell him some great secret in the language of fish. Of course I let him sit there waiting with his great stupid face in the stream while I curled up beneath a tree in the sun, but if you have a friend you trust you should try this method to get some idea of the sound.

'Trying to eat me more like; do you think me a fool?' is what I replied. Although it may have sounded different, as I had not much experience of talking underwater, and this fish seemed not to understand, and instead swam under me then rose to push me up. He was larger even than I first thought; his back was broad and long so that I could fit across it entirely, as if I were baggage slung over some underwater packdog.

Up we swam, and against the flow now; I could feel the harder force of river flotsam hitting my face. My lungs were shrunk and burning, pulsing hot like the last embers of a faggot in the hearth, and I had to fight my desperate urge to quench the fire with the ice water of the river. Just as I felt I could hold back no more, we broke the surface and I sucked in the air like life itself. A few seconds, and I could feel the wetness I had first expected, my fur clinging cold to my skin, chilled further by the wind as we sped over the ruffled brown surface of the Thames.

I coughed out a little of the stench water. 'Thank you fish, you saved my life.'

'It is no problem cat, we are a brotherhood here,' he replied, and his head, now out of the water, showed the long, viper face of a huge pike.

'A brotherhood of cats and fish? Strange brothers, but I'll accept it,' I said.

'A brotherhood of imps, cat. A guild of imps. We take care of our own here.'

And it was more than a brotherhood, more than a guild: a kingdom, it seemed, when we got there. The entrance to this kingdom's palace was through the fetid, flesh-thick, greasy ooze of a sewer they call the Fleet. An ironic name for a great slow worm of filth that slithers down through London's streets, puking the vile crop from its narrow mouth into the belly of the Thames.

You enter by a grate, a short way above the level of the river's crust. I had to climb the broken brickwork to reach it, but the walls above it showed the old markers of black grease where the water level must sometimes swell. I wondered what sort of palace this was that sucked in sewage in a wet winter.

'I can go no further here cat, but look inside and make yourself known. Tell them that Jack recommended you, and you will find no trouble in there.'

I thanked Jack, and he disappeared once again below the surface. For a second the wet dough of scum stayed parted where he had dived, so that the water could be glimpsed as it might have looked before this city chewed up its banks; then it sucked itself back into place and continued its rank, slow crawl downstream.

Standing outside the grate, I suddenly realised what an entrance I would make to this brotherhood – caked in river filth. A steady stream of cold, clean water was running down from the broken eves above and I realised it was raining now; wet as I was, I had not noticed. I stood a moment in that running water, letting it wash out the stain of the Fleet as best it could, then shook myself like some ghastly water dog. I have looked better, I must confess.

Inside, light from grates and gutters around the space shone enough that, while you would not see much, a cat like me could see well enough. I was up on the eves of a vaulted room, pillared and bare, not unlike the crypt at Fewston Church, but larger by far.

This room, I could see, led off on three sides to others that looked the same, and, I thought, must be part of a great network of rooms that covered the ground space of the vast redbrick building above.

Inges

A large, grey cat walked between two of the pillars below me; stepping briskly as if he had something important he needed to do, though not important enough to run. He disappeared again suddenly through the pillars of the opposite wall, then just as suddenly returned.

'Hello? Can I help you, cat? Do you speak?' His manner reminded me of Rev Smythson addressing the women of the back pew.

'It depends who I am talking to, cat.' I hissed the last word. 'I would speak to whoever is in charge here, and I can tell by the manner of your walking that you are one who takes orders and does not give them.'

The cat glared at me, but said nothing, and walked on. I wondered if perhaps, as this was some guild, they might have more knowledge of the city, of the men with the shells. I jumped down into the vault.

That instant the grey cat returned, this time with four more cats by his side – great toms with heads as square and solid as house bricks.

Ok, I thought, so it's going to be like that. He gestured for me to follow the bruisers.

Well, I was intrigued by now, so I took his guidance. Of course, I could have stood my ground had I wanted, but curiosity is in my nature.

'In here,' he spat, then left me alone with my guard to enter some anteroom, far smaller than the great vaults I had just left. The room was dark, save for the light that bled in under an old wooden door to the far side.

'Name?' A voice from the shadows.

'Inges.'

'What kind of cat would own that name?' the voice said.

'The kind that would prefer to see the face of a cat he is talking to.'

There was a shuffle, and then from the top of an old barrel that had been tipped on its side, a small, brown spaniel dog appeared and stepped awkwardly down. 'Despite what you might have heard, Inges, it is not all cats in this kingdom.'

'And whose kingdom is this, that treats guests so coldly?'

Inges

The dog's tail wagged briefly. 'Inges you say? Well my name is Snuff, and I am here to introduce you to the kingdom of the greatest cat – no, the greatest imp – in Christendom, The Mazger.'

'The who?'

Snuff growled slightly at the back of his throat. 'The Mazger. King of Cats. Rightful ruler of the House of Grimalikin, heir of Glascolon and Grimolochin before him.'

'Is that his full name? I hope his soul doesn't put his name around his neck; he would probably trip on it.'

Snuff snuffled, and I thought he was named well.

'He welcomes all imps, in his majestic benevolence. Are you new come to London or born of the city?'

I decided to play more gently with this simple dog, there may be advantage in it. 'I recently came here from a place far to the north; I am grateful for the welcome in your master's kingdom.'

'Not my master only – yours too, Inges. The Mazger is master of all imps.'

Well, I have no master, I thought to say, but kept that to myself for diplomacy's sake. 'Can I speak to this Mazger? I would like to meet him.'

Snuff shook his head. 'The Mazger requests one's presence, one does not request his. You may join the feast in the Great Hall this evening and be welcomed with the others. You may see His Majesty at High Table, but do not look upon him or catch his eye.'

'A cat may not look at the king then?' I quipped.

Snuff did not react, nor would I expect a dog to. Even the sharpest blade cannot leave a mark on empty air.

I remembered my fishy friend. 'Jack has recommended me to him, perhaps that earns my place at his table?'

Snuff looked up; his simple brown eyes widened. 'Jack you say? Very well, I can perhaps find a slightly better table for you.'

There were no tables, of course. We are cats. But it seemed that this Mazger must fancy himself in the mould of the human kings, and so things were named thus. This very building we were in, Snuff told me, was once a great palace of the English kings, gifted to The Mazger by one their kind named Edward. It may have been a palace, I thought, but I am sure the King Edward did not live in rooms carpeted with sewer water and hung with tapestries of green algae.

I was seated at a 'table' with six other cats. It seemed close by the High Table, which was little more than a stone bench whose feet were shaped like the paws of some great cat.

On it was laid a silk sheet that shone with spotless, iridescent blue and seemed so out of place with the room that I wondered how it could exist in such a place. Of The Mazger, there was no sign. But among my table companions I saw the grey cat who had greeted me at the grate.

'Hello again, I bet you didn't expect to be sharing with me tonight?' I said, with the right amount of teasing.

He looked down his long nose at me. He was one of those cats whose faces seem to narrow to a point, and who have the permanent look of slightly disappointed surprise.

'My name is Inges. I'm a friend of Jack's. I'm afraid I didn't catch yours.'

His expression, if it were possible, looked even more disappointed. 'Isegrim. Keeper of the Royal Latrine.'

I laughed. Perhaps I shouldn't have. It was rude of me. But still. 'And what do you do?' I sniggered. His expression, and that of his fellows, told me more than I wanted to know.

'It is one of the highest positions at court, and one I should think you would show more respect to.'

I apologised. Though I struggled to keep a face that could convince them of my sincerity, and they shuffled uneasily about, exchanging looks.

For all the pretensions to grandeur of this basement palace, the food was good. 'We fetch it down from the market at the New Gate, it is the best in London,' one of the other cats, a bright-faced young calico across the way from me, chirped.

'And how do you get it down to here without being seen, or chased for it by the kites and the dogs?' I asked, as I could imagine a great chain of cats pursued down the streets dragging the parts of a lamb in their mouths.

Inges

'Oh we come down through the conduit – you can get anywhere–'

'That's enough, Poilnoes,' Isegrim snarled. 'I'm sure Inges doesn't want to be bothered with the tedium of palace logistics. And silence now, for here comes His Majesty.'

All the cats, and the other imps – for I saw a small number of dogs, birds, toads and mice also – stood and dropped their gaze to the floor as I watched the entrance of this king. He was flanked either side by two huge ginger toms, who looked like they could put even Lord Pumpkin to flight. Behind him walked three queens, each more beautiful than the other, though none – I thought to myself then – as pleasing to my eye as Fillie.

The king himself was an old tom. Fur that had probably once been black was now washed with grey, so that it looked more like a badger's coat than a cat's. He was big, no doubt powerful in his youth, but he moved with a slowness of joints and a lifting of a back leg that clearly pained him to step upon. It seemed to me this was a kingdom that would soon be in need of another coronation.

The Mazger took his place on the azure silk, on which had been placed the heart of some poor beast – perhaps a sheep or pig; certainly enough to feed the greediest monarch. He slowly raised his paw to greet the room, then hunched down to take his first bite. The room raised their paws in answer, and – once their king began – joined the feast.

'You should raise your paw – it's the correct thing to do in His Majesty's presence,' a tabby queen sat next to Isegrim hissed. From their closeness I took her to be his mate.

'He's new here, Slickskin, he'll learn his place soon enough,' Isegrim puffed.

'Well, I'm not sure how long I will be enjoying your pleasant company,' I said with as much grace as I could manage. 'I have important things to do before I get back to my home, and very little time in which to do them.'

'Oh, what things, Inges?' Poilnoes said, seemingly excited by the prospect.

'Well, I must find a woman. Here in London. She is important to my soul.'

Isegrim looked at me down his long nose. 'To your soul? Then we must see if we can help you,' he returned a look to Slickskin. 'We must all see what we can do. Tell me, what trouble is your soul in?'

'She's to be hanged for a witch. And others too. But she has been the victim of this woman, who has turned the truth on its head, and I must see her found and my soul cleared.'

'Do you have any clues as to where she may be?' Poilnoes leaned in closer, pushing her pink nose to the inner circle where I stood.

'I have a ring. It bears the mark of a shell, and I saw the same upon a cart at Cheapside. A scallop shell, in a cross. I was following the cart when I fell into the river and your Jack found me.'

The cats at the table looked around at each other, and, despite the edict, I saw at least two look at the king.

'I will speak to the others, Inges,' Isegrim said, pulling up his shoulders and drawing the back of a paw lazily across the side of his mouth. 'In this kingdom, we take care of our own.'

I thanked Isegrim, and perhaps felt a little guilty for laughing at his royal role, though it amused me to think of it again.

Poilnoes showed me to the space where I could spend my sleeping hours. I was pleased to see it was among the crates in one of the rooms close to the Great Hall – a dry spot, and well furnished with straw that, while old, still had some softness left in it.

'I hope you find what you are looking for, Inges. You have been very brave to come to London from so far, your soul must mean a great deal to you.'

I saw in Poilnoes's eyes some shadow of sadness, and wondered if perhaps she had lost her soul and now stayed here for safety. 'Yes, she does. She is a good soul and one I would not want to lose.'

'Even to gain another...' Poilnoes's voice trailed off.

As I turned from sleep later that night, I wondered if I should have asked her what she meant by that.

I slept badly. I was troubled by dreams of Peg, of fire, of the pillory post and the man with clipped ears. I dreamt of swallowing flames and breathing water, of red kites and grey dogs.

'Wake up Inges, you are to be honoured,' it was Isegrim, pushing at me with his paw. I swiped idly at him, still with the form of a greyhound, I think, in my mind. 'The king will see you Inges. You must be a more important cat than you look.'

In his chamber, down from his stone bench, The Mazger looked even bigger and more imposing, but his guards were larger still.

'Inges, Inges! A name for a scoundrel if ever I heard one,' The Mazger boomed in a voice I felt he must save for first meetings. 'But you will find yourself in good company here; we scoundrels must watch out for each other, hey?'

I smiled politely. 'Your... Highness.'

The questioning pause in my voice must have caught his attention. 'That is acceptable, Inges. Your Majesty is better but that is acceptable.' He waited; I made the right sign of understanding.

'So Inges, I hear you are looking for a woman? Well there are many lost ones above here in this palace, but if she has a gold ring then I doubt she is one of them – unless she stole it from a customer.' The Mazger flicked his tail as is the way cats laugh, and his guards followed his gesture, forced and unnatural to them.

The king gestured for the guards to step out and for me to join him in a bowl of cow's milk. I felt it impolite to say it was too rich for my tastes. 'Tell me Inges, Isegrim said you mentioned a ring?'

'I did...' he looked up sternly from his milk and I remembered, '...Your Majesty'. He nodded for me to continue. 'It was a gold ring she had upon her finger, before my friend bit it off.'

'I like the sound of your friend. There'd be a job for him here. This ring, Isegrim tells me, it had a peculiar mark upon it?'

'Indeed,' I now felt I had Majestied enough. 'A scallop shell, and I saw the same on a cross upon the coats of two men at Cheapside. I thought they might be servants of some man–'

'Buckingham,' The Mazger said, calm but deliberate.

'Buckingham?'

'I have seen it. In my business at the palace. The cross and the shells. It is the badge of the Villiers.' He saw my expression of confusion. 'The Villiers. A family of no great importance, sheep farmers I believe, until most recently.' He stepped back from the milk bowl and stood with his face to mine. 'The English king is uncommonly fond of one of that name and has elevated him to great status. Made him the Marquess of Buckingham.'

'Villiers?'

'George Villiers.'

Suddenly there was hope.

'I must find him. Can you help me?'

The Mazger frowned, 'It is not common to ask favours of a king.' he said, and I bowed my head. 'But, I am nothing if not generous, and I like your spirit, Inges – though take care not to cross that line from confidence to irreverence, I am still your king.'

You are *a* king, I thought, but I need you now so we will play it your way. 'Your Majesty, you are too kind to a humble cat.'

The Mazger puffed out his broad, mottled chest. 'The Marquess is a powerful man, and not easy to get to. But I may be able to help. It so happens I had news only yesterday from one of the rats, who does business on the river, that there is to be a meeting two days from now at the palace of the human king, James. The king's great bishop is coming over from his place in Lambeth to discuss matters concerning Villiers. I have no direct access to Villiers, but I may be able to get someone into the chamber where the king and his bishop meet. From there, we may learn of his comings and goings. It will be risky, but if this matter is urgent to you…'

'Thank you, Your Majesty.'

'I can send an agent, someone small. A mouse perhaps? Better a vole. They could–'

'Apologies, Your Majesty, I must do this myself. Get me in that room and I will be in your debt.'

The Mazger raised his greying, rough-furred head and let out an incongruously soft mew. His great ginger guards returned to the chamber – the signal that my time there was done and matters were settled. 'It will be arranged. Be ready for instructions. Be aware though, Inges: the Royal Favour is a heavy gift to carry around.'

Of that I had no doubt, and he would expect me to relieve myself of its weight in kind at some point. But that was for the future. Now I had found George, and soon I would have the woman; and she would have the justice of Inges.

The Bishop

THE PLAN, such as it was, struck me as foolhardy, but what choice did I have? I must find the woman, force her to confess, and get back to Yorkshire in time before the trial, which – for all I knew – could be happening right now.

The palace of the Cat King had indeed once been that of the human king, though now the rooms above his royal sewer-suite were filled not with lords and ladies but with bawds and stews. The women could be taken naked and publicly whipped as a lesson to all, or else forced to work their feet in grinding corn. The whipping lessons seemed to work, as I saw a number of men who, having attended to watch the class, left seemingly keen to teach what they had learned to another hired stew.

Evidently this vast hall was too small for the grandeur of English kings. They had handed it over to these jailers and correctors – and, I suppose, to King Mazger, though I doubt they knew that – and moved wholesale to the vast city-within-a-city that was called Whitehall Palace.

Whitehall was (I learned these facts from Ferdinando, who was a most informative guide) home to some great churchman who

Inges

built a house there finer than any of his king. I suppose this must have ruffled his crown a little, as he soon had the fellow evicted and took it for himself.

Since that time it had grown to a great sprawling forest of brick and stone that must have been bigger just in itself than Harrogate or Skipton or any of the fine towns I had knowledge of. A cat could sleep in a different room each night of his life, I thought to myself, and not have seen half the palace before he died.

That in itself was our first challenge; to find our way around the palace to the room where the meeting would occur.

'Don't worry, Inges, our great king has thought of that,' Isegrim had told me in the morning as we ate our sweetbreads and reviewed the plan. Now, huddled in the footwell of the Whyte Fryers stairs, I asked to go over it again.

'We can't get you into the palace – too many people, too many rooms. We'd get lost, or caught and kicked out, or worse. So we go via Lambeth.'

'The house of the bishop, right?'

'Exactly. We have a man in there. A servant much indebted to The Mazger.' I gave a look of disapproval that Isegrim batted away. 'He will take you over the river.'

'Won't I be an odd parcel for a bishop's servant?'

'You will be hidden. The bishop takes over various books and papers – mostly for show, to make himself look busy for the king. He never reads them. You will be carried in one of the cases, in place of a book. There will be a small hole through which you can look and listen.'

'And breathe.'

'Yes, and breathe. Of course,' (It seemed to me this may have been an afterthought). 'When you are done, and have learned what you need of Villiers, the servant will bring you back to Lambeth and release you.'

'Fine. That could work,' I said. 'But I'm not sure of this first part; going with Jack to Lambeth. Could we not get ourselves a boat?'

'Do you think a wherryman will take payment from a cat? He'd sooner drown us if we spoke to him – you know the rules.'

I did know the rules, and that they applied to bishop's servants as much as to boatmen, but I would go along with this. What else was there to do? So I would go once again into those cold, fetid waters on the back of scaly Jack, like some furry cargo. Fiddle-di-di to dignity. Let's do it again.

The banks on the Lambeth side of the river are not built up like those at Bridewell, and instead I found I must make the last part of my crossing belly deep in sucking mud, as I crawled and slopped my way up and out onto the path that was set back from the shore.

'Thank you again, Jack!' I called, as he dived back down into the waters, though at that moment I felt far from thankful. I scurried across the flinty road, shaking my legs to dislodge great globules of tidal mud, and pushed through the trees and bushes that marked the perimeter of the palace. Across the clipped lawn of the palace front I ran, to the small fig tree where I was to meet The Mazger's agent. Either I was early, or he was late – so I ducked myself into its leaves and, to pass the time, and so others would know Inges was here, I pissed against its trunk.

'Cat, don't do that. The old cardinal planted that tree. Bad cat!' Our agent had arrived.

Despite the assurances of Isegrim, I was not about to talk to this human. It's just not right. It's not done. But if he calls me 'bad cat' again I'll let my claws do the talking, I said to myself. Bad cat? You have no idea.

This mission was to try my dignity once more. This young fool grabbed me by my scruff, like I was some wandering kitten, and dunked me without ceremony into a wooden box already half-filled with an old, musty book. The lid was dropped, and I planted face down into the binding. And just like that – flattened, soaked, muddied and bruised – I was carried to the boats, across the water, and into the palace of King James.

The box was badly cramped, but I found a little work with my back legs took away the cover of the book and I could crumple the pages to pad it out and soften the ride. When I was finally deposited – with less care than I would have liked – on the table of the meeting chamber, my servant got at least one thing right and my spyhole gave me a perfect view of what was to unfold.

I had expected a bishop to look more impressive. Humans – even my Peg – seem to hold holy people in high regard and, despite the poor example of our own humble vicar, I had expected the leader of them all to be a little more imposing.

He was of ordinary height for a human man, and his clothes had the look of great expense – yet they seemed more like they wore him than the other way round. A great collar ringed his neck, looking to me not unlike that contraption Maggie put about me when Quin had scratched me. I wondered if he struggled to do his toilet with it too.

The white of the lace served to frame a tired and pale face, with a natural downwards turn to his mouth. His small, soft black eyes darted back and forth to the door, so that he looked like some timid spinster awaiting a hoped-for suitor she knew would only show disappointment in their meeting.

He had a beard, which I suppose a spinster may not; though Jennit Dibble's would give it a good match, as his was thin, wispy and grey so it barely covered the weak outline of a chin that shone through in pale pink patches. He had magnificent sleeves, though, I will say that for him.

And then the king. Brought in attended by two fine boys, who he quickly waved away. No, he did not have the look of a disappointed suitor. A disappointed brother maybe? They shared a beard, that same haunted, downturned look, but the king – perhaps for his station – carried himself with an air of one who was never in doubt who the better man was, no matter what company he might keep.

'Your most serene and munificent Majesty!' The bishop's words were as puffed as his sleeves.

'Good day, Your Grace, I hope you travelled well?' (He travelled better than me, I can tell you that).

The two men's voices were the opposite of their poise. The bishop's was deep and clear; James spoke like he had a mouthful of bread.

'Indeed Your Majesty, your kindness touches me. The day has been blessed with sunlight and calm waters, as it should be when I am in service of my Lord King.'

James curled his mouth. 'Well, the water is not always so obedient to my wishes. I believe it has the same feeling for me as does Parliament – one day calmly in my service, the next billowing me about as if it wishes to throw me from my seat.'

The bishop gave what seemed a practiced laugh. 'It is in the matters of Parliament that I come to you of course, Your Majesty, and I hope that I may perhaps play the role of some ancient Greek Potamoi and calm the waters between you so you may both reach a safe harbour together.'

They talk like this, the two of them. I can't remember the half of it, though I have a fine memory, having learned a trick from that old tomcat Loki. He showed me how to store my memories around Maggie's house, each stuffed in a shrew or vole that I can bite open to release when I will.

So they talked some more of gods of this and that, and such tedious things as Commons, and Lords, and the Palatine and some fellow named Frederick who seemed to have upset a lot of people, and how the king needed money to help him out. It was something of a bore, I must be honest, and I felt a need to perhaps shut my eyes a moment, just to rest them.

I also felt the need for the toilet. Which was poor timing on my part. All the water I swallowed on my journey with Jack had worked its way through me. Fortunately there was paper enough in the box to soak it up, so it would not run out. It was unpleasant, but necessary. Then just as I had finished, I heard the words I had come for.

'Buckingham will not like it.'

'Your Majesty, rogues as they are, the Commons want his hide. We have thrown Bacon to them but still they hunger for more.'

Bacon, I thought. I would hunger for more right now too, as it had been some time since breakfast.

'Yes,' the king replied, waving his long arms, 'and Mompesson too, even his brother Sir Edward, God's Feet!'

The bishop blanched and the king patted down what might pass for an apology. 'Do you smell something? Kind of musty. Never mind, carry on.'

'My Lord King, I think if Buckingham is to press on with this match, for all that it serves you, I think it may do you – may do Buckingham – more harm.'

The king paced the room. As he stepped further from me, I could see how oddly spindly his long legs were for a man so broad in the shoulder. 'To hurt Buckingham is to hurt me.' He shook his head. 'But it is his fervent belief this match is in the best interests of us all – of me. Christ, am I not the king?'

The holy man's face now managed the great feat of looking both all-white and all-pink at the same time. 'Your Majesty, there are those in Parliament who say, "how can we on the one hand be asking for money to fight the Spanish, and the other proposing to take it from them for the wedding of our noble Prince and the Infanta". They make a show of this dilemma, and talk of doomed Spanish Matches past – of Katherine and Philip, and–'

'Am I some stock to be laughed at?' The king now raised his voice so that even his doughy words rang about the room. 'Or perhaps they fear that the dowry will free me from the need to ask for their help again? Perhaps they realise that when the soil is once more fertile I will have no need of worms to turn it?'

Now, I am a simple Yorkshire cat, and I must confess matters of state are not something I am familiar with. But here is my understanding on all this.

The king is not fond of Parliament. Rather like The Mazger, I think he sees his subjects' place as to raise their paws for him and wait for him to eat. But, also like The Mazger, he puts on a great display of wealth yet has barely a pot to piss in. And those folks he calls worms, they have the money.

So he is to wed his son to some wealthy princess, largely for the dowry, but at the same time wants Parliament to give him money to fight the girl's father.

And Buckingham is up to his lacy neckpiece in this, it seems, and both he and this Spanish girl are disliked by Parliament. They have some of the money the king needs, but he won't get it unless he gives up the match which will give him the rest of the money he needs. Good luck with that, say I. Now king, tell me where this rogue is, and we can all be on our way.

'I will speak to Buckingham this week, at the masque. I will hear what he has to say again. I will put your advice to him, but mark – I will give my own too, and I am still his king, and his best dear heart.'

'Your Majesty.' The bishop bowed and his hand rose to push back his black hat where it had slipped to show the fine polish of a balding head. 'It is my fervent wish that the masque goes well, if God wills it.'

'And why would it not?' the king grumbled, now seemingly so set on dispute that he would not leave it even for small talk.

'I hear Jonson is to oversee again.'

'And?'

'Well, I am not one to play the God-sibling, but the talk is that these days he leaves his best work less on the page and more on the floor outside The Mermaid.'

What did he say?

'I hear they sell him the eight-shilling barrel as if it were four, as he brings in the young men of means who fancy themselves great wits. Then he drinks his own wits away and fights with anyone who bests his verse; or else debases himself with some pox-ridden stew.'

The bishop clearly did not like this man Jonson. He drinks at The Mermaid. Is there more?

'Calm yourself now.' The king handed him a laced kerchief to dab at his glistening mouth. 'Jonson was a model of charm and decency at Burghley and will be again at Windsor, I am sure. He has the wit still, I think, to deport himself correctly in the face of Majesty.'

The bishop's panting was slowing now. 'Your Majesty, I forget myself.'

'Never mind, never mind,' the king patted him on the puffed sleeve and his face lit up as I thought it might were he touched by one of these debauched stews that so inflamed him. 'Besides,

Buckingham is paying him £100 I believe, so he will be on his very best behaviour for that.'

So this drunkard, this Jonson, he is in the pay of Buckingham and he will be with him at some masque, in a place called Windsor, within the week. This could be the... oh shit!

The bishop, in his great emotion at the king's touch, had paid his deep respects and been dismissed. In his fluster of leaving he went to pick up my box with an unsteady hand. And now down I fall, box and all.

'God's Hat – it's a damned cat,' the king screeched, and hopped like a startled stork, pulling up one of his long legs so that he hugged it to his chest as he bounded around the room. The bishop was staring, his sad mouth gaping like a carp, first at me then at the box.

'The beast! The foul demon! It has despoiled the Holy Book!' The reddening bishop was now in a weeping rage, and I turned to follow his gaze as it fell on the sodden, scrumpled, muddy mass of velum and hide that had been my sedan seat. In this light it looked rather old. And rather important.

'The word of the Lord, befouled by a base cat! Saint Thomas himself read from that book. You have pissed on the Bible of Becket. Oh child of Satan, curse you to a thousand Hells!'

Ah. This is unfortunate.

The king was now hopping more wildly, half stumbling, half climbing to get upon the great table that fills the better part of the room. 'It is a witch! A witch in form of cat! They have found me! Beast begone, our Lord God give me salvation!' He starts throwing candles at me, then their holders.

For a moment I am trapped, the bishop's mighty sleeves racing after me one way, the king's candles raining down the other. But in the commotion, a servant rushes in, the door is open, and I see my chance. By my great fortune the door to the courtyard has been left open too, and I slide and skitter on the tiles of the floor as I dash outside – behind me the fading roar of King James: cursing at witches and cats, promising the fires of Hell, swearing to hunt me down.

That could have gone better.

Inges

Big Ben

THE CONFUSION saved me. That and the boatman. My hasty exit had taken me out into a great garden, patterned with hedges at squares and angles, a maze for cats. I dashed between the legs of a half dozen courtiers, who turned their heads to the king's ravings but made no connection between his curses and this scrambling cat.

I was trapped, it seemed. The far end of the garden faced the river – a stone wall, a sheer drop into its airless waters. Either side of it tall buildings grew, sheer walls too steep to climb, and behind me was the king in his fury, his servants now marshalling the palace guard.

'Down here, cat – jump!' The voice came from below the river wall. I mounted to see a wherryman – squat and flat-faced, as if his nose had once been stoved with a shovel – hissing a call to me and pointing as his bow butted the masonry. I needed no second invitation.

It was a long way down and, though I fell with feline grace, due to the unnatural (and I would say ill-thought-out) layout of the boat, I landed awkwardly across its forward thwart and face-first into its watery bottom. The man laughed.

'Watch your step, cat! Now, keep yourself under the seat, I don't want to be seen with you, got it?'

I was not about to break my silence for this churl, so I let out a sharp hiss and retreated below the wooden board.

'What's the matter? Cat got your tongue?' He laughed again. I am not fond of the human laugh, I find it a little grating, if I'm honest; like when your claws catch rough stone. 'I told them it would go wrong; good job I was here, ain't it?'

Well, Shovel-Face, 'wrong' is subjective. It had not gone as smoothly as I liked, I admitted to myself, but I had the information I needed. Now I just needed to get back to Cheapside, to The Mermaid, and find this Jonson; if you could just drop me at Whyte Fryers.

A few minutes passed beneath the boards, and I felt safe enough to raise my head above the gunwale – where, to my great consternation, I saw we were now approaching the far bank, Lambeth Palace in view.

The boat was fighting against the flow of the river so that the boatman had to steer as much upriver as he did across. His thick arms were heaving at the oars as I glared at him, then back to the city side. It took him a second to get my meaning.

'That's the way I'm taking you, cat. If you want the other side you'll need to cross the bridge, or swim. It's a little walk. Maybe take in some entertainment on your way down – they'd love you at the Bear Garden.'

The boat pulled into the rise of the bank, a little way around the bend from Lambeth, and I quickly exited – stepping across the boatman's lap as I did so. If I left my claws out in stepping on him, that was entirely unintended. Across the water I could see the palace, where no doubt the king was still apoplectic over witches and the bishop still crying over his book. I took the road that followed the river's bend and watched as the city rose up before me on the other side; the tower of its high church was the beacon that would guide me back to Cheapside.

I found a little trouble with folk walking their hounds on the common road, so, by an old manor, I took a cut across country. A little way through the fields and gardens I came upon an open place in which pools had been built in perfect symmetry. They teemed with a thousand Jacks – pike, from little fry to great toothed beasts, crammed in so they could barely move, threshing against each other in anger and fear. I wondered if our Jack knew of this place.

Beyond, I found two further temples to the cruelty of man. Great open houses where signs called humans to gather and watch some poor blind bear whipped until he cannot stand, or to see dogs tear apart a horse and its beastly rider, or goad a bull and finish it with a sword. At one of these houses, through the bars to its basement, I saw a great brown bear groaning and turning on his thin straw bed, his shoulder open and running with red sores. I had a moment to talk to him, and he told me his name was Ned and that he longed for death, but his soul always called him back. I thought of Peg, and of how I had never known my own fortune until it was taken from me.

The rest of my journey was a trouble of carts, and horses and legs – but I remember little of it, my mind too distracted with the confundity of man's being. Humans spend their lives running from death: they build great temples in which they hope to hide from it, or they try to curse it off with words.

They do all they can to cling to life, but they are clinging by its very edge to a thin sheet of ice-glass. The harder they hold, no matter which way they frame it, no matter how they are schooled to grip; it will melt to nothing in their hot hands and run away from them in the end.

And yet for all they fear it, they must love it too. They invent new ways to deliver it, they drag it out for pleasure, they build whole cities and move whole countries just to harvest it. Men, beasts or imps, it seems not to matter – death is sport, spectacle, entertainment. If this is what it is to have your own soul, I am glad I was born an imp.

Ferdinando was waiting for me at The Mermaid. 'Inges, you live! I thought you were gone.' The rat put his small, clammy hands about my neck, and I thought what a sight this would seem if any street cat could see it now.

He had walked the embankment of the Thames for days, searching the falls before the bridge, or the tidal mud where children and vagrants pick the ripe treasures of the river. He must have thought me dead, yet he searched to be sure. I think of him now and I remember that embrace.

'It is a long story, which I will tell one day, but the short of it is that I know who George is, and the man to take us to him sits in this very tavern.'

Ferdinando let go of my neck and shook his whiskers excitedly. 'Do you have a name? A description?'

'I do – he is some poet, a great drunk, by the name of Jonson.'

My rat friend now skipped around, as though chasing his tail. 'Ben Jonson? ¡Madre Mia! My soul would have loved to be here for this adventure.'

'You know this man?'

'Indeed I do. All England knows him.'

I am a provincial cat of country learning. No shame in that, in fact I take pride in it. But I am well read. Peg and Maggie were not always poor cunning women. Indeed Maggie's husband had been a man of decent standing and education, before the bottle, then the cards, and then the noose, took him away – along with all he had with him. All, that is, but his books, which Peg would read, and I in secret alongside her. We read Aristotle and Caesar, some treatises of Hayward and Erasmus. History and Philosophy; but it seems her father had no taste for plays or poems, and – though Ferdinando made me think I should – I had no knowledge of this Jonson man.

'He is a fine poet, and a writer of plays. Some say the finest in England – at least since Shakespeare died, although Jonson won't hear that part and I have heard him boast, you know – borracho como una cuba – that he or Fletcher deserve that crown.'

'And whose work do you think is best?'

'I'm a rat.'

'A fair point. You have seen him then?'

He had, many times, he told me. This Ben Jonson was a great bull of a man, with a shock of black hair and a look about him that he would either crush you to death or else cry on your shoulder, depending which way his humours ran that very moment.

'You can't miss him,' he told me. 'He will be the biggest, the loudest and the drunkest in the room.'

'You may be the biggest, you're definitely the loudest and I would wager you are the drunkest fool in this whole room, Ben Jonson.' I was watching this dribbling oaf as he staggered up to the table. 'But, God's Nigs man, I love you like a brother!'

Well, if I had not known it before, that mumbling stock – now puking on the floor – had just flagged our man. He was sat at the corner table, thick fingers – like fat white puddings – wrapped around a tankard; commanding attention with a voice as deep as the Thames, calling for more beer for his fallen comrade even as the man was being carried out.

I had found a spot for myself beneath a bench seat set into the wall, safe from the rain of ale, vomit and spittle that curdled the sawdust floor.

I watched as Jonson stood, or at least pulled himself up to stand, before slumping down on his elbows on the table then half-rising again. 'Yes, my friend... where is he?' He looked around for a sign of the man now carried away. 'Never mind. Yes, I am the drunkest. And do you know why?' The company around his table, and much of the rest of the inn, shook their heads, while a few called out for him to tell them.

'I'm the drunkest, for the boundaries of my wits are set wider than can be walked by common men, and to be without them I must travel further than any of you cosksnkwhofikas.' (I may have misheard the last word, he was mumbling), 'So put me in a drunkard's cloak if you will, and march me through town in it, but first let me empty that barrel so that it may fit this frame!'

Jonson pounded his chest and raised his tankard high, before putting it to his lips and throwing his head back. Immediately he took it away and stared into its bottom, his dark, fleshy forehead furrowed with confusion and anger. 'Tapster, the bloody thing is empty. Here, get me more–' Jonson stepped forward, unaware of the table directly in front of him, tumbling himself, it, and his drinking companions across the floor in a blizzard of beer and profanities.

'Ben, there is no more for you tonight. Someone help him to his feet and put him out.' A sturdy fellow in a leather apron now moved towards the tumbled drinkers and waved at the black-browed bull who had tipped them over. 'That's enough now, Ben. Be on your way or you'll get us closed down again.'

Jonson pulled himself, in careful degrees, to face the man. He put out a great, meaty paw in friendship. 'I am sorry, John, another drink and I will be in my proper temper. Drinks for all! Buckingham is paying tonight!'

'Right, come on Ben, out you go!' The innkeeper now put an arm to Jonson's back to show him out of the door. Jonson responded by bending over to clutch his stomach and giving out a resounding fart that almost shook the pewterware off the tables. The room roared approval and one bold man called out: 'Oh Ben, I think that may be your greatest work since The Fox, I've not heard such a clamour for your name since.'

Jonson stood upright again, raised a finger, turned to the man – and all Hell broke loose.

And so there I was, outside the door of The Mermaid, sat on the cold street, looking straight at the blood-dripping nose and beer soaked lantern chin of the poet – slumped against the greenwashed wall – who must take me to see the Marquess of Buckingham in the morning.

We stared, mutually, a while, before Jonson spoke a casual acknowledgement. 'Cat.'

If not now then when? 'Ben Jonson,' I replied.

'Great grandfather's cock! A talking cat!'

'Yes. This may seem strange—'

Jonson began banging on the wooden door that had been bolted against him. 'In the name of God, open up! Open up. You must see this; this cat knows my name. Open up in the name of all that is Holy!'

'Please don't do that. It won't go well for you.'

He stared at me and his eyes narrowed. 'Good God, are you that witch's cat? That Agnes, who they hanged in Essex? Do you want me to say my Pater Noster in Latin? I will, you know. I know my prayers that way.'

The door opened enough for the innkeeper's head to fit through. 'Will you stop your banging and go home Ben; you will draw down the Watch.'

'This cat talks – he spoke my name. Speak cat!' Jonson widened his eyes to implore speech from me. The innkeeper sighed and looked wearily in my direction.

'*Prrrrrp.*'

'Eloquent. Go to bed, Jonson.' The door slammed again, and big Ben's head dropped.

'Well played, cat. What do you want of me? Is this about the recusancy, because really I'm–'

'I need your help. I need you to do something for me. I can explain.'

Jonson seemed suddenly relieved that I hadn't wanted him to pray in Latin, and his mood turned; though I wished then I had tried a little more at scaring him.

'My help? What do you need, cat? You want me to scratch your belly? Fetch you a fish from Billingsgate? Perhaps you have a desire to sit on my lap?'

'I just need–'

'I'd do it too. If you could just get me another drink.'

'I need to get into the masque, tomorrow. I need to find someone who will be there, and you are to smuggle me in.'

'Od's Bells, it's tomorrow?' Jonson looked suddenly concerned then shook his head and, away with it seemingly, his troubles. 'What's your name, cat? Do you have one?'

'Inges.'

'Ingers, Ingers. What a name, you'll go far.'

'Not Ingers; Inges.'

'Ingus? Ingis?'

'Close enough. Can you get me in–'

'Wait, wait. Ingis, Ingis, Ingis. I must honour you. Give me a moment. I will compose some heroic verse – no, better, a ballad. A ballad for a talking cat.'

'That won't be–'

He raised a thick finger and closed his eyes a moment, then cleared his throat:

Base cats use their tongues but to praise Sterquilinus
And polish the door to his temple of shit
But Ingers is not one of those arsehole cleaners
He instead puts his rough tongue to discourse and wit.'

'Marvellous.'

'I've still got it.'

And so, after some cultured to-and-fro, and a sharpening of wits between us, we came to a solemn agreement: Jonson would get me into the masque. In return, I would slip into the cellar of The Mermaid and retrieve a particular bottle of Burgundy that the poet had knowledge of. The deal was signed in blood upon a kerchief, with a warning that I personally knew Agnes's cat, who would make him recite 100 Pater Nosters in Latin if he crossed me.

Above me, the dark of the city sky now revealed the faintest hint of inky blue in its black. Somewhere across the wide ocean the sun was rolling closer to London and, in just a few hours, I must face the man who held the key to my imprisoned soul.

The Masque

'TALK TO ME, CAT. Damn your whiskers, man, talk to me!'

I was determined to keep my own counsel on matters of the night before. Ben Jonson had a note, written in blood on his kerchief, in his own hand, swearing – on the eternal damnation of his soul – that he would escort an elegant cat – white with black marks – in secret, to the performance of his celebrated masque, The Gypsies Metamorphosed.

He swears the cat made him write it, that he threatened, with his claws, to emasculate him and pickle his manhood in a witch bottle; that he had been goaded by an imp of Hell and an army of familiars. That Satan himself appeared and played catch-my-finger with the cat, before forcing his hand.

But whichever tale he tells, the writing is his, he has a headache, and he is on a wherry heading for Windsor with a cat under his gown; and he is not happy about it.

'No one wears gowns, it's not 1611 anymore. I'll be humiliated. Oh Lord, I hope that coistril Endymious Porter isn't there this time. He fancies himself a poet, you know. Which he's not. Damn you, cat. I should wear you as a hat.'

Inges

I turned a little under his gown, padding down his soft, fat belly for a warmer bed.

'You were talkative enough last night, cat Ingers. Now you try to make a fool of me.' He pushed me to the side beneath his gown, where I may have been catching my claws on his doublet. 'I don't know why you care about this masque anyway but be warned; care will kill a cat. Or else I will. I agreed to take you in, but you get yourself out. Understand?'

'*Prrrrrp.*'

'A pox on you.'

We'd taken a wherry to ourselves – apparently Ben didn't want to be seen with a gown, or a cat, or a cat in a gown. The wherryman looked over Ben's shoulder as he mumbled his complaints to me but was firmly told to keep his eyes on the river while the poet revised a few lines for tonight's performance.

'Of course, I have no need to revise any,' he whispered, and I wasn't sure if he actually was talking to himself now. He suddenly sat upright, tipping me, still under his gown, down onto his lap. 'You see that building ahead, Inges?' He nodded to Westminster Palace, and I almost let him know that I knew it better than he might think.

'There, do you see?' I had poked my head out from under his gown to look where, at one side, a huge wooden cage enclosed a towering pile of pink and yellow stone rising behind a row of older buildings.

'The king is having his great Banqueting Hall rebuilt. The last one burned down. I would wager His Majesty set the torch to it himself, as it was a vulgar forest of pillars and fancy that he detested.'

I twitched my whiskers.

'It's now being re-built to a new design by a friend of mine. Not so much a friend really, more a hanger-on, a stealer of credit – Inigo Jones. Have you heard of him? No I don't suppose you have. He does my scenery for me, a carpenter who takes my applause. I suspect, like the last building, it will in time be remodelled again, once the fashion for stolen Italian ideas turns to something new. Chinese perhaps? They will make it a pagoda.'

He seemed to be sufficiently animated at the thought of pagodas, or Inigo, that he forgot the wherryman's presence and set me down in the boat bottom where he could better lecture me. The boatman and I exchanged glances.

'You see, modern buildings – however grand, however solid – they need to be reworked, or burnt, or replaced, as the fashions of the world change. But my writing – my writing is no mere copy of antiquity; it is the continuation of its soul. Of course I don't need to rewrite it. Once it is set, it is set for eternity. Unchanging as the soul itself.'

The wherryman now seemed as much interested in Ben's address to me as he was the river ahead, mainly because the poet was now standing and causing the hull to sway from side to side.

'Within the masque itself, Inges, the same is true. The staging of the masque – the costumes, the scenes; however grandly made, whatever the cost – is like the body: ephemeral, imperfect, to be withered by age. It's the words, Inges, the words! They are the soul – the everlasting, the incorruptible: the soul. That is what I do, I create the soul.'

He waved his thick arm wildly above his head and then sat down with a thump that nearly threw the wherryman off his balance and into the Thames.

'*Prrrrrp*'

'Indeed Ingers, indeed.'

Ben steadied himself, and the boat, and we continued our journey back in our places – Ben at his seat, me under his gown, and the wherryman stealing glances at us and looking a little nervous now.

Once we had pulled into the wharf at Windsor, my escort whispered into the ear of our boatman and tipped him a coin that brightened his face. We had arrived at the palace; the masque was about to begin.

The castle rose up before us – imposing and solid. If Whitehall was designed to show the English Crown's glory, this grey bastion was the symbol of its power. And I would breach its walls to get at my enemies – Buckingham and, if my instincts were right (which, as you will see, they usually are), The Woman, too.

Inges

Ben appeared to be late. As he walked to his seat, it seemed to me he was more worried that eyes were on his attire than that I might be found. So much so that he abandoned the plan of holding on to me during the show so that I could scan the room for any sign of Buckingham and his woman. Instead, I was put under his chair, hidden by the gown which he had cast off and now stowed there. He took his seat with, I must say, a great deal of fuss: 'just stay there, don't move, don't talk, and wait for the show to end. Oh, hello Endymious, fancy seeing you here.'

If you've never been to a masque – and I can't say there was a call for them in Fewston – then let me explain them from what I learned that day. They are just like the mummers plays that the travelling players hold in the inn, only with even more alcohol, significantly more jewellery and just as many fart jokes.

'It's satire, Inges. You see, I've subtly inverted conventions of the stage and court and – tellingly – the actual metamor–'

I would have loved to have learned more about Ben Jonson's fart jokes, but right then I saw him. At first I thought him just some lowly player, as his face was covered with a layer of thick greasepaint and he was dressed like a fool. But the applause at his appearance, and the way the king smiled at him as he kissed his hand – it must be Buckingham. And if he was here, I thought, most likely his woman would be too.

I slipped carefully from below the gown and around the back of the raised platform on which the king and his guests were seated, in order to better view the other people there. One lady would be Buckingham's new wife, Katherine. Ben had told me on our boat ride that the masque was staged in her honour – so any who gave a show of being with him would not be my woman. But he would be sure to cast a look or two towards his lover, so I would follow his eyes; just as I do a vole when I must guess which way it intends to run.

At the far side of the seats there was a young woman who was clearly alone, and Buckingham seemed to have his eye on her. I watched her for a while and had made my mind to follow her when she left, but just at that moment a song finished – something about the Devil's Arse, I didn't catch it all – and the people stood to applaud. There, behind the fine lady I had been watching, and still seated, was another woman – her face in the shadow of a wide-brimmed hat – politely clapping. Only something odd about her caught my eye.

It took me a second to realise it, but her hands, gloved in white, were moving to clap with all fingers gently curved – all but one. One remained static, unbending, unnatural. She was missing a finger.

Now I recognised her. She wore her hair tied up and back under her hat so I had not seen the brightness of the yellow at first; but the dark, cold eyes – I would remember those anywhere. This was my woman; this was the one who had Peg now locked away in a filthy prison cell – or worse. It took all my considerable powers of restraint not to take out those evil eyes right there, the same way she had blinded Quin before she killed him. But you don't catch a vole by charging at it – you wait, and you stalk, and when it thinks it is safe, that is when you pounce.

So I waited, and then she moved. Buckingham had glanced again in her direction. Moments later she quietly left her seat and slipped out of a side door. I followed.

The audience's attention was drawn to the king, who was now loudly calling for a song to be sung again but with more dancing this time, so I quickly made the open space across the two banks of seating, and through the same door. About half way across I saw Ben Jonson catch sight of me, then quickly look under his chair. He appeared suddenly very white and sick in the face. It must have been the boat journey.

I caught the flash of a brocade shoe as it disappeared into one of the antechambers, and I followed, slipping gracefully through the door just as it closed, and carefully crouching under a dark wooden table to observe.

'Not enjoying the masque then, gorgeous?'

I could only see the feet of the woman and the boots of a man – too rough for a guest at this performance. The woman's voice was soft, almost musical, and quite unlike any I had heard in Yorkshire or London.

'It's a little vulgar for my tastes, as are you. Your job is to carry my words, I don't need to hear yours. You'll get paid when you get there.'

'Hold on, I was told…'

'When you get there.'

The man was silent for a moment and I saw his boots move towards my table. For a second I thought he might have spotted me, but he pulled up short and continued.

'I'm taking a risk talking to you here, there should be some consideration on that.'

'This is the safest place. We could hardly go together to his house, and mine is undoubtedly being watched. Just remember my words – do not write them down. You are being paid well enough.'

'And what words should I remember, madam?'

'Tell her George says we are ready to continue–'

'Did George say that, or is that your wish?'

'We are ready to continue. The elder girl is to be next, there are too many eyes on the younger now.'

'What of the old women?'

'They aren't ready yet. We've still got some loose ends there. But tell our friend to make sure that the same cat is seen again – she will know what to do. Is that clear? Good – because I need to get back to that execrable farce, I'll be missed.'

For a second I was unsure what to do. The man with the boots would be heading back to Fewston, and there was someone there The Woman must be in league with.

I thought first I should follow him, try to get back and discover who that was. But The Woman was clearly in charge, and if she and Buckingham were ordering it, they must be the ones to stop it – the ones to be exposed as villains. My mind was made up for me when the man left first. I couldn't follow without being seen by The Woman, so I watched her go back to her seat and made my way back to Ben.

'Inges – what in God's?… get back under the gown, go on.'

I had made my way, under chairs and between legs, back to my place. I think I might have been spotted, a couple of times. But there were chickens in the scene now on stage and I think those who saw me must have thought me part of the show. Ben was getting agitated, I could see, and I imagined he was worried about the mess the chickens were making of the set.

'What in the name of all the saints were you doing following that woman, Inges? She's a very well-connected lady – you are going to get us both killed.'

There is a way to tilt your head, if you are a cat, that lets a human know you are asking a question without you having to speak. If you know a cat, watch him carefully the next time you see him. If there is something on his mind – 'where is the food, human?' 'why are you looking at me?' – he will tilt his head, and you will know it.

'Don't you tilt your head at me like that, cat.' He let out a quiet sigh and dropped his head between his legs, closer to my ears. 'If that's the person you are looking for, she's Matilda Cheveron. She's very secretive, very beautiful and very unpopular with the other ladies at court. That's all I know. That, and some wealthy lover pays for a fine house to keep her in up on Milk Street – it's the talk of the court. Now let me watch my own masque – we're just getting to the good bit.'

Well I had no choice but to wait out the performance. The Woman – Matilda, I could barely bring myself to speak her name – would remain until the end and I would need to use all my stealth to follow her out of the room unseen. So I waited, and watched – one eye on her, the other on the show. It would be rude not to watch, with Ben seated right there.

The story of the masque had been hard to grasp before I had followed The Woman out; now, it was even more confusing. The actors – including Buckingham, who seemed overconfident in his ability to caper – had at first played the part of travelling folk. I suppose they were meant to be like those you see up Swinsty when the fair is come; but they dressed as if the inmates of Bedlam had found among themselves the services of a blind tailor.

Their faces were covered in grease and they acted the fool, pretending to steal from the king, telling flatteringly happy fortunes of the guests on the high seating, and generally prancing about in a rather unseemly manner.

Now, here at the end, they had disappeared to remove their grease and returned in their fine clothes to give back all they had stolen, having turned back to what they called civilised men. It seems to me an odd tale, with an odder thought – that the audience must hold the appearance of a man to be the reflection of his soul. I could put them straight on that, I thought. I had hoped my journey would teach me more of human understanding, but the further down that road I had travelled the further from understanding I seemed to wander.

Finally, the show drew to its end, with Buckingham capering his last caper and delivering Ben's big reveal:

'Who doth disguise his habit and his face,
And takes on a false person by his place,
The power of poetry can never fail her,
Assisted by a barber and a tailor.'

That's it? I thought, that's your pay-off, Ben? First of all: 'fail her/tailor' – seriously? And you're the best poet in England?

And then you think you need to tell them – that the audience couldn't see for themselves it was all just a bit of dress-up, a bit of grease paint? You think your storytelling is so good they might believe their friends had literally transformed themselves into someone else by some sort of... oh Inges, you have been such a fool!

There are different ways your heart can break. I've learned that now. When it truly breaks it is as if your heart was of alabaster, struck with a maul. It compacts so tightly that, for just a second, it is crushed to a point of pure, unbearable pain; then in an instant it shatters outward to grit and jagged shards that stay within you forever, turning in your chest every now and then to cut you again, even when you think they must all have passed through by now.

But at that time I had yet to know that pain. I didn't know that this feeling was just a simple crack; that it could be pieced together again, like a Delftware vase, almost as good as new. And so that, when I felt it, I thought then there were no worse ways for it to break.

'The same cat', that's what The Woman said. 'Make sure that the same cat is seen again.' And how could I be seen again, if I am here? A little grease and a storyteller. A white cat and black ointment. A drop of belladonna for the eye. The agent in Fewston: it was my Fillie.

In that moment, I am afraid I lost my famously sanguine restraint. The Woman had not only taken my soul, not only killed Quin and Gybbe and the child of Fairfax; she had set Fillie up to betray me. So, I attacked her.

Or at least I tried to – I ran from under Ben Jonson's seat and out across the stage, my fur raised and claws out ready to pounce. Unfortunately, I may have startled some of the loose chickens, who started to run about the stage. One attempted to fly but got no further than landing on Buckingham's head, and in his frantic attempt to remove it he lost his balance and sat suddenly backwards into my path; and I ran head first into his well-padded arse. The force sent me sprawling across the floor on my belly, spinning on the fine polished wood, to end at the base of a very large chair looking at a very fine pair of shoes.

'It's the cat! The witches' cat. Lord have mercy on my soul – it's come back for me. Seize him; the spawn of Beelzebub, defiler of God's Word. Somebody catch it!'

I just had time to look up and see the spidery legs of King James, his hands around his knees, perched upon a large, gilded chair. The room was in pandemonium, as actors and guests rushed to help the king, some gathering up chickens, others trying to coax him down.

Unnoticed, except by one large, still-seated man – who had his dark head buried under a rather elegant gown – I slipped out of the hall and back towards London.

Inges

The House of Grimalikin

'MATILDA CHEVERON? Yes, we know her. And Fillie, too. Come with me.' Isegrim had been waiting for my return, it seemed, and now he walked like someone who had finally found something important to do. We went side-by-side down the wide space between the rows of pillars, down into the heart of the underground palace.

'We kept eyes on her since she arrived in London. No imp comes into this city without The Mazger knowing, and certainly not one bonded to a person of importance.'

'A person of importance? Wait – bonded?' It had taken me a second to register the fullness of what he said.

'Yes, she's clearly of importance – she has wealth, friends in high places–'

'Sorry, you said she was bonded – Fillie; to The Woman?'

'Yes. Of course. Did you not know that?' He stopped our walking to look me up and down with an air of dry amusement. 'Fillie didn't tell you much, did she?'

Well, no, she didn't. Not anything I should have known, not anything she didn't want me to believe. So Anne had been a lie too. How could I not have seen that? I would have seen that.

Inges

'She arrived three years ago, on a boat from the Netherlands. They both did. Our imps at the docks saw them and passed them over to Marlinspike. He usually gets given the more interesting people.' Isegrim's tail ruffled slightly at that last part.

'Is that who we're going to see now?'

'No, unfortunately he left earlier this year for Plymouth; international mission. I'm taking you directly to His Majesty, he asked to see you on your return. We'll stop at your quarters and you can clean yourself up first.'

He had a point. My journey back from Windsor had been slow and filthy. I'd kept off the roads and made my way through rough pastures filled with the ordure of cattle, been chased by deer across a great park, crawled through the bracken and bramble of woodlands, and finally followed the greasy embankment of The Fleet back down to Bridewell. I needed a wash before I saw The Mazger – I'd alarmed enough kings for one day.

I was pleased to see Poilnoes waiting for me in my room, she was the only imp I had met in the palace who still seemed to have all four feet on the ground. The stench of self-importance around this place was almost as bad as that drifting in from The Fleet.

'Inges – I'm so glad you got back safely. I've been worried, what with all they've been saying about Buckingham.'

I could see from the way her ears dropped that she had probably said more than it was her place to do. I did not push it – The Mazger clearly wanted to be the one to debrief me, and I would let him.

'Thank you Poilnoes, and thank you for the milk,' she followed my eyes to the saucer that had been left by my bedside, 'but could I trouble you for some water instead. Rain, not river.'

She shook her tail gently, 'Of course,' then stopped to turn back as she walked away. 'They say you were close to that cat Fillie; that she's part of it all. I'm sorry.' She hesitated. 'She's very beautiful.'

'I was. She was,' I said. Poilnoes blinked sympathetically. 'Did she come here?'

'Just for a short while. The Mazger wanted her for his council, but she would not stay. I probably shouldn't say more; he did not like her I think, at the end. She was trouble you see, he says.'

She is trouble all right, I thought, but I can guess where The Mazger's dislike came from – even a king cannot always get what he wants. Now I needed to find what he wanted from me.

The Mazger seemed in an even more ebullient mood than when I last saw him. Pacing his chambers impatiently, there was now a spring, of sorts, even in that gammy leg of his. 'Inges! So good to have you back. You have had quite the adventure, I hear.'

I nodded my head respectfully. I would find out what information he already knew before I furnished him with more.

'Come with me, Inges; before we speak further I want to show you something.' The Mazger brushed his forehead against mine, and I was a little taken aback that he would show such familiarity. I could feel Isegrim's eyes burning into me.

The king showed me, alone, through a narrow doorway that led directly out of his chambers and into a small and dark adjoining space, not much taller or wider than a cat could jump. I thought it may have once been a root store, like I had seen up at New Hall. Inside, the stench was overwhelming. Not the smell of spoiled water that permeated the rest of the palace; this was more familiar – but far stronger than I had ever smelt it before. It was the scent of strength, of intimidation, of power.

'A bit overwhelming at first, Inges, but you get used to it in here.' Though my eyes were running a little, I could see – set around the room – a number of small boxes; some of carved wood and ivory, some of silver or gold, others plain timber eaten with age.

'Powerful stuff,' I said, catching my breath a little. 'Is this all you?'

The Mazger laughed. 'No, even I cannot be all these things, Inges. This is the Hall of Kings; the Pantheon, the doorway to the House of Grimalikin.'

Inside each box, he showed me, was a cloth – each soaked with the spray of a reigning monarch. This was where the kings left their presence, to be remembered, to impose and impress even beyond death.

'See this one, Inges – go on, smell it.' He had opened a small, wooden box that must once have been covered with the carved images of cats and mice but now displayed mostly the work of worms. A dull grey, tattered fragment of linen was folded carefully within. It smelt faint, but distinctive. The musk hit the back of my nose and ran through my mind like smoke taking form, showing the fleeting essence of a cat who must have been a force to be reckoned with long before even this palace was built. 'That's the oldest one I can be sure of. What you are smelling there is the claim of one of my most ancient predecessors, Muriceps. He lived before even those men who are kings above first crossed the sea to this land.'

'And here,' The Mazger was leading me around the room now, 'this one is that of Toldrum, whose soul was a great merchant and Lord Mayor above here a little while back. He was king before me. Very distinctive scent.'

'What's that one?' I asked, sniffing at the grandest box of all – a gaudy golden arc, pocked with stones of blue ice and red fire.

The king laughed. 'That is one that tells you some of my forebears may have had more faith than they had judgment. That is said to be the scent of Grimalikin himself – the God King who came out of Egypt in the time before time. One of my line parted with half his kingdom to own that cloth.'

'And I assume it is not...?'

'Well, if it is then Grimalikin must have spent his life pissing on rags, as every great house from here to the Indies has at least one of these. But it serves its purpose – it looks as it should, and it interests the more impressionable guests I have here. When I need to impress them. So perhaps it was worth the price?'

And what price must I pay for your flattery, I thought. Is it information you want, or more? 'Your Majesty, I am grateful that you show me these things. It is an impressive collection.'

The Mazger puffed out his wide, grizzled mane. 'Oh, it's not a collection, Inges. This isn't for show. This is my armoury. These boxes are my mightiest weapon, my strongest castle. This is the House of Grimalikin – here in this room is its foundations; and my scent joins them, it places me among them all.'

'You are kind to show me such a treasure.' I blinked slowly to show the expected respect.

'It is not simply kindness, Inges. I show you this because I want you to know who you are to serve, and what honour you are to have.'

I stepped back a little, enough – I hoped – not to cause offense. 'Your Majesty, I am honoured, but–'

'Hear me out, Inges, and do not be hasty. I know you are not a cat to be easily commanded – I know of what happened at Whitehall and at Windsor.'

'Your information travels faster than me, Your Majesty.'

'The advantage of having birds in your command, Inges – even if some of them are just chickens.' The Mazger padded closer. 'You are a cat I could use. A cat I could make very comfortable, in return for your service.'

I paused to collect my thoughts. I would need The Mazger, I thought, to stand any chance against Buckingham and The Woman, but I could not give my service to him while my soul needed me.

'Think about it, Inges. I will not command you – but if you give me your oath, if you take a place at my court, then I will do all I can in return to assist you in your current predicament.'

I thought deeply, but each way my mind ran – and no matter how it tried to run away – I knew I had no choice. Inges, against such powerful humans, alone, would surely mean the death of both my soul and me.

'Then I accept, Your Majesty. But I ask in return one favour.'

The king's fur bristled along his tail, from pride I thought. 'Ask, Inges, and it shall be given.'

'When it is done, when justice is delivered to The Woman and my soul is free, let me spend just a little time with Peg. The winter. Just to say goodbye. After that I will return here and take my place in court. You have my word.'

The Mazger's tail now swung wildly, and he brushed against me again. 'You have made an old king very happy and you will be, I am sure, a jewel in my collection.'

So, I thought, I have been collected by a king. That is the price. Well, if an old king can give half his kingdom for a piss-stained rag, I can give all of mine to save my soul.

Inges

I was led back into the chamber, where now the king's inner circle were gathered – those same cats that I had shared a table with before; and there we talked of what I had seen at Windsor, and what was already known.

Isegrim told me that they had suspected Buckingham's hand in what was happening to my soul. It was known, he told me, that the Villiers had a feud of sorts with the wider Fairfax family, and that Buckingham had his eye on the great hall and lands at Denton and Nun Appleton. It now seemed he meant to secure both their lands and their disgrace by drawing the weakest of their line, Edward, into a play with dark magic. This would turn the fury of James – who feared witches more than any rebel army – on the family.

'I don't know,' I said. 'What would a marquess be doing with old women in a village so remote from London? This I don't understand – there must be simpler ways to achieve the same goals?'

'Not when this way has already worked for him before.' It was Slickskin who spoke, and she fixed her pale green eyes to the floor as she did.

'He's done this before?' I asked, looking around at the stern faces of the other cats.

The king nodded at Isegrim, who now stepped forward. 'Inges, there is someone you need to meet.'

It seemed this great crumbling palace stretched further in all directions than I had imagined, and deeper down into the earth than I had thought possible. Isegrim and The Mazger's two ginger guards had shown me across the wide expanse of the columned basement to a narrow stone staircase, hidden far from the inhabited parts of the building. Down the stairs we had walked in near darkness to another flight of stairs, through a heavily bolted door and into a small room, now dimly lit by a single candle.

The room looked as if it had been carved out of the bedrock itself, and the floor was deep in water, so that we had to step across raised stone flags to a platform at the far side. Isegrim gestured to me to stand in front of what seemed to be a well, its top rising just out of the water, and covered by a heavy wooden trapdoor.

The guards, stepping belly deep into the water, heaved the door open and hauled with their strong teeth at a windlass that hung above – drawing up the rope that led down into the swallowing darkness of the black hole.

An unearthly noise echoed up from the well, a howling and hissing I at first took for the wind, but then – as it came closer – I recognised, just, as the cries of a cat. A few more turns on the windlass, and a wooden cage slowly rose above the stone well wall; then I saw him. And he saw me.

'Has yer come to kill me at last? Well I cannit die, cans I. Come in, come in, little Tommy Tittlemouse – come and be a morsel for Rutterkin!'

It seemed this... thing – this slavering, mange-riddled bundle of skin and blood-matted fur – was to be the one to tell me why my soul was imprisoned.

He was a cat, I thought, though it was hard to tell – he could just as easily have been a scrofulous rat, so small and wiry was he. The pupil of his one remaining eye, shrunk to a pin-head set in bloody amber, stared unblinking at me

'Don't get too close to the bars, Inges – he will have you with his claws, they are vicious. Give him this,' Isegrim handed me a strip of what looked like dried beef, 'and he'll tell you all you need to know.'

'So you are Rutterkin then?' I asked, somewhat redundantly, but I thought a question to which I already knew the answer might test the sanity of his replies.

'Rutterkin, Rutterkin. Rub your glove along my back, little Lord, and I will prick it with my claws. I'll kills you dead and all your little kinkin, Rutterkin.'

I took that as a yes. 'What can you tell me about the Marquess of Buckingham; about George Villiers?'

What little was left of Rutterkin's coat stood up along his back, so that he looked like some half-starved, runted boar. He leapt into the air, hitting the roof of his cage, then flew around its small space, banging and dragging his head against the bars in a whirlwind of tattered black and grey fur. 'Buckinghams, Buckinghams, where's me mouldiwarp, where's me Pretty, to kill all the little babies. Rutterkin does it, good Rutterkins.'

I could see this might take some time. 'Did you do something for Buckingham? Can you tell me what you did?'

'Gibs it.'

'Sorry?'

'Gibs meat. Gibs it.'

He was staring at the strip of dark beef by my foot, his mouth wide open to reveal nearly empty, bleeding gums dripping with drool at the sight.

'If I give you a piece, you tell me about Buckingham, ok?'

'Gibs it!' he screeched, hissing and slashing his white, needle-sharp claws through the bars of the cage; flailing wildly towards the meat that stood just out of his reach. I tore a piece off with my teeth and threw it into the cage, he fell on it and swallowed it whole almost before it hit the ground.

'Gibs more.'

'Tell me first.'

'You are mean cat, mean to Rutterkins. Rutterkins is good cat, Rutterkins do what he told.'

'And what was Rutterkin told? What did Buckingham tell you?'

'Buckinghams tells Rutterkin. Buckinghams and Pretty. Kills the little ones, kills the little lords and ladies. Tells the men it's the Flowersis, the Flowersis witches, nasty witches.'

'Flowersis?'

'The Flowersis. My soul. Oh Joanie! Oh my soul!' Rutterkin started to wail and tear at his own face with his claws. I had to throw more meat to stop him and get him back to talking. He slobbered at this piece, sucking at it with his raw gums.

'Joanie, my soul, and all her little kittens, little Maggie, little Pippie. Hang them all from a tree, bad witches kill the little lords and ladies. Buckinghams tells me, Buckinghams and Pretty.'

'Buckingham told you to kill someone? To kill someone and then frame your soul? Frame... Joanie?'

'Buckinghams kills all the little children, sends me. Moldiwarps can't do it, too small, Pretty can't do, too pretty. Rutterkins doos it.

Rutterkins gets new soul, you promises him. Promises! Rutterkins lives forever!'

The raving cat now started to tear at its own throat – as though it wanted to prove its own words.

'That's enough, he'll kill himself, take him away,' Isegrim ordered, and I nodded as the cage was lowered back down into the dark, damp hole from which it came.

'Gibs meat! Gibs meat! I eat youse bad catsis, I eat–' The heavy trapdoor shut, and Rutterkin's voice faded to nothing.

I let out a deep breath. I had heard enough, what little I hadn't worked out for myself Isegrim now told me. Buckingham had coerced Rutterkin into killing the children of a great man – the Earl of Rutford – and framing his own soul and her family for the deaths; easy scapegoats in a world afraid of women. The marquess had cleared the way to marrying the sole remaining heir of Rutland's vast estates: Katherine Manners – the woman in whose honour Ben Jonson had been paid to write the masque. I didn't ask who Pretty was. I didn't need to ask.

What a place you have found yourself in, Inges, I thought. My mind went back to the green fields of Timble, to Peg out picking wild flowers, the smell of fennel on her warm hands, the little shield bugs that would crawl out across our table and I would bat them with my paw. I thought of the white butterflies I would chase across the yard of Fewston Church when I went wandering; of the call of cuckoos rising up the hill from the woods that hung beside Timble Beck; the evening chorus of frogs at The Tarn; the heather and bilberry up on Carr Top that stained my white fur so much that hot autumn that Peg used chestnut soap on me, and I could taste it in my cleaning for at least a month.

I thought of Quin, and my life before they took his eyes. I wondered what he had seen, what last sight they stole, and I knew it must be The Woman. The Woman and Fillie. And the hand above it all was that of Buckingham. A man who had done this before. Who had killed and let poor women take his place on the gallows. A man who had built his own kingdom on the bones and souls of the innocent. A man who now did the same to my

Inges

Peg, to Maggie, to Bess Dickenson, to Jennit, to Widow Thorpe, to Mother Fletcher.

But now I wasn't in Timble. Now I wasn't chasing butterflies. Now I was hunting. And I was hunting him. At the cost of my freedom, I had bought the army of The Mazger to my side; and I would come down on Buckingham with the fury of a thousand imps. And I would think of Quin, of Gybbe, of Anne, and of the Flowers women, as I took out his eyes and tore out his throat.

INTERLUDE: *A Valediction*

IT WAS a long time before I learned all that I should have known about what happened in Timble while I was in London. What my soul went through, what my friends suffered, what was sacrificed.

I learned some of it when I returned. Some of it I sought out, some of it was offered, and some of it – I am ashamed to say – I learned too late. And that, only by chance; from those who had held the lives of others higher than I had, yet still – I now know – not as high as those lives deserved.

I cannot use my words to tell a story that does not belong to me. I do not deserve to tell this story.

Instead I will let another tell it. Someone who knew her better. Someone who would not have forgotten to ask after her, no matter how late they had returned to Timble.

❦

My name is Alexander, and your opinion of me does not concern me. I am an imp, as you might have guessed, being as I am talking to you in a book what is of imps. Now you might think me a cat, which is funny as I am not. I am, if I tell you the truth, a snail, which is as unlike any cat as you can fancy.

Inges

Now Inges has asked me to say some words on Barbara. That is, to write some words. Well not I, as I cannot write, so he has had them written down for me. And I hope they are alright words, as I am a little nervous to have them in a book what is written by Inges, who is very good with the words, as he tells me. And I expect he is, but I cannot read them so I cannot tell you for sure, and you must decide that for yourself.

He says for me to write, as I knew Barbara; but if I tell the truth I did not know her half as well as I might. I met her only once, you see, though we did spend a long time together. But it seems she had no other friends as could tell her tale, least none that knew the bit of it that Inges thinks should be told.

I think the right way with such things is to tell you a little about my situation first, so I will do that. I am bonded to a human as is called Thomas. That is all I know of his name, and is not much use to you I am sure as it seems to me most humans are called Thomas, or else Tam, or Tom, or Tommy. It might be confusing, I think, to be a human.

Now, my Thomas, he drives a cart. It is not a fast cart, say all the other Thomases as swear at him and call him names on the road. But it is a strong one, and a light one, and my Thomas, he tells them, 'I am not quick, but I can take it all the way to London and not change cart even one time.' And he carries all sorts to and from and all about Yorkshire: papers that tell of what is bought and sold, wool that blows out in the wind so that the littlest parts of it get all caught up in my trail, wood from Knaresborough or coal from Ainsty, and all such like. Sometimes he carries that saltpetre that humans use to make a great smoke and kill each other dead, and I must need be careful as it would kill me too, but not with a bang; more slowly – as is befitting for a snail.

Thomas does not know of me. What could I do for him? And what would he do if he heard me speak? Squash me, as like as not, shell and all. Not as imps should speak to their souls, that we all know – though I know some as do and I won't name them.

Most of the time I just sit. Under the carriage in the main. I'm safe there, from birds as would peck me, or spiky hyggepigs that might slurp me up out my armour. Thomas, he pulls the cart to the side of the road every so often, and there I eat until it is time to move again. It is not what you would call an exciting life, not like that Mr Inges has led. I've met no kings nor great markisses nor had none of his adventures. But that is how I like it, that is my speed – like my soul's cart, slow and steady, but I get there just the same.

So you would see it was quite an excitement to me when I met Barbara, and when I came to hear her tale, and so, by that way, I must say that I was part of a very grand adventure; though not a great part, yet still more than enough for me.

We had been taking a weight of sacks from Dob Park Mill just over the way to Fewston. On from there we were to go to Harrogate, where we would take down some old clothes and plate from a woman what had come up from London to take the waters. They do say the waters there are magical and can cure all the sickness, but notso for this lady, as she had up and died and now her rich things must go back to her home, it seemed.

Anyhow, that is by the by as we were still by Fewston now as this tale starts. We had stopped across the ford and Thomas he was complaining to some men standing about there, on account of the new bridge what they was building. He said as it was too narrow for his little cart and only good for packhorses what would take his trade, or he'd have to unhitch and go without a cart. Well, while he was grumbling about the works, who should jump up onto the cart but a little frog what I now know was Barbara. But right then, I thought she was just any old frog and that I might be her dinner.

I can't run too fast, being a snail and all, so I curled up in my shell and hid as best I could. Well, I must have called out in fear, as Barbara, now, she spoke to me, saying something like: 'Hello! Don't be scared. It's just little old me, I'm not looking to eat you, I just hopped on for a ride.'

Well she giggled and it was such a kind and soft old voice what she had that I popped a little eye out of my shell and saw her there, sitting on the wheel brace and waving a small webby hand at me.

Inges

I thought, I have never had a frog on my cart before. Nor have I had nothing but some chuckypigs or eariwigs on here – and there's none of them that can talk. So we got to yacking, and she told me such a tale, as I now know to be true, of murder and witchcraft and prisons and such, and that she must get to London with an important message for one called Inges.

Now Inges, he will have told you the main part I am sure, so I don't need to tell you that. All except she had got to York as had been his plan. And back again – all on her own, which I thought to myself was a feat for such a small frog and, though she would not have it herself, I could see she had some pride in it.

The women she had found in prison. She told me that it had been no difficulty in getting in there, for her horse had stopped right by the old castle there, and she fit right easy between the bars.

Barbara, she told me of the women and their situation there and, I do not lie, it right made me sick for I could see she cared a great deal for them and that all was as bad as can be.

They was all together of a single room, six of them in all. If I remember, Barbara's soul was called Mother Fletcher, and there was one called Maggie who it seemed played mother to the others, and then her own child – who she treated no better nor no worse than any of them – and she was called Peg and was of Inges. I hope I got that all right.

Barbara she said that at first she did not think she had her place right, for though there were six women all of a cell there were none that looked as she remembered them. Her Mother Fletcher had been a fine fat woman, red in her cheeks, and black of hair, she said. And now who was this whose skin was so grey and hung so low on fine cheekbones? Who was that as their hair was all white and half fallen? Only when she saw that necklace as had been given her by her own mother, all hung about a hollow neck, did she say, 'Oh my life, is that my soul?'

Now Barbara was afraid, for she thought her soul must die soon, and some of the others too. One who was the oldest – Jennit now I think I remember it – she thought she must already be dead for she lay there on the bare floor with her mouth hanging all loose and her eyes tight shut and facing up to the roof as if she had long watched her soul leave her body. And Peg too – I don't like to think on it too much, but Barbara said that it was sure that she must have the flux, as humans get, and her clothes were of a state I do not wish to tell you.

And Maggie, she held Peg's head in her lap and was brushing away her hair as was sticking to her forehead, and Peg all moaning and talking words that Barbara never heard before, of fire and dancing spirits and ants that were all a-crawling on her, though there were none of these things in that room.

Now I will try to bring back what Barbara said of their words, so forgive me if I maybe add some of my own where there is holes in my memory. We snails, we don't have much cause for remembering much, so I am a little out of practice on it.

'Oh mother, am I to die here?' this being Peg.

'Now my child, don't you think on it. All will be well, I will not let that happen,' that being Maggie.

But then Peg she did slip into a deep sleep so Maggie would shake her, but she did not move, and Maggie did cry, 'Oh my child do not leave me now,' and Barbara said then that she thought Peg dead, and Jennit too, and that Widow Thorpe would not be far behind.

'Well,' I said to Barbara, 'did you see all of what happened next?'

'Not all,' she said, but Jennit it seemed was not dead, as in that moment she opened her eyes and saw straight up the wall to where Barbara was sat on a coping stone as was set in just above. Jennit did hush all, and then sat up more sprightly than would seem possible and made a grab for Barbara – calling her to come to her, calling of her hunger and how angry she were that Barbara would not stay still.

Now, I believe Barbara would not want me to tell the next bit, but Inges says I must. For he says the tale must be honest, and that all must be weighed not on the action but on the intent, and Barbara's intent was good. For she spoke, as imps must not; not ever.

'Don't eat me,' she cried, 'I come from Timble and I belongs to Mrs Fletcher and I is here to help.'

Well, Jennit she just fell down and Maggie she cried. And the others, they did not move even to look at her, she said, for it seemed they could no sooner move even if the whole castle were afire and the door opened to them. Maggie just looked at her and she knew that now she must be like the dancing spirits and the ants, and all of a fever dream to them.

'And what did you do?' I had asked Barbara, and she quite surprised me with her answer, for I did not see this cunning in her.

There is a fashion about these last years, among the finer people in Harrogate and York, and London too, for some to have purses made of silk and leather so smartly as they look like a frog. Barbara had seen such on her way to York and now she had an idea that came so quick to her head as I would say frogs must be smarter than snails, and I don't mind who knows it. She left her goodwomen as they were, in such a bad way, and out she hopped towards the great church that sits there close by in York. Finding herself a fine lady, who was out at walking, she caught hold of her farthingale so as to look to all the world who saw her like a silk purse. And by this way she worked her way a little at a time, unnoticed, until she could take hold of the lady's fine brooch and then this frog purse did swallow that whole.

She laughed in telling the tale, and I was glad of it for, truth be told, I found it a dark one otherwise and I had not known of such matters before. Under my cart, I see the dead things that are on the road, but I never stop to think what put them that way, and perhaps I should, but life is short and I have always kept my mind on the sunny side even when my head is in the shade.

'That brooch,' she said, 'might buy them a little comfort in the gaol.' And I asked would not the guards say such must be stolen, and Barbara said as she could see the only difference between those who were in the cells and those without was in the surety of which ones were thieves and which might be wronged.

Now I must tell you the next part of her journey. For she was to come back to Fewston, she said, and tell all she had seen. But she was troubled, as it seemed Peg must be dead, or else she would soon be, and then poor Inges he would be in London on such a bold adventure, but with no soul for to bring him back. So she thought on how she must let Inges know all that had happened, and if he should perhaps now return.

'I had meant to get back to Fewston this day,' she said to me, 'for to talk with the others and ask their advices. But luck has played its hand and you tell me you are to London yourselves, so – if it pleases you – I will take that ride with you and deliver the message myself.'

So then no more of the adventure did she tell me but that I saw with my own eyes. We were together on the cart for a week in all. One day on to Harrogate, where we rested up, then six down to London. And I thought it the quickest journey I had ever made as we talked for hours on all manner of things. I learned so much of what was in the world; wonders as I never knew, such like lily pads as you can sit on, and snails that do live in the water, and that all the world is made of colours – though I could not understand what that were, no matter how hard it were explained to me, yet it sounded beautiful just the same.

'Barbara,' I said to her one day, as we passed down the long road they call Roman Rigg, what comes down from Doncaster. It is a long old stretch that day, for the road is good there and we keep going. I said to her: 'Barbara, I am a snail as does not worry on too much. I like to eat leaves and I like to sit under my cart, and anything else might be exciting for others but I do not have need of it. Now that is why I am a cheerful snail, on the whole, I think, yet you have seen great trouble such as I would not care to and yet you are – even if I say it myself – cheerier still.'

Well, she told me that she had a secret to that. And I was glad to hear it as my time with her had shown me things I knew nothing about, and my head, I think, was not built big enough to hold such thoughts comfortably.

'Well, Alex,' she called me Alex for short, which I did not care for at first as I thought no one has called me that. But then I thought on how no one had called me Alexander neither, and then no one had called me anything as I had never spoken to anyone before. And then I wondered if and why I even had a name. But such things are for those with quicker minds than mine, so perhaps I might ask Mr Inges.

Anyhow, she said: 'You see, Alex, there are those who would say I am just a silly old frog, but I believe in something. I believe in good. I believe we are all born good, and that those what do bad, they do so on account of they have learned it. And what can be learned can always be learned again, and better.'

She told me how things always happened for a reason, how it was not chance that she had found me but instead that it was a gift to us both; that she was helped and I was helping. She told me that when she got to London she were sure that in such a fine city, with all the clever people who keep the laws, who go to such good schools and learn – they would be the ones what had learned to be good, for she had heard that all were taught well in the ways of kindness and hope and charity.

'I think those as do bad, Alex, they just need that kindness and hope and a little charity. This is what I was shown to believe, and I will not waver from it no matter what the world shows me. For I know that if you show kindness, if your heart is good, then you will bring all over to you in the end and I believe that good will always win when it comes to the reckoning.'

And I was glad to hear it, for I do not like to think that the world is as she saw it in York Castle – and, but for what is on the road, I knew of nowhere else, so my fear had been that it was. By the time we arrived at the end of the long road from York, it was decided Barbara and I were great friends.

We stopped close by Smithfield, where we were to set off one small part of our load, and Barbara bid me farewell, in hope we meet again.

I watched her as she hopped down among the market stalls, and here and there I saw her talking to one pigeon what was pecking at some parts of suet as had fallen upon the ground.

Now we were there a good while, and then back she came all of a flutter of excitement. 'I told you,' she said, 'they is all good here. This kind imp, he knows of Inges. Not here an hour in this great city and I am already sent help.'

'Where be he?' I asked, and she said, 'Oh, he is with one who is the Cat King, and who is to help us all and save our souls. And he is in a place just a little way from here down the river that stands close by, at a great palace where he is to be one of the king's cats. You see, Alex, if you believe, then good will always find you.'

Well I was glad for her and I said, 'Well now then you should get there as soon as you can,' and she told me that she was to follow a fish named Jack as would show her the way. And when she said she was to meet him at Holburne Bridge, I said, 'Well you are right that good will show us the way, as our little cart must go by that very way in but a few minutes.'

In truth it was but a short road to the bridge, yet I wanted a minute more with her as I had found her company to my liking and would have it little while longer.

We stopped at the bridge, as is always the way, with diverse carts and horses and cattle and such on way to market there. Barbara hopped down onto the bridge wall, and below I could see the big old back of a great fish push up through the grease of that Fleet river.

'Is that you Barbara? Come on, I'll show you the way. Inges is waiting – he is excited to see you again,' called this fish.

Barbara called back, 'It is me; I am coming.' And she turned to me and said, 'Goodbye Alex, and remember to always believe.'

And she jumped down from that bridge, and Jack opened his wide mouth, and he swallowed her whole.

ACT 3: IN WESTMINSTER

'He knows not his own strength that hath not met adversity'

–Ben Jonson

Inges

The White Devil

A CAT starts to hunt at about six weeks old. We open our eyes in the first week, our ears in the second. By the third we can stand, by the fourth we can walk. One week to master balance, and then we learn to kill.

Everything we put into the first five weeks is all to prepare for the sixth. We see the prey move, we hear its cries, we walk, we crouch, we run, we hunt. This is what it is to be a cat. This is what I do.

But this is no mouse I am stalking. This is the most powerful man in England, barring the king – perhaps even including the king.

And so I remember what my mother taught me, when she brought that broken fledgling to our den. It would flutter and flap, one useless wing hanging and the other whirring in panic so that it was just a flash of dark and light, motions that set fire to my senses; shocking up my ears, widening my eyes, tightening my sinews and gripping at my guts and heart so that I no longer thought, I just did.

I would charge at it, and then I would fall back in terror as it pushed to leave the ground, or else pushed back at me with its claws and its beak. It was all instinct, untutored and wild, primal and disordered.

'Don't rush, Inges,' she had said. 'Don't let the urge overtake you, no matter how strong. Control it, be sure of your final move, release it only when you need to, and when you do, hold nothing back – make it count.'

Those words now ran in my head; and I knew that I would only have one chance, that I must be sure; that I would need to make it count.

'You are sure Buckingham will be there?' I looked at Isegrim, who seemed far too casual about the matter for my liking.

'Absolutely. We have the most reliable source. He will be there.'

'And you are sure you can get me in? I am known to him, and the king, and no doubt his guards too by now.'

'I am sure. Everything is in place. You will meet your team this evening and we will go through the briefing together then.'

He was confident, that was clear, but then he would not be the one going into Westminster Palace, nor the one who would face a full grown man in combat. Nor the one who would have to escape the guards who would fall on me in revenge for their master's death. But I had one more question, and it was the most important.

'You have sent word to Fewston? You have let them know the facts of this case. I may not… if it does not go well, I want to know that care is taken there.'

Isegrim raised a paw and casually licked it, before rubbing it behind his ears. 'We have our quickest imps on it. They are in the air right now.'

'And if I fall, The Woman – she will still be dealt with?'

'You have my word. You have the word of the king.'

I shook my tail in thanks. 'Then I am ready. Take me to The Mazger.'

The Cat King had asked to see me again, before I left. No doubt he wanted to feel part of this game, to say he commanded it, that it was he who took the life of the Marquess of Buckingham – aided by some nameless of his cats, who will be forgotten to history.

Inges

Yet I had smelt his portrait in the Hall of Kings. He was old now, yes, and slow of movement. But I saw him in that scent, as he was a younger cat – a warrior, a hunter, a killer no doubt. He had fought his battles and he had earned his fame. And, for all his age, take away his guards and still I might hesitate to fight him – crippled leg and all.

We were not to meet in his chamber, but instead I was taken once more to the far side of the palace, close by where I had descended into the personal hell hole of Rutterkin, and I thought for a moment that mad cat might be pulled up again with more that I should know of Buckingham. But, instead, I was shown to a door on the palace level – a solid wooden one, bound with steel and bolted firmly. To its bottom, a square just big enough for a cat to pass through had been cut – but this was a door for humans, a relic of the palace's past.

'You go in there. Straight through. We stay here. You leave when the king commands.' My escorts, The Mazger's charming ginger twins, were not the most cerebral of companions, nor the most eloquent, but they had a way of getting to the point.

I stepped inside and it was clear straight away that it was not just the door that had been made for humans. The walls were hung with chains and manacles, wooden chairs pushed against the stone, doors at each side of the narrow corridor – each with a small window barred across with iron. Ahead of me, one of the doors ajar and the flickering light of torches.

'Inges, my friend. Are you ready? You look ready.' The Mazger stepped out of the open door and beckoned me in. 'I would normally have Isegrim show you in but this one is just between you and me, Inges. I am not used to calling – but, for today, forget I am your king and think me your friend.'

I thought him neither, but I had made my vow to him and now I would take my part of the bargain with politeness, and I thanked him as I saw appropriate.

'No need for "Your Majesties" here my friend – there's no one to hear us. Call me cousin, it has been a long time since I felt the lightness of familiarity.'

Inges

I shook my tail, enough to say it was understood. 'Your M… cousin,' I began.

'You want to know why you are here, not in my chambers? Well, for one thing – I may be old, and I may be king, but I still like an adventure as much as the next cat, and you will indulge my boyish excitement at such a bold one. Let me play at being a stealthy warrior, right, Inges?' He pushed at me with his head in playful aggression, and I thought to myself that I was right about his strength; even in fractions it was palpable.

'Of course, well this is your plan, cousin, and so you are very much the warrior—'

'You don't need to flatter me, Inges!' His manner was almost playful, even as he scolded me. 'Come on now, I have too much of that out there already. In here, we are cats; fighters, hunters, together – sharing tales of valour, sharing a drink of milk before the battle.' He gestured to a silver bowl by the side of the door, but I politely declined.

Something had troubled me since the plan first took shape, and I thought I must address that now. If anyone knew the answer it would be this old soldier. 'May I ask you something… cousin?' I said, as he flicked his wide tongue into the rich milk. He gestured for me to continue. 'I wondered; have you ever killed a human? I have my thoughts on it, of going for the eyes, but I don't know. Is it even possible? If I were a dog—'

'Great Grimalikin's whiskers, cat! Don't you say such a thing! A dog?' The Mazger puffed out his chest and I saw a ripple of agitated fur run down his back. 'You are much more than a dog, Inges, or else I'd send Snuff or another of those dribble-jowled mutts to do this work. A dog would bark and bite and make a mess of everything. But we hunt don't we, Inges. We hunt.'

He turned past me and towards a wicker basket that was set against the leg of a human table there against the far side of the room, and behind that I saw was a deep crimson curtain that spanned from wall to wall.

'Come here.' It was a command again, and I was not cousin anymore. He gestured down into the basket to a small vessel – blue glass, little bigger than the thimble Maggie used when darning stockings for the Dickensons. In it a dark, viscous liquid shimmered with waves of iridescent colour.

'What is this?'

'This is what I brought you here to show you. This is what makes you more than a dog.' He looked at me for a second, and seemed to revel in the dramatic possibilities of my confusion. A king must be a performer too, I thought. You should meet my friend Ben Jonson; he would have a part for you.

'You ask if I have killed a human, Inges. I could tell you of those I have killed, I'd give you names if I could remember them all. But you want to know how, and I will teach you. And you know what the best way to learn is, don't you?'

A pause again, for effect. I stepped in: 'I—'

'You learn by example, Inges!' Now he had his drama – his claws were out, and he drew them firmly down the red curtain, which fell – perfectly choreographed – in heavy folds to the floor. Behind it, chained in manacles to the wall and his mouth bound with a cloth, a human man, naked but for a dirty white shirt.

I could feel my hackles rise, and The Mazger seemed pleased with the effect of his little dance. 'Here is how you kill a human,' he said, and slowly, carefully, touched the silky surface of the dark liquid with the tip of a single claw. And then he slashed – drawing angry furrows of blood across the thigh of the man, who had fallen to his knees, his eyes wide to the yolks with pleading, such as you see when you release a shrew that is too bitten to run.

I stood there a moment in silence, a thousand questions running through my mind, but only one forming into words: 'Who is that?'

'That,' he spat the word, 'is a killer of cats, Inges. That is a devil, that is a bastard son of the great Satan himself, a foul spawn of the Beast who has killed us, who has burned us and gutted us and skinned us and hanged us for 400 years!'

And now I knew I had given my oath to a mad king. He was frothing at the mouth, as I had seen a gibbering fox do once when it worried the cows up on Swinsty common and had to be cleaved with a billhook.

Inges

The poor human behind him now started to heave in his chest, and his eyes rolled back in his head as he rattled against his iron bindings.

'What has this man done?' I asked, and I saw The Mazger's tail flare out to a great brush. 'Your Majesty,' I added in haste.

'What has he done? Should we ask him? Should I take off his gag and you can ask him yourself?'

'Well—'

'No!' His words were a hiss now. 'He will spite us with his words, with his Latin and his serpent tongue. Silence is what he deserves, his words are curses, not fit for the ears of imps.'

'Is this man… is he part of Buckingham's plot?'

The Mazger laughed now, a laugh that had nothing in it but hatred and I feared a moment I had said something wrong that would bring that poison claw on me. He must have seen my reaction, as now his manner calmed a little. 'Inges, do not be afraid. You are my cat; I am here to protect you. To protect us all. No, he is not part of Buckingham's plot – Buckingham is part of his.'

The man now groaned and writhed about his waist and I could see he longed to double over and grip his belly, but his arms were held by the chains so that he could only sway and thresh like an eel in a trap.

'I am afraid I do not understand.'

'This man is a priest, Inges. Do you know what a priest is?' I did not, except that I had heard of them as something of the humans' church. 'His name is John Dorrell, but it might as well be B'aal, or Azazel, or Mephistopheles, or any other devil's name, as they are all of a kind, crawling on their bellies before their master.'

'Their—'

'The Antichrist that is in Rome!'

And now I knew where I had heard this before, at the church in Fewston. I had not understood it then and it was not getting clearer now.

The priest's eyes were now streaming with tears and he bit so hard at the gag that the blood ran down his chin and stained his white shirt a florid red. He gave out a great moan and a rattle, his body contorted and spasmed so I thought the chains would tear his limbs from their socket. He dropped suddenly – still and silent at last – suspended by his chains; his head hanging, and his arms stretched out so that he looked like the old scaredycrow that is set among Pullein's barley.

I went to speak, but now it seemed he would ask the questions for me as well as he answered them. 'You wonder why he should die so. Your eyes say it. But understand this, what I do to him, he and his kind have done ten thousand times over to us.' I was in The Mazger's theatre, and now he must set up his soliloquy.

'How old would you guess I am, Inges? 20? 30 even? In this life. And, with a good soul, in all my lives I might even be 100, is that not how you know it?'

I tilted my head as if to say, I would guess that might be so.

'I was alive, Inges, when we were loved. Before the White Devil cursed us all. I was alive when we were valued, when the laws of man protected us, when people remembered Saint Cat, when you must pay our weight in grain if you dared kill one of us. Rat catchers, mousers, friends, comrades, equals – that is what we were.

'And I was alive when that Satan threw us into the fire. When the viper, the ninth Gregory in Rome, set out his decree against us – when he plunged us into darkness and condemned us all to die. I was alive to see his priests call the slaughter of my own brothers and sisters in Cambridge, butchered before my eyes. I was alive when his wurm-begotten heir Innocent cast us out altogether, excommunicated us and burned us with our souls, condemning us to the eternal hatred of humans.

'We are hunters, Inges. It is what we are. But for 400 years we have been hunted – hunted by John Dorrel and his kind. Burned, scalded, skinned, cast from towers, drowned – pushed down so that even the greatest cat of them all must build his palace in the filthy dungeon of a human prison, while even human whores and wastrels are put above us in the windowed rooms.'

A passionate speech, I thought, but one that made little sense to me. This mad king was pulling me away from the task at hand and I must get back to that.

'What is Buckingham's part in all this?'

The king drew a deep breath. Perhaps he had expected applause. But he calmed himself now and fixed my eyes with his. They were rheumy, the colour faded dull, and I thought I could almost believe his tale of age as I looked into them.

'When you were at Westminster, in the bishop's box, you will have heard talk of the prince Charles and a Spanish Infanta.'

I did, I thought, yet I did not tell you that.

'What do you know of human understanding on religion, on government, Inges?'

Well, I confess, short of the fact that the church in Fewston has some good fat mice in it, very little. Some of it I had read in Hayward's history, but to be honest I didn't always pay as much attention to that book as I might, on account of Peg scratching me just behind the ear, you know that bit where it feels just right?

The Mazger would educate me, it seemed, his broad face now pressed close to my ear so that he could hiss his words with the proper distillation of venom. 'The Catholic Church, that corrupt body that condemned us all to death and shame, was cast out of government by the good people of this land. Buckingham – though he professes to be against them – I know to be a Papist as foul as any. He would see King James's son married to that Spanish sorceress, that whore of Rome, and fulfil his plot to return this land to the bondage of the Popes. The king is bewitched by Buckingham, he will do his bidding no matter what; no matter what Parliament or even his own bishop will say.

'He would bring down again upon us the destruction of those we love, the slaughter of the cats – not just in your little village, Inges, but across all of England. The burning of all those the Church of Rome hates – Protestants and cats alike. To stop Buckingham is the only way to stop this apocalypse. So you see, you are truly blessed; your mission is not just to save your soul, it is to save the soul of England.'

I have seen the conjurers up on Swinsty when the Summer fair comes. The travellers who wrap themselves in coloured scarves and scent the air with perfumed smoke so that your senses are already running away from you before they start. And there they cover a little ball with cups and dare men to guess which place they put it, all the while pulling their dupe's eyes in any direction but the one it should go. And in that way – with smoke, and colour, and misdirection – they take a willing fool's money.

The Mazger was a conjurer, and I his fool. He needed someone to kill Buckingham, and so he had pulled me into his game. It would be a suicide mission, that I was sure of – or else he'd have sent one of his own.

But here's the thing: I know how to play that game too. I am a cat. I hunt. I watch the ball only. I do not take my eyes off it. Everything else – the hands, the cups, the scarves, the smoke – they aren't there. It is all just the ball.

And so I see the dupes scratch their heads and I could call out to them: 'It is up his sleeve'. But I am a conjuror too, and I don't reveal my own hand until the end.

The Crouch

'NOW INGES, try again. You can't go all a mad rush. The movement will draw you in, it will coddle your mind so all you can think is kill, kill, kill. But you must fight that, you can't just give in to passion and do the first thing your hot head tells you. First you must crouch. It is not the leap, nor the claws, nor the bite: it is the crouch. Everything is in the crouch.'

My mother's words had come back to me again as I lay on my straw bed, readying my strength for the day's battle. She had been right; of course she was, she was always right. That bewildered starling, its eyes bright with terror, had no power to fly, no way to act on its instinct to escape, and so all its hope had been forced into its beak and claws. I had batted at him with my weak kitten paws, tried to snatch with my jaws, to bowl him over with a wild, headlong rush; and all I had for my trouble was the blood that ran down my cheek from where his angry claw had scratched forever the colour from my eye.

So I crouched, down into the grass, and I stopped. I did as I had seen my mother do, where she stalked so slowly you would think her a statue, then you blink and the statue has moved. Down

Inges

I went, until my belly touched the cold ground, my paw moving so slow through the air, so soft to the ground, that barely a blade of grass moved with it. The fledgling was now looking about in panic, trying to work out if the terror was gone, if the killer had fled from the fight, if there was hope. There was none – I was almost on him now, and, as he turned to look another way for another road out, I struck; a bite to the neck, a flurry of feathers, and it was over. I had killed. I was a hunter.

And so now I was in the crouch again. This was all the crouch. Get this right and the kill comes, get it wrong and you lose more than the blue of an eye. The Mazger, mad as he was, had a kingdom that ran more smoothly, it seemed to me, than any I had seen above. Everyone knew their place, everyone knew their role, everyone understood The Crouch:

Isegrim: The Brains. He is in charge of this operation, behind the front line, pulling it all together. He has hand-picked the team, studied the intelligence, mapped out the route, set the timings. Success – or failure – depends on him. Which didn't fill me with much hope, if I'm honest. The 'Brains' thing, that was his idea; he wanted us all to have special names. I'd have gone with Arse-Licker for him, but you know – let's go along with this.

Jack: The Transporter. I can't walk to the gates of the palace, not without being seen. Jack will get me in by the river, drop me at the embankment, and – if all goes well – will be my getaway when the deed is done. At the embankment, we'll wait for clearance from The Eyes.

Sutton: The Eyes. A barn owl. Silent and deadly. He would watch from the air, keeping lookout for any movement from palace guards, any obstacles in our path. He would hoot a warning – one for all clear, two to hide, three to call in The Muscle.

Vincent: The Muscle. A powerful deerhound, strong enough to take down a man if needed. He'd keep a close distance from us, just strolling around the grounds, a hunting dog out for some exercise. If things got bad – really bad – he was our last line of defence. Vincent would wait near the river until I caught up with The Guides.

Inges

Druff and Poilnoes: The Guides. These two cats are Westminster born-and-bred. They know the grounds of Whitehall Palace as well as any cat in London. We'll need to be in and across the courtyards and outhouses before a guard can blink. They'll get me in the door, where I'll meet up with The Insider.

Snuff: The Insider. The ace in our deck, a Whitehall spaniel. He knows his way around the buildings like the back of his paw, and he's well known, and well loved, there. He won't be stopped – unless someone wants to pet him. He will sweep each floor, each corridor, beating a path for The Hunter.

Inges: The Hunter. That's me. I saved the best till last. I am to get into the chapel, with Snuff, and wait under the altar cloth. At the strike of four, every Thursday, if Buckingham is at Westminster, he goes – in private – to the chapel, to pray for the soul of his father. He will kneel at the altar, he will close his eyes, and he will open them again only so the last thing he sees is my face as I send him to join his sheep-loving father in that place the humans call Hell.

After that – well then it is all about how fast I can go. No finesse – I just run. If Buckingham has died quietly, it will be easier, if he's screamed and cried like I think he will, I will need all my swerve and speed. Get out of the palace, get to the river, jump on Jack, and then back to Bridewell. After that – with her protection gone – we go for Matilda, and I will get a confession in writing even if I have to pull her eyes out myself and feed them to Vincent. The game is nearly over. I just need to get in and out of the most heavily guarded palace in England, with every guard and courtier in there on the lookout for a cat whose head the terrified King wants put on a spike upon London Bridge. Couldn't be simpler.

The rest of the team was already in place as I climbed up to the grate, the same place I had first entered into the halls of The Mazger. I looked back down to the room where I had first seen Isegrim, and there he was again. I wondered if I would ever see that ugly grey face again. And much of that depended on his planning. I shuddered.

'Good luck Inges.'

Inges

'I'll need it if we're relying on your planning, Brains!'

He shook his head, and I turned to the river, where the surface waste now parted to reveal the broad silver back of Jack. We had begun.

The Fleet never gets easier, such that it was a relief to hit the waters of the Thames, though the wind was now up, and the water flowed hard and spat up in white-tipped waves of icy wetness. When I was finally put down at the landing at Westminster, I could only imagine how I looked with my fur clinging tight to me and my whiskers dripping water. If ever a woodcut or some painting was to be done of my deeds this day, I thought, I should not wish it to be of this moment.

I had been dropped just through the entrance to the wharf at Scotland Dock; a little way from the main palace, but here would be the open space of Scotland Yard to move quickly through. Once over there, I could make my way through a dog-leg of adjoining storerooms for charcoal, wood and coal; hopefully well hidden. Then the tricky part – and here I would need my guides. I must get through the kitchen pantries, which will be busy with servants and cooks at this time, as they prepare for supper in the Royal Chambers. If I make it through there, I am in the hands of Snuff, who will take me through the Great Hall and then to the chapel. That was the plan that was unfolding, and I now saw Sutton in the air as he gave a single hoot, and there at the door of a dockyard boatshed I spotted Poilnoes and Druff gesturing for me to hurry.

'All clear so far, Inges,' Druff said. He was a stocky cat, jet black with yellow eyes. He was the mate of Poilnoes, it seemed, and had been at dinner with us that first day, though this was the first I had spoken to him.

'There's a window at the back of here that takes us straight out on Scotland Yard. I'll go first – if I'm spotted, I'm just a cat to them, but I will signal if the coast is clear then you follow. Poilnoes, you go behind to guard the rear.'

It was understood – this was Druff and Poilnoes's territory, I would stick to their lead here. Druff jumped up on the ledge and pushed at the oiled paper that filled the frame. It moved easily to the side and he was through. I followed up onto the ledge. Across the broad yard I could see the lanky frame of Vincent – some servants were walking close by him, but far enough from me that I could take my chance. I leapt down, quickly followed by Poilnoes, and was across the yard as quick as I could go.

'Ok, so far, so good,' Druff said, and he ushered us to hug ourselves close against the wall, behind a small shed that blocked the view of the greater part of the yard. 'Just round the back here is the charcoal store – get in, straight through, then you are in the wood yard. Every cat for themselves here, but we'll be hidden by the wood in the yard. Go straight down following the wall on your right, then it's the tricky part. There's a wide entrance to the yard, we must cross that to the coal store. We'll meet up again in there.'

'Don't worry Inges, I've got your back,' Poilnoes reassured me. 'I'll be following – if you get lost I'll get you back on track.'

'Thank you,' I said. 'I feel better knowing that.' And that I did.

Druff went first – in the dark of the charcoal shed he was almost invisible, and a thought quickly crossed my mind. I followed sharply, but instead of running straight through I jumped into one of the charcoal bins that stood at the side of the store, and rolled about.

Poilnoes was quick behind me, and for a second thought she had lost me and stopped. I jumped down, covered from nose to tail in black charcoal dust.

'How do I look?' I purred.

She laughed. 'Messy. And different. You are a smart cat, Inges.'

We ran together into the wood yard. It was more hectic than I'd hoped, with men and boys busying themselves in lifting and stacking timber, or chopping for the charcoal furnace. I tried to keep to the stacks of drying timber, crouching down, slowly around the wood then a quick dart between each stack. Druff was out of sight, and I thought must already be in the coal store, the entrance to which was now straight in front of us.

Unfortunately, so too was a human – a huge man with a barrel chest, his hair and clothes speckled with wood dust so that he looked like he'd been caught in a snowstorm. He had set down a great, gnarled log close by the door and was hacking at it with a two-handed axe.

'Is there another way in?' I asked Poilnoes, and she shook her head.

When you are prey, there are two options – run, or bluff, my mother taught me. 'To be a great hunter you must think like your prey, son.'

Most prey, when cornered, will try to run – this is a mistake. Your movement excites the hunter; if you are running it shows you are weak, it shows you will die easily, it shows there is no price to killing you. The clever prey, the ones that get away, they bluff. They stand up and look you in the eye, and they don't run from you, they walk past you. They say, 'here I am, kill me then; if you dare' and you think 'what do they know that I do not?'

'Walk with me, Poilnoes,' I said, and she looked at me as if I may have lost my mind. 'Walk with me, we are a black cat and a calico, strolling through the wood yard. What could be more normal?'

'You are a cat covered in charcoal, Inges,' she quietly hissed. 'That may work from a distance, but we need to go right past him. You look… a bit odd.'

I stepped out from behind the log pile. Poilnoes sighed deeply, and in a second joined me. 'Act natural,' I said.

'Really? Because I was thinking of juggling mice and reciting poetry,' she whispered. I preferred it when she had said I was smart.

We moved closer; the woodsman still focused on the stubborn log that was slowly yielding to his blows. Nearly there, the door just a short run and jump away, when of a sudden he looked up: 'Bloody cats, get out of here,' he shouted, and for a moment I thought he would bring his axe down on us, but instead he swung out a heavy boot and sent us tumbling together through the door and onto a floor gritted with black dust and coal chippings.

Druff was standing over us. 'You made it. You look a mess, Inges.'

Thanks, I thought, and so do you but mine will wash off and you'll still look like that tomorrow. I didn't say it though.

'Ok, that was the easy bit,' he said.

'Wonderful, what next – a hoop of fire to jump through?'

He ignored me and moved to show the way through the far side of the coal store. 'Out here, then into that corridor. Wait for Sutton, he's above now and will hoot when the way is clear. From there, we go into the kitchens. Be careful – they will be busy; we will be harshly dealt with if they catch us in there. From there to the pantry, then that's it – from the pantry we get access to the main palace, and we hand you over to Snuff.'

We waited at the window space for what seemed an age, but was probably mere minutes; poised and ready to go at any moment. And then we heard it, the single hoot.

'Go, go, go!' Druff mewed; no follow-the-leader now, we leapt as one. Down the narrow snicket, a hard turn right that had our claws slipping and catching at the wet flagstones, flat against the narrow opening of the kitchen door, then in.

Druff was right. It was busy. There was a long, high bench right up to the side of the door, and we had darted under it. All along its length we saw pair after pair of human legs, at least 12 in all, belonging to those who were chopping and mashing and moulding above us. And in the rest of the room, more benches, more legs, and knives, and hammers and fire. And food – food like I had never seen. Every kind of bird and beast laid out to be plucked or skinned, or else made into parcels of liver, heart, kidney, sweetbread and brain. The scent of herbs and spice – some familiar, some that had the smell of imagined lands – filled the room; carried on a heavy, hot breeze that circulated all the tastes and odours from the ovens to every corner of the kitchen.

'I should have had breakfast,' I said, though Druff silenced me with a yellow-eyed stare. He gestured for me to follow, side pushed flat against the wall, crouched low below the bench, until we reached the end closest to the pantry door. The space between our bench and the open door could not have been longer than one of the rushes that strewed the floor – we would be across it before a human could blink. But with 100 eyes in the room, it would take only one pair to stay open for that split second. I took a deep breath.

Inges

Druff was gone, I went next, then Poilnoes. Her foot caught one of the rushes which slid away from her, she tumbled slightly to her side and caught the edge of the door as she ran through. A little thud, barely audible in the rush and bluster of the busy kitchen. But 100 ears, and only one pair needed to hear.

'Oy, something just ran in the pantry there!'

'Where?'

'By the door. A big rat.'

'It wasn't a rat, it was cat. Go in there and get the bloody thing out, it will have the chicken. Take it out and drown it.'

We had hunkered down behind sacks of grain, Poilnoes was trying to signal her shame. I shook my head; it was not her fault, I knew that. But we were trapped. The way out was up and over the rafters that ran across the alleyway to the adjoining palace. There were people in the pantry now, people with long brooms and skewers. We would never make it.

Poilnoes stood up straight. I shook my head frantically, but I knew she would not back down. She stepped out from the behind the sacks and walked calmly towards the men.

'Here it is! Grab it and get rid. Stinking moggie – hands off the king's dinner.'

As they carried her out she looked back at me and mouthed 'sorry', and all I wanted to say was that she would never be as sorry as I was that I had brought her into this terrible game.

Druff was silent, and I could see his chest heave as he tried to find the power to speak again. 'We must go, Inges, before they think to look for more. Up here,' and he jumped onto a lower shelf, pulled himself up by a hanging rabbit carcass and clambered into the open roof space.

I followed, looking back for a second to the door through which Poilnoes had disappeared.

The roof space ended at a solid stone wall, and I thought for a moment we had given up Poilnoes just to find a dead end. But Druff pushed at a stone that was set low in the wall, and it moved aside more easily than it seemed it should have done. 'Rats,' he said. This plan had been made long before I showed, I thought.

'You'll see Snuff through here. Keep to the high rafters above the hall, they are wide and will hide you well. Snuff will be waiting at the far side, drop down when he signals and he will take you into the vestry. Good luck, Inges.'

'Thank you Druff. I am sorry about Poilnoes, I know—'

'I'll keep an eye on you from up here. Just make sure you do this, Inges. Just make sure that it was all for something.'

I nodded, and stepped into the Great Hall. The room was vast — far bigger than any I had seen, or even imagined. I felt the whole of Timble could have been put inside, and the highest trees of Knaresborough forest would grow lower than the roof. The walls were hung with great cloths, covered in pictures of hunters, princes, ladies and monstrous beasts. The floor was patterned with chequerwork and fine carpets. It was quite the grandest place I had seen, and it was full of grander looking humans. At the far side I saw the red-brown, lollop-eared figure of Snuff, his tail wagging furiously. He spotted me and gave a small woof. 'Get me down from here, Snuff,' I thought — there are too many people in here, I could not see a way.

But Snuff could, he started to run around in circles, chasing his tail and yelping. The grand humans in the hall turned to look at him. Then he rolled over, his feet in the air, and the humans began to bill and coo, as if he was some sugar-coated puppy-child. Up he hopped, onto his hind legs and strode along the hallway carpet, raising a front paw awkwardly as if in salute.

'Oh my stars, he is absolutely adorable!' one of the ladies below called out, and soon the room was 'ahhing' and 'ooohing' around him and paying attention to nothing but the antics of this capering hound. Smart work, Snuff. Desperately undignified, but smart. In a flash I was down, claws first, clambering one of the cloth paintings, and I slipped quietly into the vestry.

It was empty. Tables and chairs, a chest, clothes hung from a rope along the wall, that cross that all such places have. And a door. A door to the chapel. Unguarded, open. I was in.

Snuff appeared, shaking his fur that had been ruffled by a dozen sweaty human hands. 'What are you waiting for Inges, come on!'

Inges

We walked – not crouched, not slinking, not hiding – walked. Into the chapel, across to the altar, and under the cloth. Snuff pulled up his neck to show me the blue glass vial tied to his collar. I unclipped it, popped the cork with one claw, and dipped another in. I looked at the tip of my claw – the glossy liquid dulled down to a thin white, powder coating.

'Do another claw, on the other paw too,' Snuff said. 'Give you a second go, if needed.'

I nodded, and dipped again into the poison vial. I was armed, I was ready. Now we would wait, until the great bell above us struck four times, and then: One: Buckingham enters. Two: He walks to the altar. Three: He kneels. Four: He dies.

We sat in silence. Snuff closed his eyes – his nose was his guide now, and he was scenting for the approach of a perfumed lord. I stared down at my claws; the crouch was over and now it would be time to strike. Be ready, be decisive, make it count. Suddenly Snuff's nose twitched, and his eyes opened. And the first bell rang.

Inges

Death in the Chapel

ONE: The door opened, and he walked in. Dressed for an audience with his god, lace ruff like a mane around his neck, silk shirt pure white through slashes in a brocade doublet. His hair fell in long curls either side of his head, so they looked not unlike Snuff's ears at that moment. Beard and moustache waxed to fine points. He would make a pretty corpse, I thought.

Two: He stops, just short of the altar. For a moment I fear he has seen us through the thin gap in the gold-hemmed cloth. But he looks up at the cross above us and makes a sign across his chest. He steps up onto the altar platform. I can smell the sweetness of his breath, so close now.

Three: He kneels, hands together, eyes shut – and he is directly in front of me. He closes his eyes. Yes, Buckingham, it is time to say your prayers.

Four: I–

'Marquess! Oh, I am sorry, you are at prayer. Forgive me – I got your message, it sounded urgent.'

'Lady Matilda – you gave me quite a fright. There must be some mistake, I sent for no one.'

Inges

It was her. The Woman. They were both here. Snuff looked at me as if to say 'what are you waiting for'. Now was my chance, kill them both. But I need The Woman alive, I need her to stop the wheels she had put in motion.

'Kill them, Inges, kill them now – what is the matter with you?' Snuff's eyes burned into me, but something was wrong here. Something was wrong.

'It's no matter, my Lord. I must go. Give my regards to your lady wife and apologise for my absence from her dinner, I had urgent business to attend. I will see her anon.'

I am no human. But these were not the words of lovers. Nor of conspirators.

'Damn you Inges, why do you make it so difficult. Kill them! Kill them both!'

'Something isn't right, Snuff.'

The little spaniel snarled. 'You are damn right about that, cat!' He bounded out from under the altar cloth yelping at the top of his voice.

'Good lord – it's little Snuff,' Buckingham said. 'You gave me quite the fright.'

'Ah, how sweet? Is he yours?' The Woman said.

'Oh no – I'm more of a greyhound sort of man I–'

Snuff grabbed the altar cloth in his teeth and pulled it down; cross, candles and all. I stood there, underneath the bare table – bedraggled, dirty with charcoal dust, claw out ready to strike – for all the world to see.

'Oh my Lord – it's the witch cat. It's come to kill me!' Buckingham squealed like a stuck pig, turned on his well-appointed heels and ran for the door. 'It's the damned witch cat again, help, guards, help me!'

Snuff followed close at his heels, as they both disappeared hurriedly out of the chapel. Matilda stood speechless, still at the altar, as I pursued Buckingham and Snuff to the door.

I reached it just in time to see Snuff put his shoulder against it and close it on me with a heavy click. 'See you in Hell, Inges,' he snarled.

I turned, and Matilda was on me – her hand reaching out. Instinctively I struck – my claw flashed and nicked the soft skin on the back of her hand.

'Ouch – Inges. That was uncalled for. I was just going for the door. Oh…'

She had felt something, and she stared at her hand, faint drops of blood now welled like a row of red beads. She stepped back, and sat down into one of the pews. She started to laugh.

'Oh, Inges. I might have known. Well we have both been played for fools here, I think.' Her chest heaved suddenly, and she put a hand to her breast. 'Of course – this is mine, you know. My special brew. Of course it would be that. I always wondered how it felt. Now I see I shall find out. It's as it should be, in the end.'

She stood again and walked towards the altar. 'I'll pray a minute, if that's alright with you, Inges?' Her walk was stiff, and as she reached the altar she put a hand down to steady herself. 'Guards will be here in a minute I suppose, let's see if they get here before this gets me.'

'Why did you do it? Why did you kill Anne, Quin, our souls?'

'Oh Inges, I see now what Fillie saw in you. I didn't before, but yes – I see it.' I hissed at that name. 'Your poor friend Quin made the error of backing out of a deal when he learned the price. But don't hate Fillie, she cared about you. It hurt her more than you know to do what she did.'

I will hate who I want. Do not tell me how to feel. No one can tell me how to feel about her. Not even me.

'I ask again, why?'

'We've been set up, Inges. You and I. And that popinjay Buckingham – though he at least had the sense to be a coward and run. Not like us brave fools, hey?'

'Buckingham is behind this, do not lie to me. I heard you say it was him, at the masque; and Rutterkin told me.'

She laughed harder than ever now. 'Rutterkin? That crazy bag of fleas? He'll say anything if you feed him. I think he's confessed to half the crimes in England by now.'

'But you said George…'

Inges

'George? Oh, Inges, come on. And here I thought you were the clever one. There is more than one George in London, darling.' She gripped her stomach suddenly, and doubled over, falling to her knees as she did. 'Lord, it hurts. I am a cruel woman. That is true.'

I did not know what to think. This woman, who had caused so much pain, dying before my eyes, and now I did not want her to die. Not yet. Not before she had stopped that which she had started. The sound of clattering weapons and heavy feet echoed from the hall outside. We did not have long.

'Who set us up? Were you the target? Why me?'

'We were all the target, darling. Me, Buckingham, you.'

'I don't understand, why me?'

'Don't you see how easy it would have been to kill Buckingham? I could have done it. That little dog under the table could have done it, anyone in the palace could have done it. That's why.'

'No, I don't get it.'

'Because it had to be you, Inges. You had to be the one to kill him. Otherwise–' she stopped as a convulsion seized her stomach and she let out a great moan. Her mouth hung open and a gush of blood poured down her chin. In that moment the door swung open, and Buckingham stood there pointing wildly, flanked by a gaggle of armed men.

'There he is, oh Lord he has killed Lady Matilda. Get him, in the name of our Saviour, get him. Kill him.'

There was no way out. The doors to the vestries either side of us now opened and more guards appeared. This was how it would end.

Matilda turned herself towards the altar, and with an effort that seemed to shake her whole body, pushed herself up. She took hold of the golden cross that had tumbled over as Snuff pulled down the covering, and she turned to me. 'Thank you Inges, for what you have done. I know this is what should be. Go to my house in Milk Street, my bedchamber. Behind the panel – there is a book. It's all in there. God bless you Inges, and pray for my soul.'

She turned, and, with one last effort, hurled the metal cross through the coloured glass window that stood above the altar. She crashed down to spread herself across it, her last breath leaving her body in a bubble of blood that held just a second, then burst. I jumped on her back, onto the mantle of the shattered window, and I ran.

Beware of Cats

THE DROP from the window to the ground was much further on the outside than it had been within, and I span in the air, feet down, braced for a heavy landing. I hit the ground hard, knocking the wind out of my chest, but my blood was up now, and I was quick to recover.

A look one way – no good; back up into the heart of the palace grounds and now guards were running to and fro, as news of assassination spread. I looked the other way – and I thought for the first time that maybe luck was with me today.

The road outside the chapel led straight down to a long stone jetty that jutted out into the Thames. This must be the Palace Stairs, where I was to rendezvous with Jack, and the window had been a shortcut. Would he be there? If he was, he would surely be part of the plot against me, but I would deal with that.

The jetty was clear of people; if I could make it to the end I might hide aboard a wherry that was moored there, at least until the coast was clear. I ran, fast and low, and behind me I could hear the sound of clattering steel, the howl of hunting horns and the deep cries of panicked and angry men. I ran, head down, watching

Inges

the wet flags flash below my paws, straight for the jetty end – and straight into a solid wall of fur and muscle.

'Game's up Inges. Let's not make this difficult.'

There in front of me stood the towering, ragged-grey form of Vincent. Overhead I saw Sutton, circling us – his huge, unblinking eyes fixed on me.

Vincent growled at me. 'Nowhere to run, nowhere to hide. You're going to–'

I had learned this long ago – when Quin would chase me and harry me from my place by the fire: no matter how big or tough they are, their nose will be soft.

He yelped. 'You horrible little cat, I will chew you slowly you–' His leg twitched suddenly, sharply. 'What is this? What have you done to me, cat?'

Vincent's legs were now buckling, his walk unsteady, and he staggered to the side. Two claws. One for Matilda, one for you, Vincent.

'Sutton help me!' Vincent howled, and now his legs gave way and he fell down into the ground, desperately scrambling to get up again as his eyes rolled back in his head.

I just had time to feel the almost silent rush of wind and wings, and Sutton hit; his claw snatching at my shoulder, bowling me over.

He rose again, above me, claws out – long and sharp as kitchen knives – and down he came to where I lay, half dazed, on the ground. White feathers sped towards me; white feathers, white wings, white claws, a white blur. And then black.

From behind me, a black cannonball – a hissing, spitting missile – powered into Sutton. They tumbled together over wet stone and crashed into the jetty wall. Druff, his back arched and his tail raised like a great dark flag, put out his claws and crashed them down, and Sutton's eyes spilt out like jelly.

'That is for Poilnoes, you feathery bastard,' he hissed. Then he stepped back to me, putting out a paw to help me up; and Vincent lifted his head from the ground in his dying breath to bite Druff clean around the middle.

'Inges, he's got me. I'm done for!'

I stood up and put my head to his. 'You'll be fine, it's just a bite. I'll get help.'

'No,' he coughed, and a shiver ran through his body, 'don't leave me. I'm finished, Inges. I don't want to die alone.'

I looked at him, his back now at a sickening, unnatural angle. 'It will be alright, don't worry, you're not going to die,' I said, and I pushed my forehead into his, rubbing gently to let him know I would stay, until the end.

'I'm sorry, Inges. I didn't know. We didn't know. We just wanted to do the right thing.'

'I know, Druff, I know.'

'Inges – I need to tell you something,' he wheezed, and I nodded. 'The Mazger, don't trust him. He betrayed us.'

I had guessed as much. 'Why, Druff? I don't understand.'

Druff gasped for air, then blew hard from his mouth, 'I don't know, I really don't. He is mad. He is old – so old.'

'Yes, I know. He told me some fanciful tale of being 400, older even.'

'No Inges – he is mad, but he does not lie, he is that old. He swaps souls, Inges. That's all I know. He takes souls for himself. When his old soul dies he takes a new one, I know not how. And those who follow, he promises them – us – souls too, after we have given up ours; that's why we serve him. But he has done it himself too many times. Nine times, the whispers say, and no more can he do it. So he is weak, he is dying, and that is why he is mad. He is dying and he wants something – and he will kill anyone to get it. Even me, even you. Even Poilnoes.'

Even me. Even my soul. Does he want mine? It made no sense. So many cats in his kingdom, why me? Druff looked up at me and gave a cry. I hushed him gently.

'Why is it so cold? Are you cold?' He was shaking now. 'Do you think I will see her there? Do you think so, Inges?'

I saw the light in his eyes dimming fast now. 'Of course, Druff – she's waiting for you. She's…'

His chest had stopped moving, and I pushed down the lids to cover those still-beautiful yellow eyes. 'She's waiting for you, Druff.'

I looked up. The guards had still not thought to look down by the river, but even they could not be that stupid for that long. I'd need to hope Jack was waiting at the bottom of the steps, and that the dark Thames water had kept his eyes off what just happened.

I hurried down the steps. A few small boats were tied up, but no boatmen were here now. The river traffic was quiet this early evening, and the bad weather seemed to be holding people indoors. I gave the signal – my tail dropped in the water, swirling it up in a wet figure-of-eight.

At first I thought he must have fled. He seemed to take an age to appear, but then, just as I was thinking to make a den for myself in one of the boats, I spotted bubbles breaking the surface, and that long, toothy face appeared.

'Inges?' he sounded surprised, which no doubt he was. 'Is it done then?'

'Yes,' I said calmly. 'Dead – both of them. That witch Matilda was with him, scheming together. You should have seen their faces as they died.'

Jack's cold eyes looked me up and down. 'Did you get seen?'

'Oh yes, the king himself saw me. Crying out that I had killed his favourite and that he would hunt me to the end of the Earth. Send all England after me if he had to. Get me out of here quick.'

'Of course, of course – get on my back, let's go.' He moved to the side of the steps where he put his back out to me. 'Where's Vincent, Sutton? They were to meet us here.'

I reached down my paw, as if to mount his back, then my claws unsheathed and I stuck him like a fish spear, hauling him up out of the water and onto the stone quay. 'They are in Hell, Jack – where you will see them soon enough.'

His jagged mouth was gaping frantically, as his body twitched back and forth, trying to push himself back towards the water. I calmly put my paw to his side and pushed him further onto the waterless stone.

'Now Jack, you are going to tell me why I have been set up. You are going to tell me what The Mazger wants with me, with my soul.'

Inges

Jack's gills were flapping open and shut as he gulped frantically for air, but the pain he must have felt did not seem to diminish his spite. 'I'll tell you nothing, Inges. Except that you don't need to worry about your soul – she's dead. Your little frog friend told us as much. She told us your soul was dead, and so will you be when he finds you. We are all over London, Inges, you cannot cross a street unless we see you.'

I put my claw into his gill and pulled hard. 'Where is she? Where is Barbara? What have you done with her?'

'Well, cat, if you gut me like you want to, maybe you'll find a little piece of her still left in there.'

He laughed. He was still laughing as I walked away, leaving him stranded on the cold stone quay. He laughed and laughed, until at last he fell silent.

The tide was out. That was all I had going for me. The tide was out, and so I found I could walk that little way below the palace embankment, through the narrow bank of mud and slime and filth, until I reached a grand old house, a little worn by age, that dropped its feet straight into the Thames. At its base, arches allowed the water beneath, now just knee deep, and so I crawled inside and up onto the base of a stone pillar that sat just out of the water.

It would not be long before the water rose again, but I would take a moment to rest. And to think on what Jack had said, about my soul. If I am honest, I had thought it already. I had felt it. To travel far from your soul is hard. They say if you travel too far you might not get back if you die.

I was not sure if there was truth in that, but I did know you felt its presence fade with each mile. And in the last few weeks I had felt it fade further and further, until now I was not sure I felt it at all.

I could feel a great pain inside me, held down, like a fierce beast, some tyger such as Tewhit had told me of, trapped in a cage and I was sat on the lid. I would keep it down, for I knew that the moment I let it out it would tear me apart. And now, right now, I could not fight a tyger and fight The Mazger. I would keep

Inges

it caged – until my work was done, and then I would let it out, however hungry it had become.

I rested probably ten minutes, any longer and I feared I would sleep and be caught by the tide. I knew Jack was right, that The Mazger would be looking for me now and that he had eyes across the city. From the back of the old building the long Strand ran all the way to St Paul's church, and behind there would be Milk Street, and Matilda's house. But to go that road would be to run a gauntlet of imps. It would take me up above the Mazger's palace on Fleet Street, and there would be no escape from them there. It would be madness to go that way. But the world, it seemed, had gone mad, so why should I not join it? I had my claws, I had my hate, and I no longer had my soul. What did I have to lose?

The Strand is a wide open street, and I would walk it openly. I had had enough of hiding. The walk to Cheapside was long and the road was busy with evening traffic – important looking people travelling to and from Westminster and the City, or couples out walking, some looking in the frontages of the fine shops that lined part of the way. Grand houses, some almost little palaces, rose up here and there along the way, though many looked as though they might be as tired and beaten down as I now felt. In the far distance, I kept my gaze on the tower of London's church that rose above the rooftops. But now I was by another church tower, not as high, but one which let me know that here I may go no further. This was the tower of what I now know to be St Bride, and behind it, The Fleet and the door to The Mazger's palace.

I stepped more tentatively now; perhaps I had got further than my bravado had right to take me, and now doubt crept in. Should I hide? Should I rush through? Should I fight? That last option now presented itself as perhaps the only one. I was suddenly conscious of eyes on me. Many eyes, from all sides of the road, from high and low.

'Inges – you are either very brave or very stupid. You shouldn't have come this way.'

It was Isegrim, his claws drawn, and flanked by the king's ginger enforcers. All around me, the imps moved in – dozens of cats, dogs, rats; even a mouse – emboldened by numbers – who I simply glared at until he crawled back into a pothole with a whimper.

'You are a traitor to all imps, Isegrim,' I spat. 'Your name will be an insult reserved for the basest cats, and mothers will scold their kittens for using it.'

'I serve the king, don't talk to me of treachery, Inges. Get him!' Isegrim hissed.

'Inges – here, quickly. To your left, look down,' the squeaky voice turned my head just as the imps moved in. I had been standing close to a small building I had at first taken for a dog kennel in the middle of the road, with a door too small for any human to fit in. That door was now ajar, and leaning out of it I saw my little rat friend, Ferdinando. 'In here – ¡deprisa!'

I jumped suddenly to my left, into the door, and slammed it shut behind me – jarring it closed with a flat stone that would hold it for a minute at least.

'Ferdinando, am I glad to see you. What is this place? How long can we hold them off in here?'

'Inges, my friend, it is good to see you too. I must apologise, I have been following you since you passed the Strand Inn, though you would not have seen me. You see, I was down here.' He gestured to a gap in the brickwork within this kennel that seemed to lead down only into darkness.

'Where are we, Ferdinando?'

'This is the Great Conduit, Inges. We – my friends – we call it the Tube. It takes water from up on the hills out west and down into Cheapside. And we can follow it.'

The Conduit was a stonework tunnel below the pavements, in which was set a long chain of hollow logs carrying water into the heart of the city.

Between the logs and the wall was enough space to squeeze through – just – for a cat like me.

'Do the other cats know?' I asked, as we moved as quickly as I could through the tunnel.

'Oh yes, they use it all the time to raid the city shops. But I left them a little surprise.'

Inges

In the distance, I heard the sound of squeaking, of hissing and howling. I raised my whiskers at Ferdinando.

'My friends,' he said.

Tube rats – they tolerate cats if they leave them alone, he told me. But not today. Not that many cats, not trying to kill Ferdinando's friend.

'There is no room for a cat to swing its claws down here. Será una matanza – it is a slaughter – if they are foolish enough to try.'

I am glad – not just for this but for everything – that I did not eat Ferdinando when I thought to. The Mazger's, it seemed, was not the only guild in town. The rats – they have their own houses, their own army, their own spies. And I had become a brother to one of their own.

We made good time to the far end of the conduit, and startled a few old women who were busy collecting water in wooden pails as we popped out of the tunnel mouth in the far end of Cheapside Street. We ran, between the legs of evening strollers and lantern carriers, under empty carts and barrows, the short way to Milk Street.

The street ran off from the wide thoroughfare – a tall, up-and-down on each side of fine houses and wood and glass. It was just across the wide way from where Ferdinando and I had watched so many days the people of London go by. We had been so close, from the start, I thought, yet we had taken such a hard way.

'Any idea which house is Matilda's?'

'Matilda?' Ferdinando said, twitching his whiskers. Of course, he did not know.

'The Woman – I found her. Her house is here.'

'Is she rich?'

'The one who paid for the house is, I hear.'

'Then try this one,' Ferdinando beamed, and twitched his little black nose at the building that rose above us now. Three stories high, fine glass in the windows, a brickwork chimney perfectly pointed, and all backing the small church that sat at that end of the street.

'It's as good a place as any to start, I guess.'

It was easy enough to get inside, for a cat and a rat. And he was right, it seemed; this was not the house of some London merchant and his little family. Downstairs the rooms were bare, but for one that had been set aside for visitors. Functional, no sweet remembrances or keepsakes, just chairs and a desk, books and bare cabinets. The second floor was empty too, spider webs and an undisturbed carpet of dust showed this part must never be touched.

At the top, it changed. One room was set out with soft furnishings, the books there were not neatly stacked in shelves but set upon a busy table, their pages well-turned and yellowed with use. The walls were bright, and on them were paintings; of churches and little sailing boats on wide rivers, village life full of smiling faces, pictures of flower vases in a hundred different colours. And then, on a small dresser: a portrait, barely bigger than a goose egg, set in a dark wood frame. A woman, a girl really. At first I thought it must be Matilda; it looked like her, but the eyes were different, brighter. She seemed happy, this girl in the frame. She had a look on her face as though she had learned some secret that meant her heart could never be broken, nor her happiness taken away. I envied her, and I hoped that she had never let that secret go.

In the next room, it was clear we were in Matilda's chamber. The clothes were set out, just as I had seen her wear at the masque. It seems she had the best clothes, but not many. The room was sparse. A bedside table with another book on it, a newer looking one, and well read. It was in some tongue I cannot read, but some words were familiar enough to guess at: 'decision', 'reform' and what seemed some place name – 'Dordrecht'. Whatever the meaning, it was an important book to her, as I had expected one of their bibles to be in such a place.

'Do you see a loose panel, Ferdinando?' I addressed the rat who had been sniffing behind the bed, but now seemed to have located a crumb of hard cheese.

'Mmmghgsherefink.'

'Sorry?'

He gulped: 'It's here I think,' and he pulled at the corner of a panel that moved a little in his hand. I ducked below the bedstead and prized it open with my claw; and inside – that was where I found the bible. Leather bound, in English this time, and stamped on the cover, in gold lettering: '+GA'.

I turned the cover, and a dry, brittle, single sheet of paper – folded in half and in half again – fell out to the floor.

It was frayed with age, and on the front, folded towards me, was writing, so faint that I could hardly read it. The top lines only, I could just make out, with some words missing, so that they read:

'To _ brother, Charles Fairfax, _ hope _ inspire _ your heroism and the glory of England. _ darling brother, Edward. May this _ safe always'.

The rest I could not read. It seemed the words had worn with time, or else run with water off the page.

I unfolded again, and turned. On the other side the lettering was new, clear and all of an elegant hand: *'My name is Matilda Cheveron and if you are reading this you will know I am not a good woman.'*

Inges

The Revenger's Tragedy

'MY NAME is Matilda Cheveron and, if you are reading this, you will know I am not a good woman.

I can assume now one of two things has happened. If I am lucky, if all has gone well, then I have failed. My life is forfeit, and, should there be any doubt of it, the person who took my life is guilty of nothing more than delivering the justice that is due to a murderer.

If I am unlucky, then I have succeeded. And if that is the case, then the murderer will have been put to justice too, only by her own hand.

I cannot tell you which way I died; you must know that which I cannot. I can tell you little of value in how I lived. Much you may already know and, if not, little of it will be of use to you.

If I am to say the whole truth, I should say I cannot tell you how I died a second time.

For Matilda Doetinchem, who I knew as myself once, died long ago. I know that death well, for I have the place and date of it carved on the stone that has been my heart ever since: January 7th, 1602, at Ostend.

Inges

I make no excuse for my sins; I need no confession as those who follow false faith believe. I am not chosen to be with God, the Devil took my soul that day and I have been damned since

But I want you to know. I want you to know, not for me but for little Tillie, who I was. She did not deserve to die, no more than did her sister, sweet Anna. Remember her, remember Tillie; do not remember me.

If I have fulfilled my oath then the Fairfax family is dead. As I swore, on my soul, on her soul, they would die, that day I found my Anna in the sand and blood at Hell's Mouth. Just as sure as I fired the gun that took Charles Fairfax's life – as sure as he took hers – I mean to take the lives of his loving brother Edward, and those children Charles so wanted me to see. If Charles had issue of his own, they would have died; in their place I would take those he loved as his own.

And I hate myself for it. Does that sound too full of self-pity? If it is then judge me. I am already judged; I cannot be twice damned. I leave this letter here to be found – by whoever I may leave news of it with before I go. If I get that chance. My work should be done in Yorkshire soon, and if the year has now passed and they still live, then I failed, and be thankful. If they are dead, Anna is avenged.

I know Hell awaits me, but I know that, whatever terrors it holds, none can be worse than my dreams now. I cannot close my eyes but I see their faces. Anna and Anne, Anne and Anna – their names as alike as their eyes in my dreams. I am sorry Anna; I am sorry Anne. I see your eyes, and I don't know whose is whose anymore.

Enough now, with me and my shame. There is one more thing that must be known. I paid a great price to get my vengeance and I made a deal with more than one devil.

Below the palace of Bridewell there is a den of cats. Burn it. Kill them all. There is in there one who calls himself king and who promises the souls of a thousand dead to his followers. He has set his mind to provoke King James to burn witches again, alongside their pets, such as they call familiars. He killed – with my help – those poor, innocent Flowers women in Belvoir, and no doubt now the same in Fewston; and he would do the same all across England. Stop him if you can, let me at least die and not need to see all those eyes.

I read that last bit back now and think perhaps the grief and the sin has taken my mind. It seems so real. I don't know what is real anymore. Anne or Anna, Matilda or Tillie, cats or witches. I give my soul over to the one who deserves it.

Matilda Cheveron, 1621'

I stood there, in silence, staring at the letter. Unable to move. Ferdinando moved to my side and put a scaly claw gently on my paw, and in that moment all the pain of my loss – all the agony of betrayal, all the suffering of my friends, of Peg, of Maggie, of Gybbe, of Quin, of Poilnoes, of Druff – all of it burst out so that I tore the air apart with my cry.

I think I may have slept for the whole night and most of the next day.

When I awoke, Ferdinando had pulled a china saucer of water to my side, and brought up some dry ham that he may have taken from the floor under the market stalls at the end of the road. I thanked him and stretched out my legs.

Though I slept well, my dreams had been troubled. I had been chased and harried by all manner of imps, I had tried to fly but found myself swimming slowly through the air, pursued by owls with eyes of black coal. I had dreamt of children buried in sand, and birds with broken wings who ran in circles and cried out 'murder'.

But my dreams had wandered onto other things too. To questions. To why The Mazger needed me to kill Buckingham. To how he knew what he had not been told – of words spoken in my meeting with the king and the bishop. To how carelessly they put me in a box with a holy book. To how clumsily I was exposed to the king. To how easily I got in and out of the palace that day.

'Ferdinando,' I said, 'you have lived long in London, you know it well.'

'Indeed Inges, I have.'

'Do you remember my trip to the palace – the first one, when we learned of Buckingham?'

'I do, of course my friend. What of it?'

'Just a simple question really. Do you know the name of the Archbishop I met there?'

'Of course, Inges, that is well known. His name is Abbot.'

'Abbot?'

'Yes. George Abbot.'

Inges

The Puritan

I KNEW the answers, now, to my dream's questions. There is more than one George in London, and I must meet the other one again before my work is done.

And I knew, now, why I was to be the one to kill Buckingham. You may not think it, but I can be a vain cat – don't refuse it, it is true. So of course I had thought: 'why, Inges, it must be you, as who else could pull off such a daring adventure? What other cat could tweak the nose of the King of England and snatch off his favourite like a juicy capon unguarded on a kitchen top?'

I suspect it could have been Isegrim, or Druff, or any other of the cats at his command – at his disposal. He did not need Inges, he needed a dupe. He needed one who would show himself, despoiling holy books, terrifying the king and the court, making a name for himself as a menace, as a witch's cat, bent on the destruction of order and the peace of England.

So when this impetuous fool of a cat – already hunted as a witch's familiar in Yorkshire – presented himself at The Mazger's court; well it would be as if I had wrapped myself up all pretty in a bow and handed myself to him. A cat blinded by revenge? A cat daring enough to travel alone to London? A cat who looked like me: white with black spots, one eye blue, the other black? Who could forget me?

And that witch's cat would kill James's favourite, in the heart of his court. Nowhere would be safe for him in all his kingdom. Unless. Unless he burned them all – all the witches and with them their familiars, their killer cats. And then The Mazger's followers would gather at the flames to harvest their souls for their own. Was that even possible? It was at least what they believed, and they would see us dead in our thousands to fulfil his wicked promise.

I knew my way now. I had walked this road before. There was a little trouble at London Bridge, with a cat or two who might have known my face. But I am the one they sent to kill Buckingham, am I not? Dupe they may think me, but they should have sent bigger cats if they had wanted to stop me.

The rain of the last days had eased, though the cold wind from off the river still bit deep. It had been a year of ill weather, a year without a summer. I saw the poor pickings of the vegetable gardens along the riverside fields, and thought of the barley up at Fewston, and the empty larders the slandered women would soon come home to. But as I approached the palace, drifting on the wind I could smell the plump aroma of bread and sweet cakes in the stoves, the ripe tang of rich cheeses, the savour of beef and suet pastry.

There it was. The fig tree I remembered from my first visit. It seemed a long time ago. I would sniff my mark, left there on its bark. Would I even recognise my own scent now? Remember the cat I was? A figure stepped from the shadow of a sheltering eve.

'Hello Inges, I've rather been expecting you.'

The bishop looked more tired even than I remembered him, and now his great puffed sleeves were gone, replaced by a simple coat of wool that he pulled around himself against the cold.

'It's not so nice out here is it? What say we go inside, and I will tell you all you want to know.'

For a man who could afford such food as I had smelt, his own room was more sparse than I had expected. He sat on a simple wooden chair, turned away from a plain writing desk which was covered in every place by parchment, books, paper, quill and ink. The good chair – a little worn, but of fine patterned upholstery filled with horsehair – he had given to me.

'It's good to see you again, Inges. I must apologise for our last meeting; I'm afraid I rather fancied myself a stage player in my youth. It was a little over-done, wasn't it? The 'Saint's Bible' – I thought perhaps that was a step too far, but I do love the staging as much as the show.'

I had tucked my legs beneath myself, sat up on the soft chair to chase out the cold I still felt in my paws. I would let him speak.

'I am tired, Inges. Tired of it all. It's been too long, and I am too old for all this now. I am glad you have come.' I fixed my stare, unblinking. 'Not talkative today then? You don't have to worry about your laws here; I know. God knows, I have spent a lifetime talking to an imp, you won't shock me.'

'*Prrrrp?*'

'You have met him, I think. Jack is his name.'

Now I talked. 'Jack? The pike? He is dead.'

The bishop sat back in his chair – I could not read his face, it was too human. 'Dead? Hmm, you did well to do that.'

I had not told him it was I who killed Jack, though I suspect I did not need to.

'I'm an old fool, Inges. What was I thinking? Matilda. So stupid. I'm old enough to be her father, her grandfather. She's beautiful though. Was, beautiful. Have you ever been a fool for beauty, Inges?'

I did not speak.

'I hear you took the ring I gave her – rather harshly, too, from what I gather. It was nothing really – a trinket the king gave me in remembrance of St James. He is fond of his namesake. I just passed it on; she deserved more.'

I thought to myself that the ring had deceived us all then, if she had thought it a sign of his generosity.

'We met at Dordrecht, I was there on business with the Prince of Orange, Maurits. She was his, of course – or rather he was hers, I think. We had done business there on some issues of the church;

there is division in his lands over the right way to Heaven, and I was to help see matters fell the way he wished.

'And in return, he sent her to help me. To seduce Buckingham and turn him against Spain. That didn't work the way we planned it – which I could not believe; except now I think perhaps Buckingham's tastes run a little differently in that regard. So we had no choice but to try to kill him.'

The bishop sighed deeply, and put his hands to his collar, running his fingers across the small wooden cross that hung at his neck. 'You know, for all their gibbering idolatry, I sometimes understand why those Papists give confession. It is good to get things off your chest, when they have been burrowing there into your heart for so long. It is to God alone I must lay out my burden, yet I find more relief in telling you, I fear to say. Perhaps I have lost His Grace, if I ever had it.'

He must have seen my expression, or else he could not help but preach, and so he told me at length of Papists and Puritans, and the matters of Grace. That those who follow Rome must follow the priests to heaven, and those who protest must find the way in a book. That each must hate the other, and that Matilda suffered great loss from that hate.

And I thought on that thing that, to me, is the most human of all. That all humans will hate and kill another for the littlest thing that makes them different – and yet none ever see their crime as the same.

If a man steals a loaf of bread, and another steals a necklace of gold – both hang for the same crime and all will say they were thieves. Yet if a man kills for thinking one way and another kills for thinking another, each will say the other was a criminal, but they were not.

I am a simple cat, I have no great human understanding, even after all I have seen – but I know this: my Peg did no wrong, yet she suffered for the wrongs of others. And in hurting her, those who would avenge whichever crime they believe she inherited have only committed that same crime again and become that which they hate. I understand that about humans, and I understand nothing else.

'Tell me bishop,' I said at last, 'why did you and Matilda work with The Mazger? Could you not do your foul work alone?'

The Bishop put his hands together, and for a moment I thought he might pray. 'Matilda brought him to me. Her cat, Fillie, had come to know him. They said he had spies across the whole country, that he would help our enterprise. What I did not know then was that one of those spies was my Jack.'

'You knew Jack before you met The Mazger?'

'I knew him… he knew me, before I was born. You see, The Mazger collects great men. He bonds his servants with their souls, when they are young, then guides them to power. Of course, once they are there he collects his debt. Always there is a debt.'

Jack, it seemed, had promised Abbot's mother greatness for her child – all she had to do was eat a pike (some rival no doubt), and her son, then in her belly, would grow to high office. Jack, The Mazger, the great men the cat king owned: they did the rest – paid for his education, bought his place in the Church, smoothed the path to Lambeth. But for such a costly service, the debt was heavy.

'I must do his bidding. If I had moved against him, Jack would have talked. Imagine the consequences – the Archbishop in league with a satanic imp? I would have been finished. Worse, the Church would be condemned with me, and the Papists would seize their chance. I could not stop him. Or her, she knew the secret too.'

'That's why you sent her to Whitehall Chapel? You wanted me to kill her?'

The bishop hung his head. 'I just wanted to be free of it all, you understand?'

He stood up and began to pace the room, scratching at his thin beard and muttering to himself, until at last he spoke. 'Jack will be back of course, while I live.'

'Yes,' I said, 'but we are never truly back. We half-remember our past lives, they say; as if it was a story written by someone else. When we first come back it is just shadows, it takes a good while to take proper shape. And Jack will come to you before the shadow is turned to substance.'

'And?'

'And – I suggest you buy a sturdy net and a good supply of parsley butter.'

The bishop laughed, and I saw in the turn of his mouth that it must have been a long time since he had made that sound so naturally.

Then his laughter trailed away. 'Inges, I know what I must do. I cannot now see in myself any sign of God's Grace, and I must accept the path that some other has chosen for me. Matilda did give me one thing that is of use to us both, and I must use it. May God forgive me, both for what I do, and for not doing it a long time before.'

And so it was agreed. The bishop would do his part, and I mine. I would wait at Lambeth, a guest of that palace, to regather my strength and to have put down for me some words of things I would want to remember later – if memories were all I was to have after this. In the meantime, he would attend to some business in the country. Before he left, he would write and send in all haste to Fewston, to the Reverend Smythson, word that the women were innocent and that he must petition for release immediately. The Church would tend to their health and their recovery, at whatever cost it took.

'He is a good man, Inges,' he told me. 'Sometimes a little too keen in his fervour, but his heart is good. I know it pained him to see some of his flock condemned, and I do know – though he tried to hide it – that he would visit those poor wretches in prison and bring them food and comfort. He will be as happy as any man in Fewston to see their innocence confirmed.'

I had come to London to free the women, and now that work was done. But there was one more thing I must do. On the appointed day, at the appointed time, I would move against The Mazger and his army of imps. One cat against a thousand. It would be a slaughter.

De Sapientia Veterum

THE MIST hung low over the river that morning. The tops of the city – the towers and the steeples – rose up out of nowhere and there was no bank ahead of us. The water was still, and quiet; so early in the day that the sun's weak light barely broke through the fog and it felt as if all the world was kept behind a grease paper window.

'Christ, cat, you still not going to talk to me? I thought by now you might open up a bit. It's too quiet on here, I don't like it.'

Shovel-Face was rowing slowly, the less noise we made the better, and I wasn't about to break the silence. Besides, I needed to focus. This was the moment before the battle. The calm before the storming of the palace. This was Inges time.

I would be taken to Whyte Fryers – far enough from Bridewell that I may not be seen so early in the morning, but close enough that I could be there when the sun broke above the roof of St Paul's in the distance – for that was the time I would attack.

'There you go, cat,' the boatman said as our bow touched hard against the stone quay. 'I hope you know what you're doing, I hear those cats can be vicious.'

Inges

I hoped so too. This close — this late in the battle plan — was no time for doubt.

'*Prrrp.*'

'I'll take that as a thankyou, you ungrateful moggie.' The boatman slipped away, slowly enveloped by the fog, and I was all alone, standing on the quayside with only my wits and my claws, at the camp of an enemy army now waking from their sleep.

It was a short hop and jump over the wall into an open courtyard that had been the place of some other bishop, Abbot had told me. There I climbed the ivy-covered brickwork of a high wall that abutted the Cat King's palace. If they were watching at all, they would be watching the river, or the Fleet Street entrances. There was no way in here. But they would hear me. I looked up from my vantage point and, through the haze, I just saw the thin disk of the morning sun kiss the rooftop of London's great church.

'*Meeeoeoeoooooeooooow!*' I let out a caterwaul like I thought might wake the whole city. Long and loud, and filled with all the anger that had boiled inside me since the day I saw Quin hanging. A warning, a clarion call, a threat: a challenge.

I heard the faint sounds of reply below; calls in which I could hear fear, alarm, panic and dread more than any battle song of warriors. But I knew that was because the fearful are always the first to cry out, and I knew they would be coming: the guards, Isegrim, The Mazger's soldiers and enforcers.

'*Meeoooeoeooooow!*' I called again. 'Come out and face me, Mazger. Face me like a cat. Let's do it the old way, cat-to-cat, or are you a coward? I throw down my challenge.'

It was a challenge a king should accept, and so it was no surprise to me when the ivy parted at the end of the wall and a challenger stepped out. No surprise, that is, that it was not that tyrant who calls himself The Mazger; it was Isegrim, flanked by the ginger guards.

'King too afraid to face me, Isegrim? Not much of a king then, is he?'

Isegrim sneered and gestured down to where a growing circle of spitting, hissing cats was surrounding my wall. 'Kings don't fight peasants; they fight other kings. If they need filth cleaning up, kings send their army.'

'I know,' I said. 'And that is why I have sent mine.'

And at that moment, as the sun finally broke fully over the roof of the Cathedral, they came. A witch's cat had been seen at Whitehall. He had killed a great lady on the holy ground of the palace chapel. He must be destroyed. He must be that satanic King of Cats. The one poor murdered Matilda spoke of in her death letter, the letter that had found its way into Buckingham's hands. The letter that told of the Cat King's lair beneath Bridewell.

Buckingham's soldiers poured out of hiding from the buildings of Salisbury Court and Fleet Street and stormed through the doors of Bridewell. Swords, axes, bows and flaming torches – they were scouring the dank rooms of The Mazger's palace, putting to death or to flight all imps they found there. Isegrim stared in bewilderment as panicked cats ran here and there below us. For a moment he seemed frozen with fear. Then he turned to his guards: 'He's set us up, he's betrayed us all. Kill him, kill the traitor!'

But the ginger thugs had seen enough. They may not have had much wit between them, but they knew a fight they could not win. They could kill me easily enough, but they would not beat a halberd or a mace. They ran. Away across the rooftops, away to the north, to where the houses disappear into fields and woodland, away towards the horizon.

'Fine, I'll kill you myself,' he hissed, and his claws were out and on me in a second.

I knew immediately that I had picked a fight I would be lucky to win. He looked strong, but he was far stronger than I had thought. His initial hit took the wind out of me, so that when we landed I was much slower to move off than he was to raise his claw. He hit me, hard across the face, and I felt the sting and the warm rise of blood immediately.

I was down, and I knew if he got me in the death lock, if he got his paws around me and brought those powerful back legs into play on my exposed belly, it would be over. I used all the strength I had to right myself, half-dragging him with me so

Inges

that he still had a hold on me but he could not use his back legs without losing balance.

'I am going to gut you, Inges,' he panted. 'And when I am done with you...' he threw me over again and pinned me down, his powerful claw raised above my eyes, 'I will go to that cesspit you call a village and kill every last imp there, personally.'

Less talk, more fight. I got my own back legs from under me and heaved at him, knocking him off balance enough that I could get back to my feet.

'You have to kill me first, Arse-Licker,' I spat.

'With pleasure, you little–'

'Gibs.'

The voice, high-pitched, soft, came from over Isegrim's shoulder. His eyes widened and he froze, his claw still held in position.

'Gibs it.'

Slowly, carefully, he turned his head, looking round at his hind quarters, where a fat blob of pink-tinted drool had just landed.

'Gibs meat!' Rutterkin screeched, a sound from the depths of Hell – at least from that hell into which Isegrim had locked him all these years. 'Gibs meat! Rutterkins eats it! Rutterkins eats all the juicy meat!'

I had to look away. That flurry of white claws and grey fur, black blood and red flesh. I have hated few cats as much as I hated Isegrim, but no one should die that way.

Below me the battle ground was clearing. Buckingham's soldiers – steel against claw – had made swift work of The Mazger's army. But now they were looking for me, the false Cat King. And I was looking for the real one.

I thought at first to wait and search out the palace once it was clear; that The Mazger might be hiding there somewhere. But I saw that the soldiers had hunting dogs; scent hounds who would sniff out any cat down there no matter how well they hid. I thought of what they would have done to the Hall of Kings – to the history in there, that they would have smelt from a mile away.

They would also smell me if I hung around. I clambered back along my wall and through the ivy, up to the high point of the other bishop's building. And I saw him. He must have had a passage from the palace to the conduit. He should have known I was a soldier, a general, a planner. No escape that way, Mazger, had you forgotten the rats?

He was scrambling out of the little stone kennel, scratching off the rats that still clung by their teeth to his fur. He looked frantically around, and at both ends of the road were soldiers and dogs. First he seemed to want to run to the north side of the street, but there was no way into the houses there, so he turned towards the church at St Bride's, and into the door. Now I had him.

I bounded across the rooftops, leaping the gaps between the high and low peaks of the shingles with ease. The ivy grew all across the front of this old building, and I worked my way quickly down it, across the brief open ground and into the church yard. I entered the church door just in time to see the flash of a greying tail disappear up the winding steps of the tower. There was nowhere left to run.

When I reached the top, The Mazger was still catching his breath. He pressed himself against the low stone wall that surrounded the top of the tower. I looked over; it was a long way to the ground. Landing on your feet would not be enough to save you here.

'It's over, Mazger,' I said as calmly as I could. 'We can fight, and you'll die. Or you can jump, and you'll die. Pick your option, but I recommend the jump. I won't make it so quick.'

'Inges, Inges – please. I am your king. You swore an oath.'

'I swore an oath to a king, not to a snivelling murderer. Who are you king of now, Mazger? Who? Look around you – they are gone, they have abandoned you, or else they are dead like your precious Isegrim.'

He did not flinch at that, and nor do I think he cared. Not for Isegrim, nor anyone but himself.

'Please don't kill me,' he was begging now, 'I can give you things.'

'You have nothing I want, king,' I raised my claw to strike.

'I can get your soul back. I can get it back for you!'

'What?'

'I can get it back. I can do that. Get it back better.'

Inges

'Is this your nonsense about soul harvests, Mazger?' The bishop told me about that.' That name did make The Mazger flinch. 'I want my soul, not someone else's.'

'Yes, yes, Inges. Your soul, your very own soul.'

I put down my claw. 'You have a minute to explain.'

'Look at us Inges. Look at us. Look what we have done. You – you have slighted the King of England then brought his troops under your command; you have conquered a kingdom. Me – I have ruled for centuries, influencing the great men and women of England across the ages. And yet they think us mere pets, or else vermin.'

'You need to start getting to the point,' I snarled.

'We were gods, you see, Inges. Before all this. gods. Grimalikin, when he came out of Egypt. Old Bastet of legend. People worshipped us. They built great temples to us. They thought us worth more than gold, or spice, or silk or any such thing.'

'Right, time's up.'

'No – I am getting to it. You must understand first. We were gods, but then they took it. Those Christians, with their nailed god. Their greedy god, who must have all the glory and the power for himself. They took our power, and the power of all the other gods, and they gave it only to one. And then they locked him away inside their churches so that no one could get to him, no one could share his power, unless they let them through.'

He was raving now, and I would hear him out, if only to satisfy myself more when I killed him.

'But a man came to me – sent by a great prince, a friend of imps. And he told me, they lie. Their god is not locked away, he does not turn you away if you come to him without a priest. That pope that excommunicated us, Inges, he said we were outside of God's power, but he lied. We don't need a church; we just need to go to Him. And look at us, Inges, look at us! God chooses those who share his power, and he shows his choice on Earth. He has chosen us. Are we not chosen? Are we not blessed by God?'

'What has this got to do with my soul, Mazger? I am growing tired of this now.'

'Don't you see, Inges, don't you see? Go with God and you have your own soul. You need no filthy human soul; you have your own. You live in God forever. Eternal life. You become a god, like you were always meant to be. Like I am. Like I have become – when I give souls, I give life. I am not a mere king, Inges, – I am a god!'

'You are insane, and now you die.' I stepped in and The Mazger flicked at me with a claw. A soft enough hit, barely a scratch. But I knew right away.

'I may be insane, Inges, you are not the first to say it. But I still have enough wit to keep you talking while I opened that damn, fiddly bottle.'

I could feel the poison working its way through my body, and I knew it was over. The Mazger was a conjurer; smoke and colour, misdirection. And I was his dupe.

But I am a conjurer too; and I do not reveal my hand until the end.

Away, if you follow the road that heads west from here far enough, you reach the forests and fields of Hampshire. And there, in that ancient hunting ground of kings, George Abbot is crying. He needs to clear his eyes; he needs to keep them fixed ahead of him. To where his bolt is facing.

Peter Hawkins did no wrong. Just a simple gamekeeper. But the innocent sometimes pay for the crimes of others, that I have learned. His only sin was to be there all those years ago – a little boy out walking with his mother when that old lady died. When she died with her cat in the fire. He was too young to understand it. He watched with the others, and, as his mother took his hand to lead him away, an old black cat, slightly greying here and there, brushed against his legs. Peter stroked him, and he purred. He thought he saw something in the cat's eye – a glimmer, a light. It was there a second, and then it was gone.

Abbot squeezed the crossbow trigger, and the bolt flew.

On the tower the Mazger smirked. 'Did you think you could take a king's life so cheaply?'

Inges

'I have paid such a price already, Mazger, that a little more won't matter.'

Keep your eye on the ball. All else is smoke and colour – the hands, the cups, the scarves, they aren't there. It is all just the ball.

In the corner of the Mazger's eye, a flicker. Then a burst, like one of those firerockets they shoot at the heavens to mark a king's birthday. Or a king's funeral.

'What have you done Inges? What have you done?' The Mazger's paw was on his eye now, but he could not hide that dancing light. 'You stupid cat! What have you done? We could be gods. You have killed us both!'

'Not yet I haven't,' I hissed, and I threw myself at him and we fell – down, down to the hard ground far below.

IN ARCADIA

'COME ON Inges, focus. Don't go in all a rush – you need to fight that instinct. It's about patience, waiting for the moment, getting the approach right. Watch me. It's in the crouch, you see. Do you see what I'm doing? The crouch.'

I looked at the little shrew shaking and shivering in the short grass in front of me. Its small black eyes darted around looking for a road out. If it ran, it was doomed; if it stood still it was doomed. I just need to practice my crouch.

'Mum,' I said, and she looked at me with that kind concern mothers show. 'Is it ok if we don't do this today? It doesn't feel right. Can we let him go?'

'Let him go?' she mewed in soft surprise.

'I just... I feel I've seen enough death for a while.'

She wrinkled her nose. 'Oh, Inges, you have seen me kill one vole since you first opened your eyes. You are a funny boy,' and she dragged her warm, rough tongue over my head so that I rolled over and purred.

I knew I was supposed to want to kill. I would be a hunter. A great cat. But right now, I was not ready. There was a dark shadow

Inges

in my mind that I could not shake. Like a story I had been told, half remembered; a story of death and sadness.

The humans returned now, and it seemed they had brought food as well as flowers. I liked them well enough, they fed us, and they didn't hurt us, and they left us alone for the most part, which is what suited me.

'Oh do you see mother, look at the little one. He's up and about now and look at how he is. Don't you think he looks just like Inges?'

The older human looked at me. 'Oh my, Peg, so he does. He's got those same black spots, and look; the mark right over his eye just like Inges.'

'Let's call him Inges, mother. If that's ok?'

'That's ok. I know you miss him.'

I went to call out: 'hey, my name is Inges, that's funny,' but my mother stopped me with a firm paw.

'We never speak to them, Inges, no matter what. Never – that is so important.'

'Why is it important, mum?'

'Because it is bad for us, and for them. Those poor ladies, they nearly died because the secret of imps got out. And that cat, for whom you were named, that poor brave Inges...' She started to cry, and I nuzzled into her, to comfort us both. 'It's ok,' she said, 'I'm just being silly, I hardly knew him. It's just that he saved us all. We must never forget.'

'I won't mamma, I promise,' I said.

'Now,' she said, 'happier things. That yellow bird that you like, Tewhit; well he is to return to his place in India after all these years. He is a cheeky imp – he told me that since she returned he spent each night at his soul's bed, while she slept, whispering "to India, to India, to India" into her ear, until one morning she woke up and said to him: "Tewhit, I have a mind to go to India and to see all that my dear husband told me of it – we have but one life don't we?" And that made me chuckle so.'

I would miss that bird, I thought, as it felt I had known him a long time, though it had only been a few weeks.

'And you, darling. What of your soul? Have you chosen yet? I can never tell with that cheeky little black eye of yours what is going on in there. What about that sweet young baby up at New Hall that the Fairfax girl and Henry Graver had this last week? She will be well looked after.'

I stopped to think. My mind was changing so fast these days, pictures of faces I didn't know, sounds and smells that came from nowhere, dreams of rats, and frogs, of great buildings too grand to be real. And something else. Something I dare not speak of to my mother, not yet. Of a soul. A boy – a dark haired boy with the brownest eyes, out walking close by some old church. That's how I see him, in my dream. Looking up at him from the hard ground and he says: 'oh poor kitty' and he is my soul.

'No, I've not chosen yet, mum. Still deciding.'

'Well, be quick. It's not safe. I don't like the idea of you in the big bad world without a soul. That Barghest might get you.'

I twitched my whiskers in a way that felt defiant, then I pushed my head back into her soft fur.

The shrew had run away now, I saw. Another day, maybe. I followed the faint track of its escape, and my eyes met another's.

'Mum – who's that?' The strange cat seemed to be watching us from around the corner of the humans' house. White fur, quite the most beautiful blue eyes; I could not stop looking.

'Stay by me, you shouldn't talk to strangers.' I ducked behind her, peeking out around her back legs. 'Can I help you, miss?'

The pretty cat shook her head, as if we had woken her from a dream. 'Oh, I'm sorry, I was staring. You just looked so happy, the two of you, it was… sweet.'

I shook a smile with my tail.

'You have a very handsome young boy there,' the cat said.

'Yes I do, thank you,' my mother replied, and licked my ear affectionately.

'I think he will go far. I'm glad you are happy,' the cat said, and then she turned and walked away.

'She was a nice lady,' I said, and my mum twitched her nose a little.

Inges

'Mum, can I go and play with the people? Peg has a feather for me to chase.'

'Ok – but don't get too close to the fire, don't break anything. You be careful.'

'I will, mum.'

She nuzzled her soft nose into my cheek. 'I know you will Inges – you are a good cat.'

THE END

Addendum: A Veritable History

THIS IS not the first book about Inges the cat, but it is the first to tell the truth – at least as Inges sees it.

Edward Fairfax, a now obscure but once celebrated Elizabethan translator and poet, wrote his version at New Hall, in Fewston, Yorkshire, during the reign of James I.

Daemonologia: A Discourse on Witchcraft as it was Acted in the Family of Mr. Edward Fairfax of Fuystone set out his case against the 'witches' who had cursed his family:

- Peg Waite and her imp 'a white cat spotted with black and called Inges'
- Margaret Waite and her imp 'a deformed thing with many feet, black of colour, rough with hair, the bigness of a cat, the name of it unknown'
- Jennit Dibble and her imp 'in the shape of a great black cat called Gibbe, which hath attended her now above 40 years'
- Margaret Thorpe and her imp 'in the shape of a bird, yellow in colour, about the bigness of a crow – the name of it is Tewhit'
- Elizabeth Fletcher, imp unknown
- Elizabeth Dickenson, imp unknown

All six women were sent to York Prison to await charges of witchcraft brought against them by Fairfax, including accusations they had sent cats to poison his daughters' bodies and souls, had caused Lizzie a great fall, and – most damning of all – had killed Fairfax's infant daughter, Anne.

Remarkably, despite being poor village women accused by one of the greatest names in their parish, all six women were acquitted, not once but twice. This was largely down to the work of their supporters in the village, including the gentleman Henry Graver and particularly the parish minister, Nicholas Smythson, who gathered a petition of his parishioners to present at York Assizes affirming the women's innocence.

Reverend Smythson must have been a very enlightened man for that age, and Inges has been, perhaps, a little unfair on someone who could easily have been the human hero in another version of the story.

There was one more 'witch' seen by Fairfax's daughters; someone Edward Fairfax describes in his book as 'The Strange Woman'. Little is known about her, though he does tell us: 'this individum hath a spirit in the likeness of a white cat, which she calleth Fillie – she hath kept it twenty years.'

OTHER CHARACTERS

CHARLES FAIRFAX, 1567-1604: Edward's brother and an English soldier. Killed fighting the Spanish at Ostend, when a cannonball struck a French officer standing next to him; the shattered parts of his skull impacting Charles's face. Died just three days before the town surrendered.

BEN JONSON, 1572-1637: Celebrated English poet and playwright. A contemporary of Shakespeare and one of the few of that age to stand near him in the pantheon of English writers. Enjoyed a drink.

JAMES I, 1566-1625: James (also James VI of Scotland) was the first of the Stuart kings, and the first of a united English-Scottish crown. Had a deep paranoia of witches, and his reign saw many innocent women unjustly murdered over accusations of witchcraft. There was to be no Spanish Match, and his son, Charles, lost his throne – and his head – in the English Civil War.

GEORGE VILLIERS, 1592-1628: Marquess, and then first Duke, of Buckingham. The favourite, and possible lover, of James I; and the cause of much friction with Parliament. Married Katherine Manners in 1621. Assassinated at the Greyhound Pub, in Portsmouth, by a disgruntled soldier he had passed over for promotion.

GEORGE ABBOT, 1562–1633: His rise from supposed obscurity to Archbishop was attributed by some of his contemporaries to a rather fishy tale. He remains the only Archbishop of Canterbury to have killed a man while in office. He never got over the guilt of Peter Hawkins' death in a hunting incident, and died a broken man.

MAURITS, PRINCE OF ORANGE, 1567-1625: Stadtholder of the Dutch Republic during the Dutch Revolt against Spain. A brilliant military tactician, and ruthless defender of Calvinist Protestantism against both external Catholic and internal Remonstrant Protestant opposition, which he defeated with help from George Abbot at the Synod of Dordrecht.

These characters and events are recorded in history, along with many of the places and incidents within Inges's account. As with all history, you must pick your sources and decide whose version you choose to believe.

There are rumours, it is said, of two other versions of the Fewston Witches story. Ben Jonson is claimed to have written one of his very few tragedies based on the story of a gallant cat and a treacherous king. The Reverend Smythson, too, is thought to have sent the Archbishop his account of the tale, but his work was returned with an order never to publish it.

Unfortunately, the truth of these rumours is impossible to verify as – if they ever indeed existed – both documents would have been destroyed in two separate fires: the burning of Ben Jonson's library in 1623, and the destruction of Fewston Church in 1696.

There are tales from both incidents that, shortly before the fires began, a distinctive cat was seen in the vicinity of the respective buildings – a handsome cat, white, with black spots.

Some impressionable people have claimed this must have been Inges. However, this cannot be true as the Fewston fire was 75 years after the events of our book. And who ever heard of a cat who lived that long?

ABOUT THE AUTHOR

JOHN BRUNSDON is a former BBC journalist and award-winning feature writer. He is a proud descendant of cunning women, and many of the cures mentioned in *Inges* come from a 17th Century family journal passed down the years.

John lives in the Cotswolds with his partner and their cat Pi – a handsome tom, white with black spots and mismatched eyes. The resemblance to Inges – whose description is in the historic record – is almost certainly coincidental.

You can find out more about the world of Inges, and John's other writing, on the author's Facebook page: www.facebook.com/johnbrunsdonauthor

Printed in Great Britain
by Amazon